DEMON RIDGE

IN THE DARKNESS OF THE CAVE, SOMETHING MOVED.

Elliot's senses were on red alert. Since his discovery of the boneyard, he'd begun to understand the enormity of the danger that skulked down here. It was able to reach out to him from great distances and force him to see things he didn't want to see.

Now, he was in its territory, It could spring from the darkness at any time, risking the meager beams of the light it hated to fasten itself upon something it hated even more.

He made his way to the other side of the chasm, down the passage, and to the tiny opening leading to the boneyard. Once again, removing his ruck, Elliot put it to the side, and lowered himself through, this time on his back, feet first.

That's when he found himself knee-deep in a pool of water.

Unprepared for this unexpected turn of events, Elliot found himself falling forward. When he got his bearings, he looked around him and realized with a thrill of horror that this wasn't the boneyard. He had stumbled into an unfamiliar part of the cave.

That's when his light began to flicker………

ACKNOWLEDGEMENTS

This book, like any other, is not the work of one person, but rather the result of many contributors, some of whom weren't even aware they were contributing.

First, there's my dad who told me I'd never amount to anything, knowing it would make me mad enough to get off my butt and prove him wrong. You can rest knowing that you were right as always, big guy, and I love you for it.

Of course, there's my mom who always hated the fact that I grew up as an incurable horror buff. She always claimed that I'd grow up warped, and she was right. In typical mom fashion, however, she actually likes the stuff I write and encourages me to keep on keeping on. Love you, Mom.

Not to forget my son, who likes to be known by the macho name, Lance Uppercut, for providing me with ideas, then knowing when to back off and let me develop them. Love you, too, Lance.

Then, there are the members of the Garden State Speculative Fiction Writers. The group as a whole provided a wealth of knowledge and assistance, but I'd be remiss in not singling out Gabriele A. Rollé and Neil Morris. These folks really delved into my early drafts and gave me ideas that never would have occurred to me on my own. Thanks, guys.

Thanks to Victoria Strauss who I bugged with innumerable questions, but who never failed to come back with helpful feedback.

I can't forget the members of the Northern New Jersey Grotto. This is an organization dedicated to cave exploration and preservation. I've participated in a number of NNJG-led caving excursions, which provided background and inspiration for Demon Ridge.

And last, but far from least, thanks to Alan Baxter, Frank and Thom Romano, and David Collins of AB Film Publishing and Wing Spam Press for their faith, their support and their recommendations. I couldn't have done it without you guys. For real.

DEMON RIDGE

A Novel by

C. I. Kemp

PUBLISHED BY AB FILM PUBLISHING
New York, NY

ISBN: 978-0-9904852-7-8

Cover Design by Thomas Romano, USA

Published by AB Film Publishing
290 West 12 Street, Suite A
New York, New York 10014
(212) 741-1441

PREFACE

1

<u>Salem, Massachusetts; September, 1692</u>

He might have been a statue.

The only signs of movement were the spasmodic finger gestures that caused the links of his chains to jingle.

A light welcome breeze entered the windows and stirred the air in the Meeting House's vestry room. The room was filled to capacity with men whose expressions were flint and a few equally stone-faced women. They were staring at the man in chains with a hatred as palpable as the oppressive summer air. Those that could not find seating on the uncomfortable wooden benches were content to stand, even in the stultifying heat.

Such distress was a meager price to pay to see the object of their hostility sentenced to Gallows Hill.

At a raised dais to the right of the prisoner sat the Magistrate, Mr. Nathaniel Ferris, perusing the sheaves of parchment listing the crimes of the accused. It was a voluminous bundle.

It was by the will of this man that the once gentle hound of Goodman Fell turned on six-year-old Benjamin Fell, laying open the child's throat.

It was by his doing that the granary of Goodman Danbury became tainted with myriad slug like things which exuded a foul and putrid liquescence.

It was by his arcane dictate that the livestock of his neighbors shriveled and died in the brutal summer torpidity, even as his own flourished, bloated with hearty grain and good health.

The breeze ruffled the papers before Magistrate Ferris as that noteworthy gentleman turned toward the prisoner.

The finger motions of the accused were becoming increasingly active and he had begun crooning a wordless tune. These signs, Magistrate Ferris thought, betokened fear.

Never had a man more to fear, not only of his oncoming death, but of damnation everlasting.

Magistrate Ferris allowed himself a little smile. In a society where austerity was a virtue and pleasure an iniquity, Magistrate Ferris could not help but feel unwonted gratification toward the task he was to perform this day. If ever a man deserved the fate that awaited him on Gallows Hill, it was this man. His recital of those dark deeds of which he was guilty came not in the form of contrition or confession; he crowed as he declaimed, with a vaunting and ungodly pride.

The breeze from without was intensifying, but Magistrate Nathaniel Ferris took no notice of it as he faced the prisoner.

"Do you here stand, charged with sundry acts of witchcraft by you done or committed upon the bodies and properties of …"

Whatever remaining words Mr. Ferris intended were never heard. The prisoner's keening reached a screaming crescendo, drowning out the sentence that was about to be spoken. At the same time, his hands and fingers, no longer encumbered by iron fetters, were engaged in frantic gesticulations.

Mr. Ferris was struck a mighty blow in his midsection. He fell back, coughing blood, even as chaos came again in the vestry room.

The breeze that had wafted through the chamber, previously so pleasing and mild, had erupted into a veritable whirlwind. Windows shattered, and amidst shrieks of pain and terror, Magistrate Nathaniel Ferris saw Goody Fell, mother of slain Benjamin, stumbling blind, a dagger-sized shard of glass embedded in her eye.

Through all the windows, now devoid of glass, the unholy wind pummeled spectator and fixture alike. Stout Thomas Burrows was lifted off his feet and hurled into the far wall with a sickening thud, remained suspended for the space of a few seconds, then slid to the floor, his ample body a mass of crimson pulp.

Magistrate Ferris tried to rise, but could not. A weighty rafter had broken off and propelled itself upon him, pinning him to the dais, in such a position that, while he could not move, he was privy to the horror unfolding before him.

The sturdy oak benches and tables were exploding. The force of these explosions transformed their remnants into mortar with rapier-sharp edges, impaling those with whom they came in contact. Something rebounded off the wall with a violent thud, inches from Magistrate Nathaniel Ferris. That good man turned, and spewed forth his disgust on seeing the head of Samuel Fell bouncing down the floor.

Outside was the dark of night, though the actual time was just short of midday. It was as if some foul hand had covered the face of the sun with a black winding sheet.

Above, Mr. Ferris heard a loud cracking sound, and upon looking up, saw that the remaining rafters were sundering. As they broke from the ceiling, they became projectiles, hurled by an invisible giant hand, toppling those who sought futile refuge beyond the confines of the vestry.

The floor beneath him shifted and he turned his head to see it open, like a gaping maw whose tongue was flame. Those not impaled by shards of wood and glass were engulfed in that flame, falling through what was once a solid pine floor, now no more substantial than burnt tinder.

Before death took its mercy upon him, Magistrate Nathaniel Ferris witnessed a sight more terrible than anything he had seen hitherto.

The accused man was strolling through the vestry, indifferent to the agony around him, unmolested by flame or flying debris. He was walking, with no more concern than the most pious of Christians making his way to church, toward the far end of the vestry, where the upheaval of the floor was more violent than anywhere else.

From the depths, a dark shape rose to greet him.

2

The Ridge, August 9, 1997; 7:15 pm

In the shadows atop the ridge, something moved.

It squatted and focused its eyes downward on the woman.

She was a distance away. The early evening sky, which usually clung to the last traces of daylight at this hour, was darkening. A storm was coming. Yet, despite the darkness and the distance, the watcher could distinguish every strand of the woman's hair and every fiber of her clothing with perfect clarity.

It took its time shifting its position. It had no need for speed. When it was ready, it could cover the gap between the woman and itself, in fractions of a second.

The woman walked on, receding into the distance.

The watcher made its way after her, keeping to the shadows.

#

Miranda MacAuley reached into her handbag and pulled out a pack of cigarettes. She lit one and inhaled greedily. A thought, as perverse as it was satisfying, came to her: she'd smoke the whole damn pack, and when Philip came home, she'd be reeking of tobacco. Her ex-smoker husband hated the smell of the stuff and Miranda resolved that when he got home, she'd make a point of standing close to him. Let the stench, clinging to her hair and clothes, assault his delicate sensibilities. Serve him right.

Philip had done it to her again, tonight of all nights. He was with the other woman. That manipulative, domineering, bloated toad of a woman: his mother.

Miranda and Philip had planned this night out for weeks. It was a celebration, one she deserved.

After moving to Taylorville, Miranda began working for the firm of MacMillan, Sherman, and Strohm. She'd worked herself up from Administrative Assistant, which was a fancy way of saying she ran the operation. Over the years, she'd overhauled each of the firm's functions and was rewarded with a bonus, a promotion, and the promise of a bright future.

Tonight was her night to celebrate. In an area where most eateries were fast food chains, diners, or country kitchens, she and Philip had reservations at the most lavish restaurant in town. Miranda would gorge herself on the most succulent Lobster Thermidor, guzzle champagne chilled so cold it would give her brain freeze, and dance until her feet begged for mercy. She'd even planned on making hot monkey love to Philip in the wee hours until he begged for mercy.

And what did Philip do? Waited until that very morning to tell her he had to help his mother clean out his father's closet. His father had been dead for seven years; why did his mother have to pick this day of all days to attack that particular chore? Miranda knew the answer: Mama had never forgiven Miranda for taking her "schweet widdle baby boy" away from her. Philip just shrugged and assured Miranda that he'd be home in time for them to enjoy their special evening together.

Miranda's initial reaction to Philip's assurances was skepticism, but that skepticism was short-lived. After all, Philip was looking forward to this night as much as she was. He'd been the one, in fact, to suggest blowing her bonus on a night out. Surely he'd make it his business to be back in time.

She should have gone with her first reaction. An hour before their reservation, the phone rang. At first, Miranda thought there was some interference on the line. Strange sounds came out of the earpiece and it took her a few seconds to realize that they were the sounds of a woman crying.

"Hello, Miranda?"

"Philip?"

There was an embarrassed pause, after which Philip spoke. "Miranda, look, Mom's having a hard time. Looking at Dad's stuff, and, well it ..."

During the pause, Miranda heard more background blubbering, as genuine and uncontrived as a pre-election promise.

"You have to understand ... I—I can't leave her like this," Philip said. Before Miranda could protest, he went on, "I'm really sorry about this, babe. Would you mind very much calling the restaurant and making reservations for next week?"

With exaggerated sweetness, Miranda replied, "Would you mind very much fucking yourself? Babe."

She never knew who slammed down the phone first.

Thunder boomed.

The reverberation shook her out of her reverie and she realized that she was no longer walking on pavement. The sidewalk had given way to a dirt path running along the base of the ridge.

Through the dimming light, Miranda could make out the cliff towering above her, crowned with trees and bushes. In some places, it was a sheer drop, its vertical surface smooth as ice. In others, the rock was adorned with crannies. On such surfaces, the adventurous, (though not necessarily the intelligent), might free climb or scramble their precarious way up. At the base of the cliff was a deposit of scree, loose rock debris, perhaps gathering there over centuries. Below that was a slope with elms, maples, pines and eastern hemlocks. Thick and close, they were, a veritable barrier allowing for no easy passage from the base of the cliff to the path.

Miranda paused. The street was behind her and she realized how quickly and how far she had walked in her pissed off state of mind. She was a good twenty minutes from home. The path, on which people walked and kids mountain-biked, lay before her. If she followed it far enough, it would take her to a severe uphill climb, at which point all but the most physically fit turned back.

Trees on either side of her; beyond them and to her right, the ridge.

She stopped walking and looked up. Even in the darkness and through the trees, she could see clouds were flowing over each other in overlapping patterns. It was a rain sky, not a light or even a moderate rain, but a real blowdown, one that would have her drenched within seconds.

6

Lightning illuminated the sky.

Miranda turned around and started back.

The walk had not done her as much good as she'd hoped. She hadn't burned off any of the resentment she'd been feeling since Philip's call.

Another bolt of lightning and another burst of thunder. These seemed to speak to her in commanding tones not to be ignored. Stop your daydreaming. Hurry. To you, these tall trees may be majestic and beautiful. To the lightning, they are tenpins to be struck, split, and felled. Do you want to be beneath them when the lightning plays at target practice? No? Then, leave this place. Leave this place.

Miranda heeded the unspoken warning. She hastened toward the street, now that the wind was picking up. For the first time, she was aware of how different the woods looked and sounded tonight. She and Philip walked here often, mostly in the evenings. Crickets chirped, birds sang, insects buzzed. Rabbits, squirrels, chipmunks, and field mice scampered through the brush. When there was a hint of a breeze; the branches swayed and the leaves whispered secrets to each other.

On this night, however, she heard no animal sounds between the thundering booms. The birds, beasts, and bugs were safely ensconced in sheltering dens, away from the onslaught of the coming storm. *Smarter than me*, Miranda thought, *that's where I should be*. There was a different quality to the wind as well. Instead of their usual whispery softness, the rustling leaves seemed to speak in witches' voices—dry and raspy. And the trees, usually so lush and full, seemed dead and empty, courtesy of a rainless spring and summer.

There was something unnatural about these surroundings, discomfiting, almost ominous.

Miranda picked up her pace as the thunder sounded again, louder this time. She made ready to hightail back home without delay.

Rather she would have, except for one thing that gave her pause: a noise that continued after the thunder had died out. A noise that came from above her, but not from the sky.

The sound of something heavy sliding against rock. An abrasive sound with a fingernails-scraped-against-glass quality.

Miranda stopped. She reached into her handbag and pulled out the flashlight she always carried when she and Philip took their evening walks. She turned it on and aimed it toward the ridge.

The light's meager beam barely penetrated the wall of trees.

Miranda removed the cigarette from her lips, flicked the ash, and began puffing again. She scanned the upper regions of the ridge. She was sure there was something there; she'd heard it if only for just a few seconds.

Replacing the flashlight in her handbag, Miranda started her trek homeward once again, at a brisk trot.

It came again. Miranda turned in the direction of the sound and looked up toward the top of the cliff. The corner of her eye caught a movement. There was something there. It was dark, fast, and low to the ground. She saw it for a split-second then it vanished.

Miranda picked up her pace.

Could it be a bear? A cougar? Miranda had heard that there were bears in the area, but these were mere rumors. Also, she was sure that there were no feline predators in this part of the state.

Her fast walk became a run.

Or maybe there was a third possibility. Since they'd moved here, the locals had regaled her and Philip with the folk legends of the area, most of which she'd written off as superstitious nonsense. There was one, however, which resonated with her, one she found particularly unnerving. It was related to her by a neighbor who crossed himself after telling it. It had to do with this very ridge and how something dark and terrible …

Behind her, there came a loud crash, followed by loose rocks and stones being dislodged from the scree at the base of the cliff.

Startled, Miranda let out a little cry. The cigarette dropped from her mouth.

The noise resumed. The sound of scraping on loose rock followed by a rhythmic staccato beat.

Something big and weighty thudding its way toward her.

Miranda ran faster.

It wasn't a rock or a log that had fallen. Something living launched itself off the cliff and, against all logic, survived uninjured. Something lead-footed made its way through the thickness of the trees, through the brush, coming closer.

Miranda heard the sound of wood splintering and realized that it was breaking down branches, breaking through logs, breaking through any other detritus that accumulated in its path, with alarming speed and force.

It was making its way down the slope, deliberately, purposefully.

It was coming toward her

It was coming *after* her!

The sound of its footsteps continued, loud enough to be heard over the sporadic bursts of thunder as well as the rain which was now falling in torrents, dousing her. As it came closer, she heard something else mingled with the sounds of crashing and thumping.

Breathing, coming at a distance somewhere within the trees, but alongside her.

With a thrill of horror, Miranda realized that her pursuer had overtaken her.

As if some demented weather god were in charge, a burst of sheet lightning occurred and in that split second, Miranda saw.

It wasn't enough to provide a clear view of her pursuer through the trees, but what she saw was enough. It was a dark shape, large, maybe the size of a bear, but definitely not a bear. It was semi-upright, hunkered down in a sort of crouch, never falling, stumbling, or tripping over the protruding roots or wet leaves. Nothing stood in its way as it sped down the slope, past all obstacles with uncanny speed and agility. Its movements were decisive, tenacious, and as it got closer, Miranda could hear the noise again. This time, it wasn't so much breathing as snarling.

Almost stretched to her limit, Miranda forced herself to put on a final burst of speed.

Fast though the thing was, it had to weave its way through the trees. Miranda, on the other hand, was on a relatively clear path. With the head of steam she had going, she could get to the main road. Once she was in the vicinity of streetlights, houses and passing cars, she'd scream like crazy. She would get the attention of her neighbors, and hopefully scare the thing away altogether. Even as that comforting thought struck her, the first lights from her street became visible.

Behind her, she heard something break through the woods and onto the path. Adrenaline kicked in and she picked up her speed.

She was less than fifty feet from the main road. Then thirty. Fifteen.

I'm going to make it.

Her foot came down on a rut in the path and her ankle turned under her. She fell and skidded in the dirt, face down. She slid against the sandpapery ground, her cheek rubbed raw, down to the bone. The skin beneath her brow split open and her eye socket pooled with blood. She was wearing short sleeves and her forearms fared no better. Her blouse and jeans were shredded, as was the skin beneath them.

Miranda had just begun to get up when something barreled into her with the force and speed of a cannonball. She heard a cracking sound, followed by a surge of pain from a broken rib. Knocked back onto the path, her head slammed into the ground. Her vision pinwheeled and she reeled from the pain assaulting her body.

Miranda screamed and managed to turn on one side, freeing her right arm, which had been trapped beneath her. She reached out to where she thought her attacker's face should be, intending to jam her nails into its eyes. As soon as she brought her hand up, her fingers were immersed in something hot and slimy. She heard the sound of twigs splintering seconds before a new agony swept over her. Instinctively, she drew her hand back.

Where seconds ago, she had long tapering fingers with manicured, polished nails, there were now only bleeding stumps.

She screamed again, struggling to free her legs from whatever was on top of her. With pain and fear getting in the way of conscious thought, she was operating on a survivor's overdrive. Freeing her legs might allow her a few strategic kicks, perhaps even the chance to run. Her screams had become constant, but futile. She was too out-of-breath from running and they sounded more like gasps, mingling with the guttural rumblings of her assailant. They were accompanied by fetid, dead-animal exhalations that stung her eyes.

Miranda felt herself constricted in a viselike grip where the vise was studded with spikes, long and sharp, driving themselves deep into her flesh. She felt herself being lifted off the ground and felt the motion of being carried—where? She felt her body ravaged with every movement by those incredibly spiky things impaling her torso with an infinite number of excruciating wounds.

Another vise grasped her at her right shoulder with more of those spike-like things violating her. Another crack, more pain, and the vague awareness that her collarbone had been snapped.

A kaleidoscope of thoughts, memories, and impressions cascaded through her mind, as life cascaded from her veins. Some were recent, others distant recollections she hadn't thought of in decades; there was no logic to them, no connectivity. They just were.

Her anger toward Philip. Her resentment toward his mother. The time she skinned her knee falling off her two-wheeler. The clothes hanging from her like scraps off a discarded rag doll. The time a boy copped a feel off her in the back of a Chevy Nova. The succulent Lobster Thermidor and frosty champagne she'd never get to taste. Her high school graduation, where she'd been reprimanded for making rude noises during the principal's speech. The regret that there would never be a MacMillan, Sherman, Strohm, and MacAuley. The knowledge that no matter how much she struggled, her assailant was going to have its savage way with her. The folk legend she could never write off. Her neighbor crossing himself …

3

"It was a dark and stormy night…"

Even at the age of ten, Jeffrey Strickland would have considered that a pretty lame opening for a ghost story. It was, however, on just such a night that he discovered his house was haunted.

Jeff was an avid follower of ghost stories, horror movies, and monster magazines. The more bizarre and uncanny the material, the more entranced he was. His immersion in the genre rivaled that of older, more sophisticated scholars who studied it in depth.

Such an immersion could not fail to affect a youngster of Jeff's intelligence and sensitivity. What he read was there to entertain, not convince, yet, there were those rare moments when Jeff could half accept that there were worlds, realities, possibilities (call them what you will) beyond the five senses. And if this were true, was it not equally possible that they were inhabited by beings and life forms different from and possibly hostile to humanity?

It was that sensitivity, rather than any fixation on the supernatural, that found Jeff in a state of perturbed sleeplessness on this dark and stormy night. He was concerned about the move, the new house, the new neighborhood, the new school year, the whole new way of life.

In the pecking order of pre-teen society, Jeff was painfully aware that he was not one of the "cool" kids, the "popular" kids. He was often picked on by those who, unlike him, preferred rough-and-tumble forms of play over books, who saw him as "different," an easy target to be bullied and ragged upon.

Fortunately, Jeff wasn't the only kid not into sports or physical activity. There were other kids, bookish, gangling sorts, and over the years, Jeff gravitated toward them. By ten, he managed to cultivate a semi-solid circle of friends and acquaintances in his Boston elementary school. It had been a relief to reach a level of acceptance even if it was among his fellow misfits.

Small victory though it was, Jeff relished it until January. That was when his parents announced that they were moving to a town called Taylorville, more than a hundred miles from Boston. His father was offered a partnership in a law firm and his mother obtained a professorship at the local university. All in all, it was too great an opportunity to pass up.

For you, maybe, Jeff thought bitterly.

Which was why Jeff tossed and turned in his new room, (not that the lightning and thunder were helping any), still full of unpacked boxes. His overactive mind was pondering horrors not of the grave or the walking dead. His personal horrors were far more immediate to a ten-year-old boy who wanted nothing more than his peers' acceptance. His parents were not unsympathetic. They acknowledged his concerns, but emphasized that the family's needs had to be considered foremost. In the long run, the move would benefit everyone.

Yeah, right.

Despite his trepidation and resentment, Jeff wanted sleep. Not because he was tired, but because slumber would bring respite from the unpleasant, uninvited thoughts hammering at him. A new school term was less than a month away and Jeff possessed a typical ten-year-old's aversion for formal education. That the term would begin in an unfamiliar and threatening setting added to the apprehension.

After considerable fidgeting, Jeff finally found a comfortable position. He closed his eyes and tried to force himself to chill. Even at ten, he realized that fighting sleeplessness was not the way to achieve sleep. He decided he'd just lie there and relax. If that didn't work, he'd get up and read something until he felt too tired to stay awake.

He had no idea how long he'd been lying there, when he heard someone walk into his room.

No, *heard* was not precisely the right word. *Sensed* would have been more accurate, since Jeff didn't actually hear anything. Nor was *walk* any more appropriate; there were no footfalls, but he did feel that he was not alone in the room.

He opened his eyes and saw nothing. The darkness of the room was—what was that word writers used to describe total darkness? Stih-something. Stih- sty-

Stygian.

Jeff's first though was that Rusty, the family dog, a loveable Heinz-57-variety, had padded in. He whispered the dog's name, waited, whispered it again, then put out his hand.

Then drew it back.

The sensation lasted for a fraction of a second, not unpleasant, but certainly unexpected.

From his many readings, Jeff knew that coldness often characterized fictional encounters with ghosts—a cold spot in a room, a cold touch at the nape of the neck, or that old standby, a cold chill.

But this was none of those. Where he reached out, he felt—warmth.

In slow motion, Jeff put his hand out again.

Nothing.

He waited, leaving his hand outstretched, squinting into the darkness.

Nothing. Not even indistinct shapes.

Jeff continued squinting, waiting for his eyes to adjust to the dark and pick out something. A shape. A movement. Anything.

Once again, Jeff whispered Rusty's name, all the while certain that the presence in the room was not the dog.

In the utter silence of the room, the whispered word sounded like normal spoken speech.

Jeff drew back his hand and sat up.

Could he be dreaming? Could he have fallen asleep and entered into a dream where he was in his own room, alone, yet not alone? Jeff had had dreams in which he knew something was going to happen before it did. How different was such a dream from what he was going through right now—knowing that his room held an inhabitant other than himself? If this was a dream, it certainly was more vivid than any he'd ever had. Plus, on those rare occasions when he'd realized he was dreaming within the dream, he'd awakened abruptly. That wasn't happening now.

Suddenly, it occurred to Jeff that he might be in danger. Of course it wasn't a ghost that was in his room any more than it was Rusty. Perhaps some bad person had gotten into the house. That would mean that they got past his parents, past Rusty, maybe even injured them. Now that bad person was in his room, preparing to do God-knows-what.

Jeff began to shake. He scrunched up toward the head of his bed, wishing he had a baseball bat or something like that within reach.

Don't be afraid.

Again, it wasn't something Jeff heard, so much as sensed in his mind's ear, something not transmitted in words.

Put out your hand.

Jeff did, and once again a warm sensation caressed his hand and lower arm, then withdrew.

Don't be afraid.

I'm not.

There was a presence in the room. This presence meant him no harm. It was there to reassure him and bolster him. He lay back in bed, immobile, no longer dwelling upon the anxieties he'd felt earlier. Now, he was both curious and fascinated. He stared at a point in the darkness, waiting for a sound, a movement, anything coming from the presence itself.

Then an idea came to him. Why hadn't he thought of it before? Why not just get up, get out of bed, and turn on the light? Surely, there was no danger, and the curiosity was overwhelming. Yes, that's what he'd do.

Jeff swung his feet out of the bed, estimated where the wall switch would be and began moving toward that spot.

Something caught at his foot and he felt himself moving, not toward the light switch, but downward into the darkness, halted by an impact and a deafening *whomp.*

"OWWW."

Waves of pain pulsed up his right arm and in his head, lights flashed. It didn't take a genius to figure what happened.

In his enthusiasm, Jeff had tripped over one of the many boxes strewn throughout the room, holding his unpacked belongings. He'd stumbled and taken a fall, landing right on his funny bone, then bumping his forehead on the floor.

Feeling sheepish, Jeff got to his knees, then rose to his feet, and felt his way back to bed. Stupid idea anyway. Even if he could negotiate his way to the light switch among all those boxes, what would be the point? The presence would probably dematerialize with the illumination.

Jeff got back into bed and waited, trying to determine if it was still there.

It was, and Jeff somehow sensed that it was amused.

Jeff lay back, trying to open his mind, trying to gauge the temperament and intentions of this nocturnal visitor. Something remained in close proximity, but it did not emit any vibrations or impressions. It just *was*.

So it remained until Jeff fell into a dreamless slumber.

#

"'Morning."

Mom and Dad were seated at breakfast and Rusty was slurping at his water dish when Jeff came into the kitchen the next morning.

"Good morning."

"Good morning, dear. Sleep well?"

"OK, I guess." Jeff decided he wasn't going to tell his parents about his experience of the previous night. Besides, in the light of day, he was halfway back to convincing himself that it had been a dream after all.

"I don't see how you could have," replied his father. "What with the lightning and thunder going on till all hours. You mean to tell me you didn't hear any of that?"

"No."

His mother had just put down a bowl of kibbles for the dog. "You didn't hear poor Rusty? Every time there was thunder, he'd practically jump out of his skin."

"He was crying and yowling half the night. You didn't hear him?" asked Dad.

"No." Jeff sat down and placed his elbow on the table. "OW."

"What's the matter?" asked Mom. "What happened? Are you all right?"

"What's wrong with your elbow? Let me see that." Dad got up from his chair and took his son's elbow. "How did it get so black and blue?"

"I don't know," Jeff answered, not really hearing or paying attention to his parents' gaze or attention to his bruised elbow. His mind was veering in a completely different direction.

His parents said there was lightning last night, yet the darkness in his room was … *stygian*.

With lighting came thunder, yet his room was completely silent. He didn't even hear Rusty yelping.

Shouldn't his parents have heard the sound when he tripped and fell? He *did* fall, his bruised elbow was proof. So, come to think of it, was the throbbing in his head.

For the second time, Jeff Strickland decided that what happened last night was real. Something other than his family and himself lived in that house. Something forceful, yet benign. Something that didn't want him to be afraid.

He wasn't. Nor would he be.

4

Bergen County, New Jersey; August 9, 1997

It was 8:00 pm, raining like a son of a bitch. The coffee was lukewarm and bitter. All was *not* well.

The rain and the coffee were minor annoyances. What ate at Police Lieutenant Anselmo Irrizarry was that eight-year old Kathie Machlan was still missing after nearly three days to the hour.

Anselmo raised the coffee to his lips again, then threw it down in disgust. It landed in the wastepaper basket by his desk, drenching the papers that had accumulated there over the last three days. Anselmo couldn't care less.

Conventional police wisdom held that the best chances for finding a missing child were within the first forty-eight hours. For Kathie Machlan, that deadline had passed. Anselmo had a daughter of his own, about Kathie's age, upon whom he absolutely doted. He tried not to imagine how he'd feel if she went out one day and didn't come back.

Which was why Anselmo was at his desk after hours, taking calls on the confidential 1-800 line from anyone who might have information leading to Kathie's safe return.

Three days ago, Veronica Machlan's call came in. Her daughter was missing. The top brass announced that no effort would be spared in bringing little Kathie Machlan home safely. Anselmo got on it and within an hour, came up with two suspects.

Veronica Machlan was divorced, with an ex-husband living outside of Tamaqua, Pennsylvania. She had a current boyfriend named George Hull, who was no kind of nice guy. Hull was clean since moving to New Jersey, but he had a rap sheet in other states for petty theft, vandalism, and domestic violence. Still, Veronica was devoted to him, despite his temper and tendency to raise his voice in Kathie's presence. Had he ever been violent toward her or her daughter? Had he ever threatened either of them? No, never. Still, she admitted that Hull intimidated Kathie and Kathie resented him. Hull suspected as much and did not take kindly to it.

The next step had been to question Hull. To say that Hull was uncooperative would be an understatement. When two of Anselmo's men came to his door, Hull was in a foul mood, disrespectful, and uncooperative. When the officers pressed him, he started swinging at them and ended up with a broken jaw and a charge of assaulting an officer. Hull had been in the local lockup since then, sullen, refusing to speak. Threats, entreaties, and persuasion were all futile. If George Hull knew anything, he was keeping it to himself out of spite.

The other possibility was Kathie's father, Leonard Machlan. Leonard knew about Hull, knew that Veronica had kept company with several men since their divorce, and was bitter about it. Whether this attitude stemmed from a perceived slur on his manhood or whether he felt that this form of socializing was inappropriate in front of Kathie was immaterial. What Anselmo did discover was that Leonard and Veronica had had several loud arguments over the phone on the subject. Leonard had accused Veronica of being an unfit mother and threatened to take Kathie away from her. Anselmo asked Veronica if she though Leonard was capable of kidnapping their daughter. Veronica's emphatic answer was, "Fuckin' A he is!"

Several attempts were made to reach Leonard Machlan at work and at home. At work, his voice mail instructed the caller to leave a message. Many messages were left. None were returned. At home, the phone kept ringing and no answering machine responded. Anselmo had been in frequent contact with the Tamaqua police, who couldn't have been more helpful. They made frequent stops at Leonard's home address and consistently reported that the place seemed deserted.

Anselmo had been taking calls for the last six hours. As always happened in cases of this nature, many of the calls fell into the category of cranks and pranks. Of the pranks, there was a wiseass who called to order a pizza and another who wanted to speak to Mike Rotch. On these, Anselmo slammed down the phone. Of the cranks, one claimed that Kathie was in the hold of a ship bound for a third-world country where little girls were sold as sexual commodities. One man suggested that the police use bloodhounds to scour the Hackensack River and that he'd be glad to volunteer his dogs for that purpose. A lady said she saw Kathie with a bunch of other little girls at the Willowbrook Mall, in the company of two women, probably lesbians. Others who called just for the sake of calling were neither helpful nor disruptive; they just wanted to be part of something important.

Anselmo was debating taking a quick run to the vending machine to get another cup of coffee when the phone rang. *Here we go again.*

"Irrizarry."

A brief pause, then, "You are in charge of the Kathie Machlan investigation, yes?"

An accent. One Anselmo couldn't place. "Yes, sir, how can I help you?"

"Lieutenant, I want to assure you that Kathie Machlan is very safe as we speak. I can tell you where to find her."

Crank? Prank? Other? Anselmo couldn't be sure. "Do you know where she is, sir?"

"Not precisely. Please listen carefully, Lieutenant. She is in a place where there are many small horses."

That did it. A prank, and Anselmo was in no mood for pranks.

"Listen, buddy, I think you'd …"

"Kathie Machlan loves Snoopy; her room is full of Snoopy paraphernalia. She also is devoted to a character on TV show whom I believe is called Elmo. She has also recently been to the Big Apple Circus and enjoys watching the New York Yankees."

Anselmo froze. Prank or not, this guy was 100% on the money. When Anselmo and his men questioned Veronica Machlan, they'd searched Kathie's room. It was full of Snoopy-related items: posters, stuffed Snoopys, and a shelf full of Peanuts books featuring Charlie Brown's anthropomorphic dancing beagle. The only plush toy that wasn't

Snoopy was a huge Elmo doll along with several videos featuring the furry Muppet's best *Sesame Street* moments. Also a Yankees' pennant and a souvenir program from the Big Apple Circus.

None of which had been relayed to the media. That meant this guy knew something.

Struggling to keep emotion out of his voice, Anselmo asked, "Sir, what is your relationship to the Machlan family?"

"I have never met any member of the Machlan family."

"Then how do you come by this information?"

Pause. "I realize that you will be skeptical upon hearing this, Lieutenant, but sometimes I can see things."

This time, the pause came from Anselmo. He'd heard stories about how police sometimes used psychics and mediums to solve difficult cases, but he'd always regarded such tales as dubious. Yet here was this guy, claiming to be a just that …

…who knew things that the media had not reported and, come to think of it, addressed him by title, when Anselmo had only identified himself by name.

What the hell was going on here?

"I know you must be skeptical," the voice repeated, "but I assure you, I have assisted many police organizations throughout the country in various investigations of a similar nature. I will be glad to furnish you with contact names and phone numbers …"

"Sir," Anselmo interrupted. "What did you mean by 'a place where there are many small horses.'?"

"I am sorry, Lieutenant. Sometimes what I know is rather cryptic. It is not as clear as I would wish it to be. Perhaps if you asked the mother or the D'Elia woman?"

The D'Elia woman. That would be Doris D'Elia, the elderly neighbor lady who'd been at the Machlan house, comforting Veronica, when the police arrived. Mrs. D'Elia was obviously devoted to the mother and daughter. Her presence was the only thing that kept Veronica from going completely to pieces.

Was Doris D'Elia mentioned in the media? Anselmo wasn't sure.

"Sir, would you be willing to come in and …"

"I am sorry. I am calling long distance. I just happened to read about the Machlan case and thought I should call with what I know."

"Is there a number where I can reach you?"

"Again. I am sorry. No, I am calling from a public phone and I have to catch a plane in a few minutes. If you are tracing this call, I'm afraid it would do you no good."

Trace the call. Stupid! Too late, Anselmo realized that was the first thing he should have done! The truth was that this guy was so riveting, the thought hadn't even occurred to him.

"Can I at least have your name, sir?" Confidential line or no, Anselmo just *had* to get some kind of handle on this guy.

"My name is Baumann. Henrik Baumann. I am sorry, Lieutenant, but I am very pressed for time. Please. Remember. A place where there are many small horses. Good luck."

"Hello? HELLO?"

It was no use. The line was dead.

Anselmo stared at the phone. What had just happened? Who was this Henrik Baumann? Baumann. That explained one thing, at least. The accent. Come to think of it, it did sound German.

But what to do with the information Baumann provided? The man sounded sincere, for all his eccentricity. Clearly, he knew things about Kathie Machlan that none of the other callers did. No, writing him off was not an option.

A place where there are many small horses.

Anselmo dialed Veronica Machlan's number. He had no idea what he was going to say, but follow through he must.

Veronica answered on the first ring.

"Mrs. Machlan? This is Lieutenant Anselmo Irrizarry. I was one of the officers taking your statement a few days ago. Listen, Mrs. Machlan, I have a very odd question to ask you. It may not make sense, and I don't want to get your hopes up, but it may be a lead of sorts, so please think very carefully before you answer.

"I've received a tip to look for Kathie in a place where there are many small horses. Does that mean anything to you?"

A pause, longer and more uncomfortable than any that had occurred during Anselmo's conversation with Baumann. In that pause, Anselmo awaited for Veronica Machlan's reaction. It could be anything: tears, frustration, or fury at having been asked so ridiculous a question at so traumatic a time.

But it wasn't. After several iterations of "Oh, my God," Veronica claimed she knew exactly what that meant.

Within fifteen minutes, a patrol car was parked in front of Veronica Machlan's house.

Within thirty minutes, Veronica Machlan was hugging her daughter who was indeed safe after being found in a place with many small horses.

Within sixty minutes, Anselmo Irrizarry was making statements to the press, relieved and confident on the outside. On the inside, however, he had more questions about Henrik Baumann than he'd ever had about Kathie Machlan.

5

The Ridge; August 9, 1997; 7:15 pm

The three things sixteen-year-old Elliot Ryan loved most in this world were working with his hands, being outdoors, and smoking weed.

Elliot was currently engaged in the second of these, shortly to begin the third.

He had just left one of the many trails that crisscrossed these woods, like so many veins and arteries. His walk along the old carriage road was purposeful, deliberate; he had a specific destination in mind.

In the distance, Elliot heard the sound of thunder and sped up. All day, the air was heavy, the threat of a downpour looming in the wet heat that blanketed Taylorville. Elliot didn't give a rat's ass about the rain. He just wanted to get to where he was going and pick up his stash before it started coming down. Besides, he was in a mood to indulge.

Another round of thunder, and Elliot decided he was probably OK, timewise. The storm sounded far enough away for him to get to the ruins and pick up his stash. Maybe he could even smoke a joint or two, then get home before his parents did. His mom was at some sort of churchy-type function and wouldn't be home till way later. The old man? He was doing a job on Simpson's Mustang down in Stockton. Elliot knew that when he and Simpson got together, they'd toss back some suds and play a few rounds of poker. No, the old man wouldn't be back till after midnight, which suited Elliot just fine. They'd had another fight before the old man left for Stockton.

24

It was the usual bullshit. Elliot's attitude toward school, work, authority. He'd heard it before, many times, and he was fucking sick of it. The old man had never finished high school, so where did he get off lecturing Elliot on the virtues of education? And the old lady was no better. She'd finished high school, but what did she do with her life? Marry some beer-swilling grease jockey and go to church seven days a week. The only times she ever talked to him was to lecture him on how he should be living a good Christian life.

They made him sick. Elliot resolved that as soon as he was eighteen, he was going to leave this freakin' town. Get away from Joe Ryan's constant disapproval, away from Emily Ryan's unending preaching. There were even those moments of extreme anger (like now) where he visualized himself standing before his parents' graves without shedding a tear.

The carriage road curved and in the semi-darkness, Elliot could make out the remains of a stone structure, set back about ten feet from the road. It was reputed to be an old way station or supply depot from the Revolution. Elliot didn't know or care who built it or why, or what it was doing in the middle of this vast wooded area, far from the nearest town.

The structure was composed of stone and mortar, and measured about forty by thirty feet, the longer dimension facing the road. Many of the outside walls had collapsed except for some straggling remnants of stone on either side, allowing for easy entrance. The sides had one window each, the glass long gone, but vestiges of wooden casing remained affixed to the stone itself. The back wall had two such windows of equal size. There was no roof and no remains of what might have been within the interior of the structure itself. The height of the walls was approximately fifteen feet, which led many to believe the place had only one story. There were remains of interior walls, large chunks of stone embedded in mortar from the wall that divided the structure into two chambers. There was no floor and the ground dipped like the bottom of a huge round bowl. It was as if some impossibly heavy object was placed there for a long time, then removed, altering the configuration of the earth. Scattered along the ground was all manner of debris: broken glass, beer cans, cigarette butts, used condoms (some of which had been Elliot's).

Elliot reached the structure and pulled himself up to a standing position on one of the side windowsills. From the outside, the sill was maybe four feet from the ground, easy for an agile, long-legged sixteen-year-old to reach. Given the angle of the ground, the sill was less accessible from the interior, which was why Elliot had chosen this method of entry. Besides, Elliot didn't want to go in just yet.

Bracing himself against one side casement with his right hand, Elliot reached along the other with his left. It had been weeks since he'd been here. He was confident that the object of his search was where he'd left it, but he wasn't sure of the exact spot. His hand made a slow sweep along the surface where there were no vestiges of wooden casement. What he wanted would be revealed when his hand touched stone.

Elliot ran a careful hand along the stony surface of the wall, testing, and prodding. Soon, he'd find …

There.

Elliot pivoted so that he was facing the side of the window toward the back. This time, using both hands on a loose stone, he worked it back and forth, with patience, without haste. The stone fragment was irregularly shaped, about the size of a football. It proved to be resistant and heavy, but Elliot was a strong kid and he knew he would move it before long.

It took a few minutes to dislodge the stone. Rather than let it fall on the ground, Elliot rested it on the sill by his feet. He then turned to the opening in the wall. Reaching inside, he pulled out an object wrapped in heavy-duty plastic. He tucked it into his T-shirt, picked up the stone he'd dislodged and carefully replaced it.

Elliot then jumped down from the sill, to the outside of the structure and entered through the front opening, carrying his bundle. He cradled it, like a new-born in the arms of a first-time mother. Finding a spot on the ground inside near the rear wall, laden with less debris than elsewhere, Elliot sat and undid the package.

The package consisted of a cigar box that held two joints and a lighter.

Placing the joint in his mouth Elliot flicked the lighter, lit the joint and inhaled deeply. He kept the smoke in his lungs for more than a minute, before exhaling in a controlled and steady breath. The immediate result was a relaxed and mellow feeling. Geary had really outdone himself with this batch; he'd have to remember to thank the fat bastard next time he made a score.

Elliot finished the first joint and was beginning the second when he noticed several things he'd never experienced before, even under Geary's best.

His vision. Though it was dark, he could still make out indistinct shapes in the old stone structure. He could make out the walls, the windows, the beams used in constructing the site, now fallen to the ground. As he watched, they began fading into a darkness not of the night or the coming storm. Instead, they faded away altogether. In their place loomed different structures, semi-jagged/semi-rounded shapes which were, at the same time, formidable and beautiful.

The cold. The day had been stultifying, and the night had brought little relief. Elliot had been sweaty from the walk. The effort he'd exerted to dislodge his stash only made him sweat that much more. Now, however, as he leaned against the inner wall, he felt his whole body enveloped in a refreshing coolness. His T-shirt no longer clung to his back. His jeans no longer chafed at his thighs and calves. His boots no longer weighed down his feet. In fact, he couldn't even feel his T-shirt, his jeans, or his boots. It was as if he were naked. Nor could he feel the wall he was leaning against.

Empowerment. By rights, Elliot realized that he should have been afraid, undergoing what was happening to him, yet he wasn't. Marijuana was no hallucinogen, yet what was he doing right now if not hallucinating? He knew he was Elliot Ryan, clothed, sitting in some old, dilapidated stone ruins. Yet, his senses were telling him something different, something that his rational mind *knew* not to be true: he was somewhere else, doing something else, and being *someone* else. *Someone* else who didn't have to tolerate the old man's bullshit, his mom's holier-than-thou moralizing, sanctimonious lectures from Parsons, or shit from the Corey brothers. No, this was a *someone* else who could make all that unpleasantness disappear, and not in a nice way.

Movement. The contours began a slow and subtle shifting, and Elliot realized that this *someone* was moving. He began feeling aware of a soft wet surface beneath the soles of his bare feet and his palms bracing against something similar. Then the sensation of moving sideways, up, down, sideways again, passing the jagged/rounded shapes, through variations of the darkness.

The movement took all forms. Sometimes climbing, sometimes crawling, sometimes walking upright. Once, he felt himself squeezing through a narrow opening, before he was able to crawl, then climb into a larger chamber. This chamber was filled with the same odd shapes, which he now recognized as stalagmites and stalactites.

He was in a cave.

He was pausing, but only for a moment, then moving again, this time into a side tunnel which widened, then narrowed. At one point, he had to move sideways. When the passage widened again, he found himself facing a wide lateral gash bisecting the passage. To his surprise, he leaped across the chasm, landed on all fours, then launched into a run without breaking stride. At last, he reached a wall, which blocked any farther forward motion.

He began to climb. There were a number of hand and footholds as the upward passage began to narrow, like a chimney. At times, he needed to brace himself with his back pressed against one wall as he pulled himself up along the other. The whole process was quick and effortless as if he'd done it innumerable times before.

How long had he been climbing? He had no idea, then he realized that he was out in the open air again. The surface on which he was resting his hand was no longer a moist hybrid between mud and clay, but actual rock. Above him were two high walls, also of rock, above that, a sky full of shifting rumbling clouds and an occasional burst of lightning.

The light offended his senses, even in the narrow cleft of rock.

Once again, he began climbing. The fact that the rock was now hard, no longer soft like the cave walls, presented no obstacle. His fingers were strong and sure and once they found a place to grasp, no matter how slight, they held with an unyielding tenacity. He was able to pull himself up and out of the steep cleft with no more effort than it would take to climb stairs.

At the top of the cleft, he paused. He was atop a high escarpment overlooking a valley of trees and mountains. It was a vista he'd never seen before, and he'd been hiking and exploring these woods for years.

He walked to the edge of the escarpment and looked down and to his right. He could see a clearing, and beyond that a road. Across the road was a farm he recognized—McSweeney's. He could see the farmhouse and beyond that a pile of timbers. He was surprised when his nostrils picked up something that smoldered. McSweeney's barn. It had burned down.

Below him, about a hundred feet to his left was a mountain lake. He stood there, studying it with uncanny clarity.

More than clarity. He found his vision shifting, as it had when he first saw the shapes in the cave. He was now looking at the surface of the lake, not from a distant promontory, but from a height of a few feet. He could see a water snake coiled on a rock alongside the lake. There was water glistening off the snake's scales, as if it had moved through underbrush, still moist from an earlier drizzle. He could see its forked tongue flicking, sniffing the air. As if aware of danger, the snake uncoiled and launched itself into the lake.

Another shift.

Now he saw the snake's undulating form skimming the lake bottom, sending up clouds of mud, obliterating it from a predator's eyes, but not his.

Sheet lightning filled the sky, and he felt an angry sound come from a throat that was his yet not his. The snake was forgotten. He found himself running from the promontory into the trees. There was no trail, yet he ran unerringly through the trees down the slope, never tripping or losing balance. Again, he had the sense that he'd done this before; many, many times.

For how many seconds, how many minutes had been running? How many miles? No way of knowing and what did he care anyway? All he knew was that he was outdoors, in the open, feeling an unparalleled sense of freedom and supremacy. He was going to enjoy it as long as he could. Maybe forever.

He paused in his run and was surprised to find himself in another area he recognized. He was perched midway on the incline between the ridge's apex and North Rim Circle. He recognized it by the street lights and the cul-de-sac where a bunch of new houses were being built. The streetlights were distant so that they did not bother him, yet, he receded into the shadows and remained there, immobile.

Another burst of sheet lightning lit up the sky. Another guttural sound from his throat.

That's when he saw the woman.

She was on the dirt road below him, walking with a fixed and resolute stride. He shifted in the shadows, watching as she walked past him, emitting a scent of strong emotion. He followed, keeping to the shadows.

Another burst of lightning illuminated the sky, at which point, the unwelcome light made him stop in his tracks. This time, though, no sound came from the throat.

He saw the woman stop and reach for something. He stopped as well, squatting in the shadows, watching. Then there was a scent of something else coming from the woman, something burning.

Another bolt of lightning, another burst of thunder. Startled, he shifted from a squatting position to a standing one. In doing so, he put his weight on a protruding root which snapped like a gunshot in the night.

The woman stopped. Had she heard the sound? She appeared more vigilant, more aware. Had she seen him? Did she know he was there?

The woman reached for something again and when she faced the ridge this time, there was light coming from her. It wasn't strong or as painful as the lightning, but it irritated. He hunkered back down among the trees and the brush.

The woman moved the light along the ridge, coming close to his hiding place. He averted his eyes. The scent of something burning was still there.

Thunder rumbled, and the woman began moving again, rounding a curve in the dirt road.

He began to run, this time, quickly and without stealth

The woman quickened her pace.

He continued to run, no longer caring whether he was breaking branches and dislodging dirt, stones, plus any other detritus that might have accumulated in his path.

Then he stopped, hunkered down again, and watched.

Again, strong emotion emanated from the woman, but slightly different, as though the first scent had been joined by, and co-mingled with another. Again, she turned and beamed the light onto the ridge.

A noise came from her.

The noise meant nothing to him; it was just noise. Silence. Then noise again.

The woman swung the light slowly along the ridge again. The scent of something burning was gone.

A fine rain began to fall.

The woman began to move again.

He was getting ready to move again, then he …

… found himself back in the old stone structure, leaning against the rear wall, the remains of a joint dangling from his mouth.

He was clothed and sweating like a pig on a spit. The fine rain on his face felt good and cooling, but he knew that it would be hammering him within a few minutes.

He stood up, just barely steady on his feet and took a few shaky steps.

Man, what was that all about?

One minute, he'd been here, feeling all kinds of placid, happy, and peaceful.

The next minute, he'd been having some weird out-of-body experience, boppin' through the woods at the speed of light and following some chick on the other side of the ridge.

Now he was back.

Elliot giggled. He was still laughing when he made his way back to the carriage road. In spite of the darkness and the rain, Elliot felt like running. He broke into a fast jog which would take him back to the trail, which, in turn, would get him back to the main road, and back into town. It shouldn't take more than fifteen minutes and if he was drenched so what?

He'd just been on the best damn trip of his life.

1997 – PRESENT

1

Throughout his pre-teen and adolescent years, Jeff Strickland would dwell on the first days at 1604 Crow's Nest Pike; Taylorville, Massachusetts. He'd remember how elated Anne Strickland was with the anthropology professorship at the university. He'd remember Peter Strickland coming home late every night, bringing piles of work with him. In spite of this, he'd never seen his father happier. Of course, he'd remember the glorious secret he discovered the first night in his new room.

That night wasn't the only event that revolved around *The Presence*, as Jeff came to think of it. There were other incidents. Most were benign, some neutral, a few rather disturbing, and only one overtly threatening. Throughout it all, Jeff protected his secret the way a parent might protect a beloved and fragile child. He felt a bond with *The Presence,* as if it had singled him out to share knowledge of its existence. To speak of it was unthinkable. Besides, he was certain his parents had no idea that there was anything unusual about 1604 Crow's Nest Pike. Even Rusty, with his finely tuned canine instincts, seemed oblivious to anyone or anything inhabiting his house other than his own personal humans. Unlike the finely tuned dog of innumerable ghost stories, Rusty never sniffed at corners or barked at shadows. Rather he remained his good-natured, goofy self, as per the unique wiring of his doggy brain.

But Jeff knew. All through his elementary, middle, and high school years, he flowed with the events that began in his dark and silent room. At no time did he regard these events as anything more than a series of random incidents. They had no more rhyme or reason than the subtle shiftings of a summer breeze.

It was not until the final horror that he would question whether or not they were as arbitrary as he first thought. Only then would he wonder whether there was some devious and hideous connection between them and the shattering occurrences that engulfed him and others.

But that bit of introspection was years and years away. For now, Jeff Strickland was a ten-year-old boy on the verge of a great and wonderful change.

#

If Jeff expected another visit from *The Presence* his second night in his new house, he was to be disappointed. He was also to be disappointed on his third, fourth, fifth night and so on into his second week.

Jeff discovered that when he turned out the lights on any normal night, the combination of streetlights and moonlight illuminated his room. He could discern vague forms, such as his desk, chair, bookshelves, TV set, and anything strewn on the floor. Also, since Crow's Nest Pike was a truck route, the sounds of passing vehicles were audible at all hours. In short, if his first night was any indication, no visitation would occur unless the room was engulfed in absolute darkness and silence.

It was not until the second week that Jeff awoke from a dreamless sleep to find his room in just such a state save for the glowing dial of his digital clock. Squinting, Jeff could make out that it was 3:33 in the morning. He waited for some manifestation of *The Presence*, only to have drowsiness win over anticipation, and by 3:50, Jeff was asleep again.

His mom woke him the following morning. She wanted to know if he wanted to go with her to run some errands in Stockton. To sweeten the pot, she suggested a stop at the Yankee Trader, a used book store with an awesome selection of out-of-print books of the occult. Any other time, Jeff would have jumped at this opportunity, but today, he surprised his mother (and himself) by begging off. Anne Strickland, knowing her son's literary tastes, chalked up Jeff's refusal to the unpredictable moods of the ten-year-old mind.

"So what'll you be doing with yourself all day?" she asked.

"I still got some unpacking left," Jeff replied. "And maybe I'll take a run to the library later."

"OK. Just be careful, and make sure you're home before two."

"OK, Ma."

"Oh, and don't forget to take Rusty for a run."

"OK."

The site of Rusty's run was the spacious Strickland back yard. The front of the house faced a main road. As a result, the Stricklands took turns keeping an eye on Rusty, and cleaning up as he did his business out back and make sure he didn't go off on his own into the woods which bordered the far end of the yard. Anne was concerned about critters in the woods, particularly snakes and skunks. Peter Strickland assured his wife that as soon as the family got settled, he'd have the yard fenced in. For now, Rusty's romps were supervised as a matter of family policy.

Because he was the only one home this particular morning, that task fell to Jeff. As he oversaw the dog's meanderings, he pondered his own agenda for the day. It was quite different from what he told his mother.

He made up his mind he was going to explore the woods. Snakes, skunks and any other critters be damned.

Jeff wasn't sure exactly when the urge struck him. He was not, by nature, an adventuresome boy, and he certainly was not a rebellious one. Yet, he felt no qualms about deceiving his mother or embarking on an enterprise of which she would surely disapprove. He also recognized that the urge did not originate from within him but from someplace else.

Don't be afraid.

It was irresistible.

Once alone in the house, and having done his duty by Rusty, Jeff put on his Phantom of the Opera T-shirt, and his grungiest cutoffs. He threw a candy bar and a couple of Cokes into his rucksack, walked across his backyard and entered the woods.

#

After about fifty feet of thrashing his way through brambles and low-hanging branches, Jeff came to a path. He followed it to a clearing, beyond which was a clump of trees through which the path continued.

To get through the clearing, Jeff had to pick his way through an expanse of calf-high Timothy grass. Occasionally the grass was broken up with smaller expanses of yellow and purple flowers. The field was literally abuzz with life; flying, buzzing things surrounding Jeff's head. At his feet, movements in the grass caught his attention as crickets skittered out of his way. Bumblebees hovered lazily. They paid him no mind unless he stepped too close, in which case, they buzzed farther away, continued to hover lazily, and paid him no mind. Once, a large bird, which looked too big to be a crow hovered overhead, a black silhouette against the sun. A hawk? An eagle, maybe? At the edge of the clearing, something larger than a cricket skittered into the woods and Jeff got a glimpse of a furry shape close to the ground. A woodchuck, maybe. Or a raccoon.

Attentive, but unconcerned, Jeff made his way across the clearing where the woods resumed. There was a path, but through the trees, and Jeff could see another creek with a large wooden log fallen, or perhaps placed across it. He headed for the log and noticed that the creek was maybe ten feet across and only a few inches deep. On the other side of the creek was a trail which led up a slight rocky incline.

Jeff stepped onto the log, which shifted under his weight. A bit taken aback, Jeff adjusted his balance and continued to walk along the log. He supposed that he could have removed his sneakers and waded through the creek, but this was more fun. How often does a kid from the suburbs of Boston get to walk across a makeshift bridge in the middle of the woods? His parents weren't outdoorsy types. He'd been to the Boston National Historical Park and various sites along the Emerald Necklace, but those visits were few and infrequent. Besides, they were nothing like this. This place was a veritable wilderness in spite of the insects that seemed to find his head so fascinating.

On the other side of the creek, Jeff followed the trail and began a gentle climb, sidestepping the stones that pockmarked the trail. In several places, the trail was wet from the intermittent rains of the previous week (none as fierce as that first dark and stormy night). Anxious to see what lay at the top of the trail, Jeff walked a bit faster. In doing so, he stepped on a rock that was wet from the runoff, and slipped. He stopped his fall before sprawling face-down on the wet trail, but his palms were caked with mud and his right one was scraped. After wiping them on his cutoffs and making sure there was no blood, Jeff hiked on.

At the top of the rise, the trail veered off to the right under a canopy of trees. The trail narrowed and twisted but as long as Jeff could see the red markers, he felt confident. After about a mile, a disconcerting thought occurred to him: would he be able to find his way back? He'd been following the markers up till now, but what if they weren't so clear on the return trip?

Don't be afraid.

Jeff stopped and looked back. About a hundred feet from where he stood, he could see a red marker below the branch of a large oak. Beyond that, another. Relieved, Jeff trudged forward, observant of any landmarks on the trail itself, rather than relying on the markers alone.

He went on for another mile when he heard the sound of fast running water. A waterfall. Even a city slicker like him couldn't mistake that sound. Forgetting his earlier slip, Jeff began to jog, then run along the trail toward the sound. The trail started to slope upward again, which forced Jeff to slow his pace a little. When he got to the top, he saw it.

There was the waterfall, feeding into a good-sized lake. Surrounding on three sides were sheer rock faces. The trail ended and gave way to a sandy-gravelly beach which surrounded the lake.

Jeff stepped onto the beach, intending to hike the perimeter of the lake. He had just gotten to the base of one of the cliffs when he found himself facing another boy.

The boy, roughly the same age as he, was taken by surprise just as Jeff was. It was Jeff, however, who took a step back. He was on this kid's turf, and the kid didn't look all that friendly.

"Who are you? What are you doing here?"

Without realizing it, Jeff clenched his fists at his side.

"Where did you come from?"

Jeff sized up the other kid. He was about his own height with curly-red-hair, a pug nose and a shock of freckles, clad in bathing trunks and bare-chested. Jeff figured that the boy had been swimming in the lake and was resentful of him, as an intruder.

What to do? Come up with a smart-ass answer? Start swinging? Run away?

"Yeee-HAWWWWW."

Following that was a booming sound, a cross between a thud and a splash. Jeff turned and found himself drenched by a veritable tidal wave, hitting him in the face.

"Neil, you dumbass!" shouted the red-haired kid, equally drenched.

From the lake emerged a pudgy kid with close-cropped hair. This newcomer was Jeff's size, but considerably broader, his pudginess stemming not from fat, but sheer solidity. This kid looked like a future NFL pick. He was laughing at his friend's discomfort when he first saw Jeff.

"Hey, who are you?"

But Jeff was no longer looking at Pudgy or Red. He was looking at the top of the cliff, the spot from which the pudgy kid must have jumped.

It was high. *Real* high.

"Hey, new kid …"

Jeff turned back and faced Pudgy directly. "You jump from up there?"

"Yeah. *You* wanna try it?"

Jeff looked back at the cliff. It seemed so *high*. Yet Pudgy, (wait—Red called him Neil), had done it, so why couldn't …?

"Hey, new kid, I'm talkin' to you. You wanna try it or not?"

No two ways about it. This was a challenge.

Don't be afraid.

Jeff turned back to Neil. "Yeah. Sure."

"Awesome, come on!"

Jeff kicked off his sneakers, removed his shirt and socks, and followed the others up a narrow path leading to the top of the cliff. Neil was in the lead, followed by Red, with Jeff bringing up the rear. Where the path ended, there was a wall of rock, over which the boys scrambled before getting to a flat rocky bluff overlooking the lake.

Still, it seemed so *high*.

"This is it?"

"Yeah," Red answered. "It's real easy. You just stand back and take a running leap …" Both he and Neil stepped back about ten feet from the edge and ran in unison right off the bluff. Seconds later, there were two loud splashes from below, and a cry of "Come on!"

This was the moment of truth. He walked over to where Red had stood and made ready to jump. At the last second, he slowed to a stop. No way would he do this. So what if these kids called him a wimp? It wouldn't be the first time. It was better that than getting his neck broken.

"Well? You gonna do it or not?"

Don't be afraid.

Suddenly, the fear was gone. Jeff backed up and started his run once again toward the open nothingness past the edge of the bluff. One second, there was a rocky surface beneath his bare feet, the next, he was in the open air plummeting toward …

… a rock! A huge jagged rock!

They'd set him up. Beneath the surface of the lake was a rock and the other boys knew about it. They knew to avoid it, and they were using it to have some fun with the nerdy new kid. They …

Don't be afraid.

Jeff hit the water and sank below its surface. It was like diving into a sea of ice cubes. And there was no rock.

That was a mystery to be solved later. Right now, Jeff was running out of air, so he kicked his way upward. No sooner did his head break the surface than he heard the sounds of clapping and cheering.

"All RIGHT. Way to go!"

"New kid's OK!"

"Come on, we can't keep calling him 'new kid.' What's your name?"

Jeff stepped out of the water, onto the bank "Jeff. Jeff Strickland. I just moved into town. On Crow's Nest Pike."

Red put out his hand. "I'm Andy. Andy Buchanan. The Incredible Bulk over here is Neil Coleman."

Neil stepped forward. "Bite me, Donkey-Breath."

Andy took a fighter's stance and Neil did the same. "Yeah?"

"Yeah."

"What are you gonna do about it?"

"This." With a speed Jeff found surprising in so big a kid, Neil tackled Andy and they both fell back into the lake.

Andy broke free, grabbed the elastic of Neil's swim trunks and pulled down. "Full moon!"

Neil pulled up his trunks and made for Andy. "You are *so* dead, Donkey-Breath."

"It's *Mister* Donkey-Breath to you and don't you forget it."

By this time, both boys were grinning even as they tussled, and what Jeff at first took to be a fight in the making, had materialized into a game of good-natured roughhousing.

"I don't know about you guys, but I'm gonna jump again."

"Cool."

The "fight" ended and the three boys raced each other to the top of the cliff. Jeff came in first, but to him, the real victory was gaining something in minutes that had previously taken years.

Acceptance.

#

"The rock? Yeah. Sorry, man. I should have told you about it before." Neil said. "This is a quarry, see? It's, like, over a hundred feet deep in some spots. It's also really clear, so you look at something like that rock over there? It looks real close to the surface, but it's really far down."

"How far?"

"I dunno."

"Fifty feet, maybe?" Andy guessed.

"No, more." This from Neil.

Jeff viewed the rock from his vantage point on the bluff. It sure did look like it was close to the surface, but having done several jumps from that height, he knew it was not. It was a neat optical illusion, though. It would be interesting to know …

"Watch it, you guys, I'm going to jump again."

Jeff backed up to get a good running start while the others moved away from the brink. He paused, filled his lungs with air, then started his approach. This time, instead of jumping from a running start, he reached the edge in three long, deliberate strides. He then jumped up, as if from a diving board, and arched his body, head down, hands poised to hit the water first.

No sooner was his body immersed in the icy water than he began a fast scissor-kicking motion while pushing the water backward with his arms. This, along with the momentum from his dive, drove him farther and faster beneath the surface. He opened his eyes and could make out the shape of something large and gray, looming closer.

Jeff's kicks and strokes became more aggressive as he felt the water grow colder the deeper he got. He also knew that he was running out of air.

Kick. Stroke. Harder. Faster.

Closer.

Bubbles started to spew from his mouth. He was able to check his exhalation, but he didn't know for how much longer he could do so. The rock really was deeper than it looked and if he didn't reach it soon, he'd have to give up.

Kick. Stroke. Harder. Faster. Closer. Closer.

His hand reached out and touched something solid.

He'd made it!

He twisted his body around so that his legs were on the rock, bent his knees, scrunched his body, and kicked upward, hard. The next thing he knew he was rocketing upward through the water, exhaling, no longer able to keep the air in his lungs. He kicked and stroked harder than ever until his head broke the surface.

Jeff stayed where he was, treading water and gulping in the air, only half aware of the attention he was getting from the others.

"Did you do it?"

"How far was it?

Still panting, Jeff made his way to the beach, and just lay there on his back, spent. He was aware of the two successive splashes and he wondered if any of the others had tried also to touch the rock. Having done it once, he had no desire to do it again.

As he lay there, his gaze happened to fall on the bluff, where he saw a quick and sudden movement. He sat up to a reclining position, never taking his eyes from that spot. Then he saw it again.

Someone was standing on the bluff, staring down at him.

Jeff squinted, trying to make out details, but could not. That it was a man, a tall man, was the only thing he could tell. The man's back was to the sun, which put the sun in Jeff's eyes, so all he could make out was a shadowy outline.

Then it was gone.

Jeff stood up and called to the others "Hey you guys." Neil was the first to clamber to shore, and seeing Jeff's gaze, looked up at the bluff.

"What is it?"

"You see him?"

"See who?"

"There was a guy up there."

Neil shook his head. Andy, having made it to shore, did likewise.

"Maybe it's the demon," said Andy.

Jeff was all attention. "Demon?"

"Sure," Andy said. "Dontcha know, these woods are …" He lowered his voice to a tone of dramatic menace, "… haaaauuuunnnnnnted."

"Haunted?"

"Yeah," Andy went on in the same tone. "By the ghosts of Dunbar's Raiders …" He lowered his voice still further to a near whisper, " … and the demon."

"What are you talking about?"

"You don't know?" snorted Neil.

"He just moved here," Andy pointed out. "Give him a break.

"Anyhow, Isaac Dunbar was a hero in the Revolution," Andy went on, "and Taylorville was the place where the Americans kept all their guns and cannons and stuff. So the British were gonna sneak into Taylorville from the old carriage road in these woods. They were gonna come in the dead of night and burn it to the ground. General Burgess had over a hundred troops and he ordered his men to torch every house in Taylorville. Kill every man, woman, and child.

"But Isaac Dunbar knew they were coming, and he got a bunch of the farmers together and they hid in the woods and waited for Burgess and his men. That night, when Burgess and his men came down the old carriage road, Dunbar and his guys were waiting for them. Even though there were maybe thirty of them, they wiped out Burgess and all his troops. You ever hear of Dunbar's Massacre?"

"Nope."

"Well, that was it. Not one of Dunbar's men was killed. Not one of the British troops survived. To this day, they say that when there's a full moon, if you listen very carefully, you can hear the sounds of troops marching in the woods."

"Yeah, right," snorted Neil.

"They also say," Andy went on, paying him no attention, "that if you listen *really* carefully, you can hear the sounds of men screaming for their lives. That's because the ghosts of Burgess and his men are still trying to destroy Taylorville. But they can't because the ghosts of Dunbar's raiders are there to stop them."

Neil blew a raspberry, then pretended to snore. Jeff didn't join in on the teasing. He was enjoying himself. "What about the demon?"

"The Backwoods Demon," Andy replied. "Since the days of the witch trials, there's this legend that these woods are haunted by this demon from hell. Kind of like Bigfoot.

"People who've been in the woods at night claim they've heard something big crashing through the woods. Of course, no one's ever seen the thing 'cause the people who've seen it never come out of the woods alive," Andy went on, resuming the exaggerated dramatic tone he'd adopted earlier.

"'Course not, there's no such thing," said Neil.

"Still, people have disappeared in the woods," ventured Andy.

"There's a few million acres of woods out there, Donkey Breath," answered Neil. "You go deep enough into those woods, you ain't never gonna come out of there, demon or no demon."

"You really believe in that stuff, Andy?" asked Jeff.

Andy paused. "No, not really. But you gotta admit. It's pretty creepy what happened to that lady a couple weeks ago."

"What lady?"

"Some lady was walking by the ridge a couple weeks ago. They found her handbag, but the rest of her just disappeared."

"Probably a bear," Neil said.

"There haven't been bears in these woods for years," Andy retorted.

"I'd believe a bear before I'd believe a demon."

"Whatever. We'd better head out of here before Parsons comes around."

"Who's Parsons?"

"Police Chief. If he catches you here, he'll take you down to the station and make your parents come get you. If it's a ranger, they'll just chase you away."

The boys put on their sneakers and began gathering their clothes. Jeff reached for his Phantom of the Opera shirt. Andy said, "You see that show?"

"Yeah, last year in Boston."

"Me too. Hey, you ever see the movie?"

"Which one?" Jeff had read the Gaston Leroux classic and knew that it had inspired numerous film versions.

"The original," replied Andy. "That's the only one worth a damn."

Jeff was impressed. Kids his age didn't go in for classic movies. His interest in old horror movies was one of the things that had set him apart from his age mates. Now that he'd found someone else who shared his interest, he had to ask: "You like any of the other old horror films?"

"Oh, yeah. You?"

"Sure."

If Jeff was impressed, Neil was not. "Oh great. Two geeks. Bad enough I had to deal with Donkey-Breath there. Now I got Strickland, I mean Geekland."

"It's *Mister* Geekland to you and don't you forget it!"

Jeff took a fighter's stance, Neil did the same and both boys began pummeling each other with mock blows. Andy had picked up a sneaker and was using it as a microphone. "And Geekland lands a blow to the Bulk's gut. The Bulk is down, no he's up and he comes back swinging. What a fight, folks, WHAT A FIGHT."

The "fight" continued until all three boys could no longer contain themselves. Laughing, they resumed dressing, sure that Parsons or the rangers would be by shortly.

When Jeff mentioned the trails he'd followed and how he'd come upon this place. Neil laughed and told him there was a quicker way to Crow's Nest Pike. Jeff tagged along with them, glad to prolong the time with his new friends. He knew that it was past the two o'clock be-home-by curfew his mother had set. He was fully aware that he was in for a tongue-lashing and a possible grounding. After the events of the day, however, he decided it was worth any wrath his mother might send his way.

He'd actually made friends and won their respect.

Not only that, but he'd been treated to the kind of local color any young horror buff couldn't help but relish. Haunted woods and a--a demon from hell. Neat!

43

2

"What you had is a Spirit Quest, my man."

"A what?"

"A Spirit Quest."

Elliot Ryan was standing in "I-Can-Get-It-For-You" Geary's yard while Geary was rummaging through the trunk of a rusted Plymouth Duster. The Duster looked to have been old even before Elliot was in diapers. The whole of Geary's property, in fact, looked like a junk yard. Elliot wondered what else Geary had stashed around the place. Word was that Geary dealt in all kinds of stuff you didn't dare ask for at your local Kmart, not just drugs.

Old tires, discarded appliances, car parts, and other rusty and smelly stuff were strewn all over the place. The neighbors might be expected to complain, except there were no neighbors. Geary's place was set back nearly a quarter of a mile from the road. There was a stretch of trees on both sides and the Ridge adjoined the rear of the property. There was even a junkyard dog in a penned-up area, the only metal structure in the place not covered with rust. It was a huge mean-looking black and brown *thing* which was all teeth, sinew, and meanness. Ever since Elliot had ridden onto the grounds, it had barked and growled at full volume, throwing itself at the wire walls of its enclosure. Elliot wasn't sure it couldn't get out, but Geary didn't seem to care. Bastard was probably tickled at the grief he was causing.

"Spirit Quest?"

"GODDAMN. Don't they teach you kids nothing' in that school you go to? Yeah, that's what them Injun tribes out west used to do. When a kid was, oh, maybe a little younger than you, he went out into the desert, all alone. No food. No water. Just a little …" Here, Geary pinched his thumb and index finger together and tapped them to his lips. "And he stayed out there till he had a vision."

"What kind of vision?" Elliot had elected to tell Geary about his dream (that's what he's decided it had been). He figured Geary might get a kick out of the story, but the dealer seemed to be taking it quite seriously.

"Oh, any kind. Maybe some heap big Great Spirit come down, tell him that him be heap big great warrior. Kill many white-eyes. Ugh." Geary started laughing, and Elliot wondered whether Geary was making a joke at his expense.

"Or maybe the totem animal of the tribe would appear and speak to him," Geary continued, serious again. "Kid would go back, talk to the medicine man of the tribe, find out what it meant, and that would tell him what to do with the rest of his life."

"Might he …" Elliot hesitated. How should he word this? "Might he actually see through the eyes of the animal?"

"Sure," Geary replied as he stopped rummaging through the trunk and faced Elliot with a look the boy didn't like. "There's only one problem with your story, kid."

"What's that?"

"For you to have a vision like that, you'd have to be on something a lot stronger than what I've been selling you. You ain't been gettin' that shit from me, so you must be gettin' it from somewhere else." He took a step forward. Elliot now saw that Geary had removed a jack handle from the trunk and was clenching it in a way that seemed very menacing.

"So tell me, kid, you getting' it from somewhere else?"

Elliot took a step back. He was no coward and had no fear of confrontation, physical or otherwise. He'd licked Desmond Corey and held his own against Howard Corey. Both the Coreys had half a head on him, plus a good twenty pounds. But this guy was *different*. Geary was big and muscular. He looked like Bluto from the old Popeye cartoons, if Bluto ever had the crazed look of a rabid rat.

"No, way man! Come on Geary, you know …"

Geary dropped the jack handle and started laughing. He stepped forward and gave Elliot a playful (though not painless) punch in the shoulder. "I was just yankin' your chain, kid, relax!"

Elliot had backed up to within a few feet of the dog's pen and the beast renewed its barrage of angry inhuman sounds. This made Elliot jump and Geary laugh all the harder, as he turned back to the remains of the Duster.

"Here ya go." He pulled out a cellophane bag which held a baggie full of "the best shit you'll get anywhere." Elliot handed him his money and Geary grabbed the neckline of Elliot's T-shirt and dropped the bag down his shirt. "Enjoy. Y'all come back, now, y'hear?"

"Thanks, Geary."

Elliot hopped on his bike and pedaled hard. He was always glad to finish his business with Geary and get away fast, never more so than today. For a second, he thought that Geary might even loose the dog on him. Elliot pedaled faster and over the clicking of his gears, he could still hear Geary's shrill and sickening laugh.

#

Just when the whim hit, Elliot couldn't say, but at some point, he decided to ride home via Sand Point Road rather than through the main drag of Dunbar's Crossing. It was a more rural and relaxing ride, despite a couple of steep hills. Besides, Elliot felt the need to unwind and burn something off after the unpleasant encounter with Geary.

Sand Point Road was dotted with a number of farms, sparsely spaced, and very little traffic. Occasionally, he might smell cow or pig shit, but it was still a pleasant ride. Anyway, Elliot didn't object to the four-legged pigs who might make their presence known on this road. He did object to the two-legged ones who'd hassle him every chance they got. Particularly if they knew what was tucked in his shirt. Particularly Parsons.

This was why Elliot chose the road that took him past the McSweeney farm.

It wasn't until he'd ridden a hundred yards past the property that it dawned on him. He braked the bike hard, nearly skidding off the road, then headed back to make sure he really saw what he thought he did.

Sure enough. Right behind the farmhouse, with its VOTE RAND COREY sign was a pile of burnt-out timbers.

He stood there, straddling the bike, staring, when he noticed a woman and a little kid in the yard. The kid was about four, and the woman, a mousy-haired, tired-looking farmwife, was chasing him. She looked up and noticed Elliot.

"Yeah?"

"Uh." Elliot wasn't sure how to ask what he wanted to know, so he just let the words spill out. "What happened over there? Your barn I mean ...?"

"Burned down."

"Uh. When?"

"'Bout two weeks ago. Why?"

"Oh, uh, nothin. It's OK. Thanks."

The woman went back to chasing the kid. Elliot got back on his bike, and began thinking.

The last time he'd been down Sand Point Road was when he and the old man did that job on Kurwen's Caddy about a month back. Not that he'd paid much attention, but he was sure the barn was standing back then. He'd have remembered seeing it burnt down. Besides, the farm wife said it happened two weeks ago.

Yet, he'd seen the remnants of that barn about two weeks ago. During his dream, or hallucination. Or Spirit Quest.

In other words, the last time Elliot was *physically* in this spot, the barn was standing. When he was here on his "Spirit Quest" it was a pile of still-smoking ruins.

Two weeks ago.

Elliot reasoned that if you saw something that wasn't there, you were hallucinating. Even a dream was a kind of hallucination, one you had when you were asleep. On the other hand, if you saw something that *was* there, *was* real, that was no hallucination. To take it a step further, if you saw something that *was* there when you *weren't*, that was something on a whole new level.

He had been on that level.

Like most casual drug users, Elliot was aware that narcotics like coke and heroin supposedly stimulated the senses. Was it possible that weed did the same thing?

First things first, though, and the first thing was to stash his latest purchase. Elliot never kept his weed at home; he had many little hidey-holes throughout the woods. The window casement in the ruins beside the carriage road was only one of those. There was a nearer one.

About a mile past McSweeney's was a side road that led to a trail head. This was Elliot's immediate destination. When he got there, he locked up the bike and made for the woods. The path he took was barely discernible through a growth of thorns and brambles, but Elliot negotiated it effortlessly and unerringly. His bare arms would be covered with blood and scratches, but he didn't care. These obstacles kept others off the trail, which meant fewer chances of him being spotted or his stash found by some casual hiker.

The path eventually gave way to a heavily wooded area. It was only because he'd done this so many times that Elliot could spot the narrow and unmarked trail that led deeper into the woods. He jogged it, never breaking stride, even when it turned into a semi-steep incline, before giving way to a rocky outcropping.

Here, Elliot paused for the first time in his run, looking for something very specific. He hadn't used this hiding place for a while, so maybe it was …

No, there it was, a large tree, fallen on its side. It had been farther away from the outcropping than he'd remembered, but there it was.

Stepping up to the tree, Elliot kneeled and with painstaking slowness, ran his hand along the under-surface of the wood. Somewhere toward the base, he could recall—yes, here it was, a hole in the trunk. He'd almost missed it. It was well hidden beneath some ground vegetation, which made it all the better as a hiding place.

After poking gently into the hole with a stick he'd picked up, Elliot determined that there were no critters hiding inside. It was a deep hole and Elliot could wedge the cellophane bag in it so that it wouldn't be dislodged unless he himself removed it. In fact, a smoke right now might be nice.

Elliot was about to remove the bag and indulge, when he heard voices shouting, coming from past the outcropping. He made his way back onto the rocky surface which ended in a drop-off. Looking over the edge of the bluff, he noticed the three boys.

Two of them were splashing in the quarry below. One of them was lying on the shore and seemed to be staring directly at him.

Elliot stepped back, suddenly uncomfortable.

No one had seen him hide the package, of that he was certain. Still, it seemed wisest not to linger. He stepped away from the outcropping and ran back down the trail to his bike.

Now that these things were out of the way, Elliot could devote more thought to something else. If this Spirit Quest, or whatever it was, told him the truth about McSweeney's barn, might it not have revealed other truths as well? The cave for instance? Although Elliot considered himself familiar with the woods and all their trails, he never heard of a cave anywhere on Dunbar's Ridge.

But if that part of his vision was accurate, Elliot had a pretty good idea how to go about finding it. Man, wouldn't that be something?

3

Excerpt from the Taylorville News, October 19, 1997:

Toll of Animal Deaths Increasing
Officials Recommend Caution

ANIMAL Control officials expressed caution earlier today over the large number of dead animals found in recent weeks throughout the tri-county area.

"An inordinately large number of animal corpses have been found along Dunbar's Ridge as well as the adjoining wooded areas," stated Animal Control Officer Theresa Boorman.

"The dead animals were woodchucks, squirrels, snakes, raccoons, and even a skunk."

Boorman went on to emphasize that these deaths were not attributable to natural causes or hunting.

"They seem to be acts of extreme predation," Boorman went on to say. "The bodies of these animals were torn and mangled."

When asked what type of predator might be expected to produce such devastation, Boorman declined to comment.

The bodies of the animals are being brought to local veterinary facilities for analysis.

Residents are asked to keep their pets indoors and to report any instances of dead animals to their local Department of Animal Control.

4

Elliot leaned back, drew a long breath into his lungs. He held the smoke down for as long as he could before beginning a measured, unhurried exhalation. He repeated the process and waited.

It was two months since he'd seen things through eyes other than his own. For two months, he'd been trying to repeat the experience. He was beginning to think that it had been a fluke, a by-product of some mutant lot that Geary had sold him. Still, getting high was one of the things he loved doing so, worst case, he'd get a good buzz if nothing else.

Tonight especially, he needed to get high. He'd had a hell of an argument with the old man over something stupid. The old man had misplaced a tool and blamed Elliot for taking it and not putting it back properly. Elliot proclaimed his innocence, which got the old man even madder, which in turn, got Elliot even madder. Within minutes, they were yelling at each other. Elliot told his father what he could do with the tool once he found it. The old man was close to laying his ham-hock-sized hand on the kid. The old lady was clutching her Bible and crying about Elliot not getting along with his father. Finally, Elliot just stomped out.

He took another long toke and noticed that the joint, his second, was almost spent. He was debating whether to light up a third when his eyes started doing funny things.

Though it was late dusk and the light was fading, Elliot could still make out the trees through the ruined walls with some clarity. Overhead, the stars were clear and bright, not like the last time. He remembered how that summer storm broke and drenched him before he got home. All of a sudden, the stars and the trees morphed into those other funky uneven shapes he'd seen last time.

He was back in the cave. He was moving.

Once again, he felt the coolness all over his body, through his flannel shirt, windbreaker, jeans, thick crew socks, and Gore-Tex boots. Once again, he had a sense of extreme power, gliding through the darkness into the night. A night that was his.

A night when no one would accuse him of misplacing a tool, or threatening him with ham-hock-sized hands, or crying to him about not getting along with his old man. A night when he'd tear the Coreys, or anyone else who messed with him, a new one—literally.

Familiar sensations coming back to him. A soft wet surface. Moving sideways. Up, then down. Sideways again. Shapes. Variations of the darkness. Climbing. Crawling. Walking upright. Squeezing through a mail drop of an opening, then crawling again. Climbing. A side tunnel which widened and narrowed. A wide chasm, an effortless leap. A wall with hand and footholds. A chimney-like passage leading upward. Everything quick, unforced, and natural.

Finally, open air. Rock, two high walls of it. A sky with no bursts of lightning to affront the eyes. Climbing. Atop a recognizable escarpment looking down upon trees, a clearing, a road and McSweeney's. He saw that the remains of the old barn were gone and that a new one was in the process of being built.

Suddenly, this vista ripped from his sight, giving way to a sensation of incredible speed. He was a passenger in a body that made an abrupt change in direction and was running from the escarpment into a thick wooded area. Solid, low-lying branches broke as he crashed through them, feeling the impact, but no pain.

The trees cleared and fifty feet ahead was a drop-off and the runner was making for it without slackening its speed. It leaped off the edge of the escarpment into what looked like a hundred feet of open air.

There was no fear, just a sense of power that was as inexorable as it was inexplicable. A sense of invulnerability. Falling through the air, crashing into trees, breaking branches, scattering birds and other high-climbing critters. Scraping against the trunks of trees on a maddening downward plunge. Impact, but no pain. True invincibility.

Hitting the ground, the fall broken only slightly from the trees. Then, running again through the trailless stretches of the woods. Sometimes going around obstacles, other times, just crashing past them.

Shapes speeding by so fast as to be indistinguishable. Nothing recognizable like the McSweeney farm, everything totally unfamiliar.

Sheer exhilaration.

Moving with less speed, going uphill. Coming to a fallen tree where an angry sixteen-year old had hidden his stash. Leaping upward, impossibly high, and coming down on the tree, smashing it in two at the point where he landed.

Running off the edge of the bluff, falling into icy water with a hard and delightful shock. Seeing shapes in the water, far away and below, yet as clear as if they were before from his face. Old tires. The remains of an old car. An old refrigerator. And natural formations including a rock which jutted from the far bottom …

Undulating, jetting through the water, his limbs not moving, but making rapid progress all the same. No fear of drowning.

Breaking the surface and reaching shore. Half-running, half-loping along the beach to a trail.

More speed. More crashing through branches. Very little sense of direction or whereabouts.

Wait. Something else.

A sense of destination. Movements no longer random, now purposeful.

Slow following the trail. Zeroing in on something. What?

Trail ended. The carriage road. No longer running. Walking.

Then he saw …

Pain!

Elliot Ryan saw a flash of light that faded to reveal the walls of the ruins. He was aware of holding a played joint in one hand while the other rubbed the back of his throbbing head.

He realized what happened. He saw through another's eyes as if in some half-remembered dream something so unexpected, that he jumped back, startled, bumping his head on the ruin's wall.

Elliot stood up, shaky, the effects of the weed, no doubt. Gingerly, he walked to the entrance of the ruin and looked out on the carriage road.

It was no longer dusk. It was full-fledged night now. His vision was no longer what it was when he was looking through someone (something?) else's eyes. He could not see what he was looking for.

But he knew it was there.

The last thing he saw before he bumped his head was the ruined way station where he, Elliot Ryan, had faded into the consciousness of another while smoking one of Geary's more potent offerings.

"Hello?" Nothing. "Who are you?' A little louder; still nothing.

There was no movement, but Elliot could not be certain he was alone out there. He took a step out and onto the carriage road. Suddenly, he wanted to be out of there more than anything, even if it meant being home with the old man bitching and the old lady preaching. He turned to his left and began walking, listening, but hearing nothing.

Even in the dark, Elliot knew that there was a main trail intersecting with the carriage road. It was not the one he'd been on before, out of body, but one which led to a main road. He kept walking, ever vigilant, but hearing nothing.

By the time he got to the trail, he'd convinced himself that it was what he thought it was all along. Not Geary's Spirit Quest bullshit—no way he bought into that. No, it was what he'd thought it was initially—an out-of-body experience during which he'd seen things that were real as opposed to a dream where the mind made up all kinds of weird shit. Who knows? Maybe some people did have certain extrasensory abilities that drugs were able to stimulate.

By the time he got to the main road, he was feeling fine once again. That he was one of the unique few who could have such an experience filled him with elation. OK, he was freaked out for a moment there, but so what? He'd been through something awesome, something other people couldn't begin to understand. Would he do it again? Damn straight he would.

But first, he was going to find the cave.

\#

Elliot had a policy of never going to the same hidey-hole twice in a row. Last time, he used the one in the ruins. This time, it would be the fallen tree overlooking the quarry.

It was early afternoon and Elliot knew the old man was expecting him at home to work on an engine job. Elliot wanted to be on time, not because he enjoyed the old man's company or because they were getting along any better. It was just that he didn't want the old man to become suspicious. So he had cut out of school early on his errand of vital importance.

The first thing he noted as he approached the tree was that it was reclining at an unusual angle. He supposed that it had somehow shifted its position, though he couldn't imagine how. Like all the local youths, he'd been coming to this spot for as long as he could remember. In all that time, the tree had lain in precisely the same position.

When he got closer, he saw that just below the upper branches, the tree was broken in two. As if something inordinately heavy had landed on it.

Or leaped on it.

Elliot crouched down and examined the spot where the break occurred. There was no doubt. The trunk was shattered at that point, changing the angle at which it lay on the ground.

His first instinct was to look for a logical explanation, as he did after his visions under the influence. He had been ready to write them off as particularly vivid dreams. The vision of the destroyed barn, he attributed to some undiscovered sense-heightening properties of the herb that science might one day explain.

The tree? Well, it had been there since God-knows-when and had just rotted through, that's all.

Then how to explain the *other* thing he saw?

Looking down past the tree, he noted that the vegetation was crushed flat and that low-hanging tree branches were broken, not just haphazardly, but systematically. It was as if something huge and heavy had barreled up the slope, indifferent to the obstacles in its path, blazing a trail of destruction.

Elliot ran his hand along the underside of the fallen trunk until he found his stash. He stuck it in his windbreaker pocket, no longer interested in copping a smoke.

He walked to the edge of the bluff. His eyes began a slow and patient scan of the opposite shore. It was impossible to be sure, but at one point along the beach, it looked as if there was a break in the trees. Had it been there before? Again, Elliot couldn't be sure.

He focused on that spot, squinting. Was it power of suggestion or did the trees beyond that part of the beach actually have fewer branches? Had something large trampled the ground, forging a path where none had been previously? If you followed that path, wouldn't you emerge on the carriage road, which in turn would lead to the ruins?

Elliot stood on the brink, not only of the quarry, but of a new insight. It was one thing for one's mind to veer off on some astral plane, to see sights, and undergo sensations in which one's body was not participating. But this was no insubstantial, out-of-body occurrence. It was decidedly in-body, but not his own.

Besides, when he emerged from the ruins, didn't he have a sense of being watched? That there was something *there*? Not some spook, some will-o'-the-wisp, but something *solid*?

Elliot couldn't quite decide how he felt about this revelation. It was weird, no question. But it was also exciting. The roller coaster rush of racing across the landscape at undreamed-of velocity — it was awesome beyond belief. Did he want to give that up because of a few misgivings?

He turned back and began walking along the trail to the main road. He had a lot of thinking to do. For once, Elliot actually looked forward to spending the afternoon with the old man, working on cars, and doing that thinking.

5

It was the first week in November. Jeff awoke in the cold night air. Opening his eyes, he found some things wrong with this picture.

He was fully dressed in his parka, flannel shirt, jeans, thermal socks, and boots.

He wasn't in his bed; he was on the wooden bench on the back deck.

The back yard looked exactly as it did when the Stricklands first moved in. The wooden fence that Dad had had built to keep Rusty from the woods, and vice versa, was gone. A stretch of trees bordered the back yard. Beyond the trees lay the thick of the woods, the entire scene covered with a light dusting of snow,

Jeff was puzzled, but delighted, having become, by this time, used to unusual nocturnal occurrences. He got up and walked to the rail, watching his breath as he exhaled in the chill winter air. Whatever vision was being bestowed upon him was essentially true-to-life, despite the lack of the fence. It *had* snowed earlier in the evening, a wispy, powdery dusting. It lasted only a few hours, but long enough to transform everything it touched into a surreal vista of whiteness. It *had* been pretty darn cold; when Jeff took Rusty for his evening run, both boy and dog couldn't wait to get back indoors. This was unusual for Rusty, who normally took his time about doing his business.

A cold breeze blew and Jeff put his hands in his coat pockets for warmth. His right hand closed on an object, and he pulled out his

Swiss Army knife, a gift from his father, and his pride and joy. He'd even taken one of those label-making guns and affixed his initials JSS (Jeffrey Steven Strickland) to the handle. He replaced the knife and began pacing the length of the deck for warmth.

Despite the unpleasant cold, Jeff had no desire to go back in the house. In the past, any manifestation of *The Presence* brought with it some reward. It might be an insight, an impression, or just a brain fart that panned out for the best. If not for that urge he had months ago to take a walk in the woods, he wouldn't have befriended Neil and Andy. It turned out that they both went to his school and without their camaraderie, he'd have had a much harder time adjusting. So Jeff was certain he was here for a purpose and resolved to stick around to learn just what that purpose was.

He'd been pacing the deck when something in the woods drew his attention.

Someone was out there.

It was a man, Jeff was sure of that. If he strained his eyes, he thought he could see the outline of a man standing there. If he strained his ears, he thought he could hear the sound of breathing.

"Hello?"

There was no answer. The only response was a tentative movement, as if the visitor was undecided whether to approach or retreat.

"What do you want?"

No response, no movement.

"What are you doing out there?"

For a split second, Jeff supposed that his parents might hear him. But no, they wouldn't hear him, because he wasn't in the house, not really. The house had a backyard with a wooden fence. Jeff was—well, in a *different* place, somehow. He could yell his head off and neither his parents nor Rusty would hear a thing.

Strangely, he also felt *safe*. If he were alone in the house during waking hours with a strange man in his yard, he'd be scared and on the phone to Chief Parsons in a heartbeat. But now, he knew that he was protected and that this intruder had no power to harm him. He was the vampire hunter, Van Helsing, in a bunker filled with garlic, wolfsbane, and crucifixes. He was impervious to the nefarious machinations of Count Dracula who could only wait and seethe in anger at a distance.

Emboldened, he shouted, "You'd better get out of here!"

To his surprise, there was movement, less tentative this time. A dark shape emerged from the trees for the briefest of seconds before fading back in the darkness. Then, there were the sounds of footsteps, slow at first, then more rapid, and less distinct.

The intruder was departing.

He'd done it, frightened away the monster without succumbing to fear!

Suddenly, he was back in the house and there was a noise.

Had the intruder of the night somehow doubled back? Had he had gotten *inside* the house?

No. This was the sound of someone crying, not a sound of a furtive prowler intent on wickedness.

Jeff moved slowly toward the sound, suddenly aware that the house was immersed in absolute darkness. He dared not move too quickly. He still recalled the pain when he tripped over the box on that first night. He was now familiar enough with the house and furniture to move, if not with speed, with confidence toward the living room. The sound emanated from there.

Feeling his way, Jeff found himself beneath the arch that separated the dining area from the living room. He stopped and listened. Sure enough, it was coming from this room; to be more specific, from the couch. It sounded like someone burying his face in something soft and plush.

"Are you OK?" Jeff whispered.

The cries stopped momentarily, then resumed in a spasm of sobs, of someone in severe physical or emotional distress. Jeff took a step forward and whispered, "It's OK. Don't be scared. No one's going to hurt you."

As he walked forward gradually, the darkness seemed to dispel ever so slightly, and Jeff began to make out the contours of the couch. Less distinct was the form huddled on the couch and Jeff could not tell whether it was a boy or a girl. It was definitely a kid and the kid was huddled over, facing away. His or her body convulsed too quickly for Jeff to get a fix on it in the sparse light.

"Can I help you?" Jeff whispered.

No sooner had Jeff spoken than the miniscule amount of light faded, as did the sound of crying. Jeff stood there, unmoving in the darkness, wondering what he'd just experienced. He was ready to make for his bedroom, when he found himself standing on the threshold of that very room. The house was no longer dark. Moonlight streamed through his window and outside, the breeze gave way to a fierce and keening wind.

Whatever the house at 1604 Crow's Nest Pike had meant to show him, it was over. He was back in his room, now dressed in his pajamas. Everything else in the room was as he'd left it before going to bed.

Jeff got back into bed and spent the rest of the night in a deep and dreamless sleep. In the morning, he'd wake up and find the parka, flannel shirt, jeans, thermal socks, and boots he'd worn the night before draped on the chair.

The only difference, and he wouldn't notice it until a few days later, was that his Swiss Army knife was gone.

6

From the end of the summer through the fall, Elliot grabbed every opportunity he could to go off into the woods. He remembered that the cave was situated between two walls; at the top was a high escarpment, overlooking trees. There was a clearing, a road, and McSweeney's farm. Below was a mountain lake. What he had to do, therefore, was find an escarpment by a lake, using McSweeney's as a starting point. It took Elliot several treks over these trails to realize that this strategy wasn't going to be easy. After several promising, but false starts, Elliot had been forced to turn back.

Toward the end of December, Taylorville was in the midst of a thaw, a break from the early and fierce winters typical of New England; Taylorville being no exception. It was a balmy forty degrees, which Elliot used to his advantage.

Once again, with the McSweeney farm as a point of reference, he headed for the woods. After a few miles, he saw something off-trail in the distance that looked promising. An outcropping of rocks. Elliot headed in its direction.

The outcropping looked to be between fifty and seventy-five feet high, as Elliot approached. There was no sign of a lake, but this did not discourage him. The outcropping extended in both directions and Elliot figured that by circling it, he'd find a lake if there was one.

He'd gone perhaps a quarter of a mile when he came to a crevice in the face of the rock. Remembering that there was such a gap when he emerged from the cave, Elliot decided that this find called for further exploration.

At first, the crevice was wide enough for him to pass through with ease. After a few curves, it became clear he could only make progress by going sideways. This proved to be difficult, due to the fleece parka he was wearing, so he simply took it off and wedged it between the two rock walls before proceeding.

The narrow channel continued for another twenty feet. It curved to the right, and then opened up for another ten feet, only to be blocked. A wall of rock loomed in front of him. Elliot was about to turn back. It was getting cold and his progress appeared to be halted, when he noticed that there was a crawlspace under the rock.

Maybe this was it?

The channel afforded him enough space to get on his hands and knees for a closer look. Yes, there was definitely a passage here. He lowered himself onto his belly and wormed his way under the huge rocky barrier. Once in the crawlspace, he was surprised at how spacious it was, allowing him to move forward more quickly than he'd originally supposed. Elliot resisted the temptation to move quickly, however. He recalled climbing up a steep vertical passage before reaching outside air. He had no desire to be taken by surprise and end up falling down, through that very same opening. He forced himself to move at a literal crawl. Then he saw sunlight.

The crawlspace ended and Elliot found himself in a continuation of the cleft. Above him was a chill, cloudless sky, framed against walls of rock, which, in warmer weather, Elliot might deem climbable. Ahead of him, the crevice continued for another twenty feet, before curving off to the right. The chill in the air was starting to get to him, and he was just debating making his way back, when he noticed something.

Just short of the curve, there was a gap between the floor and the left-hand wall of the crevice. Elliot approached it, got down on his belly and looked inside.

It was wide enough to accommodate his head and shoulders and when Elliot felt for a floor, he felt none. He reached as far down as he could into the open space below ground level, and felt nothing. He emerged from the opening, took his lighter out of his pocket, stuck his head in the hole again, and flicked. The light was not strong, but he could see a passage leading down and a draft of air coming from below. He touched the sides of the wall and touched a surface which felt like a moist fusion of mud and clay.

This was it!

Elliot cursed himself for not bringing a flashlight. This was really it, and all he could do was stand on the outside like a schmuck. That he could find the place again, he had no doubt, but the day was half over, and he'd never make it back before dark. Besides, he wanted to explore the cave; really explore it. Who knows? It might even serve as another place to hide his stash. It might even be fun to get high in here; he'd never done it in a cave before.

Elliot made his way back to where he'd left his parka. Yes, he'd definitely be back. He'd make his way out of the cleft, check out the promontory further (there was just enough daylight for that). He'd find out if there was a lake at its base (there was, a frozen one), and if so, make his way back at his earliest convenience.

#

Between jobs for the old man as well as weather delays, his earliest convenience turned out to be late next April.

On a brisk Saturday morning, Elliot was traipsing through the woods. In his rucksack were a cellophane bag of weed, a jackknife, two flashlights, and four skeins of clothesline, 250 feet each.

Once again, he found the outcropping of rock, the crevice in the face of the rock, and the narrow channel leading to the crawlspace. This time, he wore a light cloth jacket and was able to negotiate the narrowness without difficulty.

Once again, he wormed his way through the crawlspace, moving with more confidence, knowing he wouldn't fall through some hole in the earth.

Once again, he saw sunlight, then the gap between the floor and the left-hand wall of the crevice.

Removing his rucksack, he took one skein of clothesline and cut a three-foot length. He then took one of the flashlights and tied the clothesline around it. He knotted the two ends together and looped it around his neck. He took the other flashlight, and inserting his head and shoulders into the opening, turned it on, and aimed it downward into the darkness.

It was a vertical passage, narrow on top, wider at the bottom, about fifteen feet altogether. There were sufficient hand and footholds; he could climb it easily, both ways. In the narrower parts, he might need to brace himself with his back pressed against one wall, but it was doable. The trick was getting his gear down there. To do that, Elliot simply replaced the extra flashlight in the rucksack, tied one of the straps to the end of the clothesline, then lowered it gently. Using the flashlight around his neck, Elliot determined that the rucksack made it to the cave floor below, at which time, he let go his end of the clothesline. He turned on the flashlight and proceeded to climb down the passageway.

Elliot proceeded with wariness even though he'd done rock climbing (it was impossible to grow up in the vicinity of Dunbar's Ridge and *not* do rock climbing) on more challenging routes. The hand and footholds of the passage were not hard, like rock. They were firm, but gave the impression that they might yield under his weight. At each step, Elliot made sure his hands and feet had four points of contact on a solid surface. Only when he had those points of contact did he move a limb to another hand or foothold, or aim the flashlight in another direction. In this manner, he reached the bottom of the passage. He found a protruding rock and tied one end of clothesline to it. He then took the flashlight from around his neck and aimed it ahead of him, making his way forward through the cool subterranean air. As he progressed, he fed out the remainder of the clothesline as he went.

From this point on, all of Elliot's preconceived notions about caves got shot to hell. Years ago, he'd seen *Journey to the Center of the Earth* on cable. The characters walked upright through underground passages. He'd also seen the movie where Tom Sawyer and Becky Thatcher made their way through the lighted movie-set simulated passages of McDougal's Cave. They'd walked upright also. While Elliot didn't expect illumination, he did expect to stand upright. Instead, he found himself crawling; walking hunched over; snaking through low passages on his belly; alternating between clay, mud, and puddles of water, inches deep. Through such passages, he had to remove the rucksack and push it in front of him to keep it dry. This was not always easy.

Nor were the tunnels consistent; one moment they were wide, then narrow. After one stretch during which he had to move sideways, he found himself facing a wide lateral gash bisecting the passage. For a moment, he contemplated broad-jumping it, but on aiming the flashlight down, and seeing no bottom, he decided against it. This was it, he figured. No way to go forward, he'd have to go back.

Then he noticed that the passage extended into a short side tunnel to his right. In that tunnel, the chasm tapered considerably, and on the other side was a ledge onto which he could easily step. This would enable him to continue going forward.

On the other side of the chasm was a passage through which he could walk upright. He did so for about fifty feet before it narrowed to a tiny slot through which Elliot wasn't certain he could fit. He got down on his belly, aimed the flashlight through it, and saw, just beyond a four-foot drop, a spacious chamber filled with stalagmites and stalactites.

On closer examination of the slot, Elliot decided he could get through it, but not head first. It would be wiser to get on his back, and lower himself gradually down. Once again, he placed the flashlight around his neck and lay on his back. Using his hands alternately against the floor, the walls, and the low ceiling, he inched himself forward. For the longest time, his feet were dangling in midair, and for a while, Elliot was certain he'd misjudged the depth of the chamber, until his feet touched a solid floor. He then used his heels to move forward, and soon he was through. He reached back, grabbed his rucksack, and surveyed his surroundings.

Once in the chamber, Elliot paused to get his bearings. His eyes swept the chamber. The ceiling was a massive dome, and like the walls, it was peppered with formations that reminded him of candle drippings suspended in midair. Freakin' awesome, man! Had anyone else ever seen what he was seeing? Was he the first to be in this place? Wouldn't it be great to get stoned in here? Wouldn't it be even greater to bring a chick down here and ...?

No, it wouldn't.

There was something about this place that set it apart from all the other hidey-holes and screw-spots Elliot had used in the past. To use it for such purposes somehow seemed wrong.

A movement overhead caught his eye. He looked up, but there was nothing there. He took the flashlight and moved it along the ceiling. He was just starting his second sweep when he saw it again.

A bat.

"Cool."

Its flapping appeared frantic, and Elliot swung the light downward a bit. While the bat wasn't in the direct glare of the beam, it was still visible in its periphery. This seemed to soothe the animal and its motions became less frenetic. A second one joined it and the two flapped away into the darkness.

Elliot was tempted to follow their progress with the light, but decided against it. If he had a soft spot, it was for animals, and he liked them better than people. Besides, he knew that the bats posed no threat to him, why should he pose one to them? They were harmless, delicate eaters of fruit and insects, and, despite old wives' tales, too timid of humans to enmesh themselves in unsuspecting ladies' hair.

Elliot aimed his light along the sides of the chamber. If memory served correctly, there was a passage beyond this one. He made his way toward the wall of the chamber, moving the beam along the wall at the base of the cave floor.

The chamber was circular and Elliot had to trace its circumference twice before finding the passage he was looking for.

For the first time, the tunnel branched in two directions. He chose the left one.

The passage curved within a few feet and beyond the curve was a chasm far wider than the one Elliot had come across earlier. The other side was not even visible. Elliot aimed the light downward. There was no bottom to be seen and no way across.

Making his way back to the fork, Elliot decided to check the right-hand tunnel. This one led to another a rounded chamber before continuing. It was here that Elliot came to an abrupt halt.

Inside the rounded chamber was a pile of bones, bones of all sizes. Elliot recognized the remains of squirrels and woodchucks. Another set of bones was attached to an elongated spine, one that belonged to a snake. There were smaller ones, which Elliot supposed came from bats. There was also a larger set of bones and Elliot looked closer and saw a circular object, a dog collar. Someone's pooch wasn't coming home again.

Some of the bones were even larger.

Suddenly, Elliot wanted to be out of there. He no longer felt a sense of awe. Whatever lived in this cave was a predator. A squirrel or a chuck might wander in here, but certainly not a dog.

Except for the bats, these things were taken on the outside and brought here, dragged here, maybe even killed here.

Elliot grabbed hold of the clothesline and began to retrace his steps. Through the slot. Into the spacious bat chamber. Tunnels that widened, narrowed, then widened and narrowed again. Across the chasm. Through passages, alternately crawling on his belly, crawling on hands and feet, walking while hunched over, walking upright. Carrying his rucksack, pushing his rucksack, carrying it again, then pushing it again. Arriving at the wall from which no further forward motion was possible. Then the climb. Wearing the flashlight pendant as he climbed, with one end of clothesline tied to his belt loop, the other tied to the rucksack. Reaching open air and pulling his rucksack along with him.

Once outside, edging away from the gap between the floor and the left-hand wall of the crevice. Worming his way through the crawlspace with haste borne of past experience and newfound apprehension. Emerging from the cleft in the rock. Finally, running through the woods, not stopping until, looking over his shoulder, the high outcropping of rock was no longer visible.

It was only then that Elliot stopped. Was this what he'd waited so long to find? This cave was a place of darkness not only physically, but spiritually as well. What was it that lived down there? What was it that *killed* down there? Elliot had no idea, and was just as happy to keep it that way.

But as he walked back toward the main road, a cold, cold fear began to take shape in his mind, uninvited.

7

"Rusty's gone."

"Huh?" Jeff said groggily, rubbing his eyes. "What do you mean, 'gone'?"

His mom sat on the edge of her son's bed and took his hand. "Last night, your father let him out into the yard. All of a sudden we heard him barking, and when we went to let him in, he was gone."

Jeff didn't respond. Anne Strickland couldn't tell whether he was still drowsy or in shock—probably a bit of both. "We went out to look for him, we called him, but he didn't come back. We don't know where he was."

"Wasn't the gate closed?" As soon as Jeff asked the question and looked at his mother's tearful face, he felt guilty. The question sounded like an accusation to his own ears and the last thing he wanted to do right now was make his mom feel any worse than she already did.

But she just shook her head. "That's the first thing your father checked. The latch was *broken*. The gate was closed, but the latch was broken."

It was too much for Jeff to take in. "How ..." he started, then stopped. That was a foolish question. His mother wouldn't know how the latch was broken; how could she? It was intact the day before. Rusty's afternoon run was his responsibility and he performed it when he came home from school. In fact, he let himself in via the backyard entrance, and to do that, he used the gate. He'd even double-checked the latch, as always, before he let Rusty have the run of the yard.

He sat up and swung his legs out of bed. "Where's Dad?"

"He's out in the car looking for Rusty. Your poor father was up till all hours of the night driving around trying to find him. Didn't you hear us calling him?" Jeff shook his head. "Well, we need your help now. Get dressed and come on downstairs."

Jeff dressed hurriedly, his mind still trying to register the terrible news. The family adopted Rusty when Jeff was three, and he couldn't remember a time when the dog wasn't part of the family. He remembered how they all laughed when Rusty ran at lightning speed from one room to the next without any apparent reason. He remembered the expression of sheepish embarrassment on Rusty's bedraggled face whenever he was given a bath, which never failed to rouse Jeff to hysterics. He remembered how Rusty had growled when he and Neil were horsing around, and Neil had gotten Jeff in a wrestling hold. Family protector that he was, he was ready to attack anyone who dared mess with his human.

When he got downstairs, Dad was sitting at the kitchen table, looking like a man who hardly got any sleep the night before. His head was drooping, his hair unkempt, circles under his eyes, and a beaten look kept those circles company. He was wearing the same green sweater he'd been wearing the night before. If it were anyone else, Jeff would have said that the person looked like shit. Under the circumstances, he couldn't bring himself to even think that because of what his father was going through and how he was feeling.

"Dad?" Jeff ventured. "You OK?"

Peter looked up and nodded to his son. "Hi, son. I guess your mother told you what happened. I'm sorry."

Jeff went to his father and hugged him. His mom was right, the man had had a hell of night. He undoubtedly felt terrible because the dog had disappeared on his watch and he'd spent half the night scouring the area, in an attempt to compensate. "It's OK, Dad," Jeff said, hugging him tighter, and relishing the fact that his father was hugging back. "It's OK. We'll find him."

Mom immediately took charge. "Look, you two. I'm going to call the police. Peter, you take a shower and try to get some sleep. Jeff, have yourself some breakfast, then check the woods. Then come back and I'll drive around some more and you can help me look."

Peter asked. "Why are you going to bother with the police, anyway?"

"Because," answered Anne, that soul of practicality, "if the latch was broken, it might be vandalism, and I want that on record."

"OK, fine. While you're waiting, I'll drive around some more."

"Uh-uh, mister! You stay put. I want you at least semi-rested, home, and awake in case Rusty does come back. I don't want him coming home to an empty house and wandering off again. Any questions?"

Peter agreed, and Jeff threw on his parka, a pair of thermal socks, and ankle-high hiking boots. He went to the front door and looked out. His mother was right. It did look like snow was coming, and a lot of it. He'd have to get going now if he hoped to get back before it started. "I'm going out to check the woods, Mom."

"All right, but be back soon, and be careful."

Outside the season's first ice storm was in its earliest stages and it was no different from any other New England winter storm. The sky was a patchwork of low clouds, ranging from a dreary off-white to an angry threatening grayness just short of black. Gradually, the motley discoloration of the sky would give way to a consistent eggshell color along with a moist coldness in the air. Both of these were a sure sign that the heavens would pelt the earth with some very heavy and very nasty wetness.

No sooner had Jeff stepped out than he was struck by a frosty blast hitting him full in the face. He pulled up the hood of his parka and he made for the woods where he and Rusty romped. Throughout the summer and early fall, boy and dog would make for the quarry by way of the Crow's Nest Pike trail head. Once there, boy would let dog off leash. Boy and dog would race through woods to quarry (boy always coming in second). Boy would join other boys who would get a kick out of dog's wet and bedraggled expression when dog emerged from water. More than once, boy would have to prevent dog from joining him as boy jumped off twenty-foot-high bluff into water.

Slowly, an unpleasant awareness began to materialize in his gut, like a dark, venomous snake, coiling its body in anticipation of a pre-emptive strike. The process was unhurried and measured; the snake had all the time in the world. Its prey would surely come within range, not in *its* own good time, but rather the snake's.

Jeff had told his father that they'd find Rusty, but what if they didn't?

Jeff began to run, slackening his pace only after slipping on some wet leaves. Even then, his gait was faster than an ordinary walk. If Rusty was anywhere in these woods, it would be at the quarry where the two of them had spent so many fun-filled hours. Why the silly mutt might even be splashing around in the water.

When he got to the quarry, Jeff called the dog's name several times with no results other than a faint echo. He skirted the rim of the quarry, slipping again, this time nearly falling into the water. Jeff slowed, making a full circle around the quarry. He climbed to the top of the bluff, and called some more. Once again, no Rusty. Once again, only a faded echo, which somehow seemed mocking.

After a second lap around the quarry, then a third, Jeff felt the first sting of ice against his face. The storm was starting, and remembering his mother's warning, Jeff made the reluctant decision to start back. The storm was slow in building, but when Jeff got back to Crow's Nest Pike, the ice was blowing horizontally, stinging him like so many nettles. Jeff pulled his hood tighter and ran as fast as he dared.

When he reached his house, he saw his mother standing by the broken latch talking with one of Chief Parsons' officers. They could hardly be heard above the wind but Jeff could make out the gist of the conversation. They were talking about the animals that were apparently carried off and mutilated over the last few months; the work of some unknown predator. When they saw him coming, they stopped talking.

His mother walked up to him and he just shook his head. She put her arm around him, excused herself to the officer and led him inside.

"There's some hot chocolate in the microwave, honey. Why don't you heat it up for yourself?"

"Are we going out to look for him?"

She looked at the sky. "I don't think that'd be safe, honey. But don't worry. We've called Animal Control and they'll be on the lookout for him. It'll turn out OK. You'll see."

But it won't turn out OK, Jeff thought. Hearing his mom's conversation with the officer reminded him of a similar discussion with some of the kids in school. Andy had mentioned how some old lady's cat got out and when they found it, it didn't look like a cat anymore.

Jeff took off his coat and flopped down on the couch. He hadn't realized until just now how weary he was. Or how sad.

71

Suddenly, the dark, venomous snake in his gut uncoiled. It opened its hinged, fanged jaws to their fullest and in one lightning strike, buried those fangs in Jeff's heart. At that instant, Jeff knew Rusty was gone. Not just gone, but *gone*. Permanently, with no hope.

Jeff buried his head in the plush cushions of the couch and began to cry in a spasm of body-wracking sobs. If Anne or Peter Strickland noticed, they were good enough to stand aloof, allowing their son to grieve for his best friend in peace and solitude.

8

Excerpt from The Taylorville News, August 15, 1998:

POLICE BLOTTER
Assault

TAYLORVILLE - On August 8, Howard and Desmond Corey were assaulted by a Taylorville youth in the parking lot of the 7-Eleven on Route 29. During the altercation, Desmond Corey was struck in the mouth and sustained a broken jaw. Howard Corey sustained a broken rib. The assailant received only minor scrapes. The Coreys were taken to Mercy Hospital in Stockton where they were treated and released. The name of the assailant, a minor, is being withheld.

9

Police Chief Linus Parsons was a firm believer in a sixth sense. Not the Jeanne Dixon or Edgar Cayce variety; but the kind a man develops after being a cop for twenty-plus years. This stone-faced black man had been a cop for twenty-plus years. He believed he had such a sixth sense, and he was about to test his theory.

Parsons was witness to a strained tableau, unfolding in the Ryan kitchen. At the table, sat Elliot Ryan, sullen, unmoving, leaning his folded arms on the table. On one side was Emily Ryan, thin-faced, careworn, almost tearful, also unmoving, except to fidget with the cross around her neck. In contrast to his wife's immobility was big, angry Joe Ryan, pacing behind his son. Every so often, Joe opened his mouth to say something then closed it, not trusting himself to speak. Finally, he came up behind his son, poked Elliot in the back of the neck, and said, "The man asked you a question, boy."

The gesture was more of a nudge than a smack, but Parsons noted Elliot's fists clench. Other than that, Elliot remained silent and unmoving.

"What happened, Elliot?" Parsons prodded.

"I already told you," Elliot answered.

"Well, tell me again."

Elliot told the story again, making no effort to hide his exasperation. He'd been riding his bike along Route 29 when some idiot began blaring his horn behind him. Elliot had steered well onto the shoulder of the road, but the idiot kept honking at him. When he turned around, he saw it was the Corey brothers in their battered pickup bearing down on him. He tried to get onto the grass, but the pickup just kept coming, swerving at the last second. It was enough to cause him to lose control of the bike and take a header into the grass. The Coreys then sped past him, blaring the horn and laughing like a pair of hyenas on uppers.

Elliot picked up the undamaged bike and continued riding. To his surprise, he caught up with the pickup at the 7-Eleven where Howard and Desmond had just made a beer stop. He rode up to the driver's side, just as Desmond was getting ready to pull out, and propelled his fist through the open window into Desmond's jaw. Desmond screamed "like a little girl," according to Elliot, and the truck stalled. Howard then burst out of the passenger side, wielding a hammer overhead and making for Elliot.

Elliot surprised the hell out of Howard, who expected the boy to turn tail and run in the opposite direction. Instead, Elliot ran toward Howard and drove his shoulder into the bigger man's armpit with enough force to send the hammer flying. Elliot punched madly at Howard's back and if he hadn't pivoted, Elliot would have fractured Howard's spine. As it happened, the blow had enough force to break a rib. The combatants fell, rolling to the ground, with Desmond, dancing around them, spitting blood and teeth, looking for an opening. That, at least had been Desmond's story. Bystanders claimed he was doing nothing more than egging Howard on, at a safe distance to boot. Finally, a police car pulled up and two officers separated the fighters. Howard and Desmond, having sustained obvious injuries, were taken to the nearest emergency room and Elliot taken into custody.

It wasn't long before the brothers' father, Randall Corey, phoned Chief Parsons, demanding that Elliot be charged with assault and arrested. Parsons listened to Corey's rant with as much patience as he could muster. This was a situation to be handled with diplomacy. Rand Corey had connections in this town and political aspirations as well, so he was not a man to dismiss. Technically, he was on firm ground. Elliot *did* attack Desmond Corey without apparent provocation; numerous witnesses would attest to that. On the other hand (and this was where the Parsons sixth sense kicked in), it was unlikely that the Coreys were blameless. Howard and Desmond Corey were hell raisers and bullies with whom the police had had frequent run-ins. They'd gotten away with many a slap on the wrist due to their father's influence, which galled Parsons. Parsons felt a perverse satisfaction in knowing that they'd gotten at least a modicum of comeuppance this day.

Still, there was the matter of what to do about Elliot. Parsons had no doubt that there was an element of truth in Elliot's version of the events. Rand Corey was pressing for action, though, and it was not wise to disregard the wishes of Rand Corey.

Elliot had turned as he spoke and was staring at the lawman with a look of annoyed condescension. It was a look Parsons had seen often, from the time he was pounding a beat, back in Newark, New Jersey. He'd learned that by asking the same questions over and over again, Colombo-style, and keeping his expression impassive, folks assumed that he was slow on the uptake. The truth was that Parsons didn't give a damn so much about *what* folks were saying. What interested him was the way they responded—their expressions, body language, and interpersonal dynamics revealed more than their words.

Parsons stepped forward and tapped Elliot on the shoulder. "Let's step outside. I think we need to talk."

"Alone," he added as Joe Ryan attempted to follow.

#

On the front porch of the Ryan house, away from his father, Elliot was still dour, but more relaxed, as Parsons expected he would be.

Parsons had known Joe Ryan for years. Joe had a reputation in this town. How often had Parsons driven by Joe's garage and seen Joe and Elliot working on vintage cars from out of state? People trusted Joe and for good reason. The man was not only the best damn mechanic/fix-it guy in three counties, but the most honest.

Elliot also had a reputation in this town. A misfit? For sure. A rebel? Definitely. Angry? Oh, yeah. But a bad kid? Parsons thought not. Sure, kids who were abused or neglected might go bad, but that didn't seem to be the case here. Parson's instinct told him that Joe Ryan was gasoline to Elliot's flame.

Joe certainly wasn't a bad man, probably, by most accounts, not even a bad father. It stood to reason, however, that a man who'd built up the clientele and standing of a Joe Ryan was a man with exacting standards. He would expect anyone working for him, including his son, to abide by those standards, with no leeway given.

Somewhere along the line, Elliot had picked up a sensitive gene which required the type of stroking that he didn't get from his father. Parsons knew that Elliot liked working on cars and was good at it. He could envision Elliot fixing a sputtering engine, making it hum like it did when it got off the assembly line. He could also envision Joe taking his son's accomplishment as a matter of course, with no acknowledgement of the achievement.

That's what made Elliot so angry and defiant. He would run with a bad crowd. He would get into fights. He might even turn to drugs. Such a kid was at a crossroads and it was up to Parsons to make sure he didn't take the wrong path.

"You realize that you could be sitting in jail cell right about now, don't you Elliot?" Parsons said. No response. *"Don't you?"*

Elliot nodded, eyes to the ground.

"Look at me, Elliot."

Elliot looked up. Parsons locked his gaze with the boy's before continuing. "I think I can get Rand Corey to drop the charges."

For the first time, an expression other than surliness crossed Elliot's face. "Yeah?"

"Yeah."

Parsons had a plan he was sure Rand Corey would go for. Earlier, he'd dropped off Howard and Desmond at home where he found a very pissed off Randall Corey. Corey Senior's first love was politics where, if a man who could not control what went on in his own house, he could not be expected to control what went on in his community, his town, or his state. This was why Rand Corey laced into his sons with such fury. He backhanded Desmond across the room and reduced Howard to a fit of blubbering. He then told them to pick up stakes and get out of Taylorville the next morning. Parsons could not help grinning as Howard and Desmond Corey "Yes-sirred" their father with all the bravado of a mouse cornered by a snake.

Once he wiped the smirk off his face, Parsons pointed out to Rand Corey that he *could* have Elliot arrested and charged. If he did, however, this incident would remain on everyone's lips for a long time. It would call attention to the many lawless escapades of the Corey brothers. Did the man who wanted to be the next governor really want that, or would he prefer this incident to die a quiet death? That was when Parsons proposed his plan, and Rand Corey reluctantly agreed to it.

"I worked things out with Rand Corey," Parsons went on. "I told him that I'd put the fear of God into you and that you're going to do a hundred hours of community service."

Elliot was immediately wary. "What do you mean, community service?"

"You show up at my office tomorrow morning at ten, and I'll show you what I mean."

"OK."

"OK. Remember. Ten o'clock. My office."

Elliot turned to go back into the house, when Parsons said, "Wait."

Elliot turned back.

"Are you doing drugs?" Parsons demanded.

Elliot shook his head.

"That's good," Parsons continued, "because if I ever find you using or selling in this town, your ass is grass, and I'm John Deere. Do we understand each other?" Elliot nodded.

"Good. Remember. Ten o'clock."

#

So it was that at 10:30 the next day, Elliot Ryan was dropped off at the waiting room of Dr. Marvin Pressman, Doctor of Veterinary Medicine. There he found himself in the presence of a pretty auburn-haired receptionist whose name tag read "Susan" and saying to her, "You work here?"

Susan looked up from her paperwork and gave him a look, which, for all its quickness spoke volumes. It said, "No, it's my *hobby* to sit at this desk and answer dumbass questions which are really lame attempts at pickup lines from dumbass geeks like you." So Elliot, who was normally not shy around girls, found himself fishing for another line and finally came up with:

"So what's this Pressman guy like, anyhow?"

Before Susan could answer, the phone rang. "Dr. Pressman's office. Susan speaking." She appeared to be explaining the boarding policies and services to some lady who apparently wanted only the *absolute* best for her cat. Elliot was hoping to get another shot at befriending the fetching Susan, when a tall, gaunt man in his mid-fifties in a white lab coat entered.

"Elliot Ryan?" Elliot nodded. "I'm Dr. Pressman. If you're finished making goo-goo eyes at my niece, you can come with me. I'll explain what you'll be doing here."

With a final glance at Susan, Elliot followed Dr. Pressman. They went into a small closet of an office containing bookshelves bulging with medical tomes and periodicals. There was a desk stacked high with paperwork and a leather chair in front of the desk. Various pictures of cats and dogs adorned the walls, plus a horse, a rabbit, and a monkey. The picture of the monkey was crooked. Dr. Pressman sat behind the desk and gestured to the chair.

Elliot sat and Dr. Pressman began speaking. "As you can see, I'm up to my neck in work here. I'm going to need someone to help out with some of the more non-technical duties around here. You like animals?"

"I guess."

Dr. Pressman continued. "I have a contract with the county. Any time Animal Control finds a sick or injured animal, they bring it to me. I examine it, make sure it presents no danger, such as rabies, or any other contagious disease, and treat it if that's called for. If not ..." Dr. Pressman shrugged. Elliot got the idea.

"Unfortunately," Dr. Pressman went on, "that doesn't leave me much time to take care of some of the other animals that are left in my care. One of the things I don't get to do is to exercise the animals that people board here. They pay me for the service, they're entitled to it, but I just can't get to it. You follow me?"

Elliot nodded again. Dr. Pressman had intended to go into greater detail as to *why* he couldn't discharge some of his regular duties, but decided against it. No sense scaring the kid.

"Chief Parsons knows the situation. He knows I need some help around here and you need to do some community service. He suggested we hook up and help each other out. That sound OK to you?"

"I guess."

Dr. Pressman sighed. This kid was turning out to be some conversationalist. "OK," he said. "Follow me." He grabbed a leash from somewhere on the desk and led Elliot to a door which led outside to a row of pens containing several barking dogs. He pointed to one at the far end, containing a very loud, very large, and very hyper German Shepherd. "We'll start you with Killer."

"Killer?"

Dr. Pressman allowed himself a puckish grin. "Don't worry. That's just Cal Johnson's sense of humor. Come on, you'll see what I mean." He walked up to the cage, noting that Elliot was following, but at a distance. He pulled a set of keys from his pocket, and opened the padlock to Killer's pen. All the while, the dog was making noises which, Elliot swore, weren't natural to anything in the animal kingdom.

Dr. Pressman stepped into the pen and the dog leaped upon him, its massive paws on the vet's shoulders. The dog's weight caught the doctor off-balance, pushing him into the wall of the pen, his tongue washing Dr. Pressman's face furiously. Dr. Pressman grabbed Killer's front paws, and the two of them looked like a pair of spastic dance partners.

Dr. Pressman turned to Elliot, who was standing outside the pen, shaking. "It's OK, son. The only danger you're in from this dog is that he's likely to slobber you to death. Come on in. Don't be scared."

"I'm not scared." Elliot was no longer shaking, but neither was he eager to make the acquaintance of this behemoth. Nonetheless, he entered the pen tentatively, upon which Killer turned his attention from man to boy, jumped on Elliot's shoulders and began giving him the same facial bath he'd given the vet. Elliot managed to hold his ground and keep from being thrust back into the wall. What he couldn't keep from doing was grinning, perhaps from relief, perhaps from the absurdity of the situation.

"DOWN," Dr. Pressman shouted, and Killer was immediately on all fours again, tongue out, panting happily. "Just put this on him," he said, handing the leash to Elliot, "and run him around out there," gesturing to an open field just beyond the pens. "Give him about ten minutes. If he still seems bouncy, run him around some more. Think you can handle that?"

"Sure," Elliot said, putting the leash on the dog, and then starting to run.

Watching the two, Dr. Pressman was hard put to decide who was running whom. If he were a betting man, he'd say it was the dog running the boy. He was equally hard put to decide who was wearing the sillier grin. If he were a betting man, he'd say it was the boy.

10

"So these two guys hated each other, I mean, they *really* hated each other.

"But the one guy's son loved the other guy's daughter, and they wanted to get married, see? But they knew they couldn't 'cause their fathers hated each other so much. So they decided to run away together. So the first guy's son told the other guy's daughter that he was gonna steal his father's horse and coach and that he'd meet her at midnight at the old carriage house on the Ridge and that they'd run away together, and they did.

"The next day, the first guy saw that his son was missing and so was his horse and coach and the other guy saw that his daughter was missing, and they realized what their kids did, and they were real mad at each other. But they followed the tracks of the horse and coach on the carriage road until they just *disappeared*. No one ever saw either of them ever again.

"But if you're in the woods on certain nights of the year, they say that you'll be able to hear the sound of a horse and coach moving along the old carriage road. If the moon is full, you'll see a coach being drawn by a big black horse and in the coach is a man and a woman."

Andy paused dramatically, waiting for responses. He got them.

Neil faked snoring.

Jeff let off a loud burp.

"OK, OK," said Andy, also laughing in spite of himself. "But that's supposed to be a true story."

"We *know* it's supposed to be a true story," replied Neil, throwing a twig into the campfire. "We've been hearing it since we were in diapers."

"In your case, that's only a week ago," said Jeff.

"Bite me, Strickland."

The boys broke up laughing. Their banter was old hat, but somehow, it seemed funnier by a campfire.

The boys were observing a Taylorville tradition. The last weekend before Halloween, a group of parents took their kids to the Taylor Creek Campgrounds for an overnight camp-out. The first year he'd lived in town, Neil and Andy invited Jeff to join them. They all shared a site at the edge of the campgrounds. Several of the fathers were on an adjoining site, listening with half an ear, but mostly allowing their sons the luxury of privacy and independence.

Jeff soon realized that most of the fun lay, not in the traditional campsite activity of telling ghost stories, but in razzing each other over them. As far as spook tales went, there was nothing original under the sun (or full moon as the case may be). Most of the stories were pretty clichéd, and the wisecracks were more enjoyable than the tales themselves.

It was the boys' second Halloween campout together and the sessions were becoming rowdier and bawdier. Lame ghost stories were interspersed with dirty jokes, told in hushed tones under the auditory radar of the chaperoning parents, several campsites away.

"OK, I've got one," said Jeff. "I'm going to tell you the true story about Isaac Dunbar and Dunbar's Massacre."

"We know the true story, Donkey-Breath," Andy interrupted. "We've lived here all our lives, remember?"

"You only *think* you know it," Jeff answered, and he launched into a tale that had come to him in a dark and silent room the night before.

"Did you ever wonder how Isaac Dunbar knew the British were coming to Taylorville? Did you ever wonder how he and thirty men were able to whup an army of over one hundred trained fighting men? Well, it was because Isaac Dunbar was a *warlock*."

"A what?"

"Warlock. A wizard. A male witch." Jeff lowered his voice to a dramatic pitch. "Someone versed in the dark arts." He paused, waiting

82

for the inevitable wiseass comments, but none came. Even Neil was quiet, not exactly spellbound, just waiting to see where this story was going.

"Anyhow, Isaac Dunbar had been tried in Salem years ago, during the time of the witch trials for supposedly trafficking with the devil. See, anyone who pissed him off or looked at him the wrong way had some kind of horrible misfortune. Their crops died, their livestock died, or if Isaac was *really* pissed off with them, *they* died."

"Whoa, whoa, hold it right there," Andy interrupted. "The Salem witch trials were in the late 1600's. Dunbar's Massacre was in 1771. If Isaac Dunbar was in Salem back then, he'd have to be over a hundred when he led the Massacre."

"But he was a warlock," Jeff explained, "he might have been over a hundred. He might have been *ancient* by the time he led the Massacre."

"Yeah, right," said Neil, blowing a raspberry.

"Chill, I want to hear the rest of this."

"Anyhow, Isaac Dunbar found out about the British, so he went into the woods by the old carriage house and called upon his dark gods to help him. They did, too. If you look at the ground in that place, you'll see that it's all caved in. Like something came out of the ground one night, but the ground never settled right after that."

Neil blew another raspberry, but Jeff was gratified to note that it was more halfhearted than his earlier one. He was doubly gratified when Andy elbowed Neil again and told him to chill.

"Dunbar promised the dark gods of the forest that there'd be lots and lots of blood if they helped him, see, and that's why they did. They reached down into the pits of hell for the most evil and vicious thing they could find.

"They sent the Backwoods Demon."

"No way!" Neil exclaimed.

"OK. Where did the Demon come from?"

"There is no Demon, Jeff. It's a legend. "

Jeff sighed. "OK, brainiac. Where's the Demon *supposed* to have come from?"

"It's—it's just something that lives on the Ridge. I don't know!" Neil replied, exasperated. "What's that got to do with anything?"

"Well, if you don't know, how do you know it didn't happen the way I'm telling you?"

No answer.

Jeff continued, "So General Burgess was leading his men along the carriage road. It was dark and it was starting to thunder, and they wanted to burn the town before it started raining." Jeff paused. "Funny thing was, it was clear all day. Anyhow, they were just getting to the edge of town when it started with the lightning and the thunder. They moved quicker, hoping to get to the town when this burst of sheet lightning hit.

"That's when they saw it.

"A hundred men, armed with muskets and bayonets, and General Burgess himself, one of the toughest and meanest men in King George's army, terrified by the *thing* that faced them down in the woods that night. Some of them ran, some fell to their knees, and others started firing into the night, but it didn't do them any good. The ones that tried fighting back were gutted where they stood. The ones that just gave up were torn to pieces, if they didn't die of fright first. The ones that tried to run were cut down. All that was found the next day was blood and body parts. The men whose faces weren't shredded to pieces had this look of terror on them. No one could ever figure out why.

"But Isaac Dunbar knew, and the thirty men who were out there that night knew. They saw what happened to the British troops, and they took an oath never to speak of what they saw because they were afraid that Dunbar's Demon might come after them. That's why, to this day, people believe that the Backwoods Demon still haunts Dunbar's Ridge and is still hungry for blood and is still ready to kill any unsuspecting traveler who ventures too far into the woods."

Jeff paused, waiting for responses.

Andy spoke first. "Where did you get this stuff from, anyhow?"

Jeff shrugged. "I don't know. I just figured it would be an improvement over the lame stuff you guys have been telling."

"Wait a minute," Neil objected, "if Dunbar was such a badass—what did you call him, a warlock?—why would he help the farmers? Why wouldn't he just let Burgess burn the place to the ground?"

"He didn't care about the farmers or Taylorville, or anything," answered Jeff. "He just wanted to summon the Demon and he needed a blood sacrifice. Why do you think they call it a Massacre? Do you think a few farmers with muskets and farm tools could wipe out a whole troop of soldiers without a single casualty?"

"Sure," said Neil. "They knew the area, Burgess didn't. They knew where to set up an ambush. They knew how to sneak up on Burgess."

"But then, you'd have a bunch of bodies with bullets and shells in them," Jeff replied. "Burgess' men were *slashed* to death."

"Says you."

"No, he's right about that," said Andy. "Burgess and his men had their throats cut. It was supposed to be a warning to any other British who wanted to attack Taylorville."

"That's the watered-down version," whispered Jeff darkly. "Cutting their throats would have been tame compared to what happened to those guys."

There was a pause and Jeff threw another log on the fire. He took satisfaction knowing that his story did not elicit the usual ridicule or abuse, albeit good-natured. The teasing that followed the spook tales was tradition and Jeff's story seemed to have broken that tradition.

"Well, I gotta say this for you, Jeff," said Andy. "It's different. I mean every story we've ever told was older than these hills. This one at least is new."

"Yeah, and that's all I give it," said Neil, regaining his characteristic scorn. "Nice try, Jeff."

Jeff was in no way fooled by Neil's attitude. He had watched the faces of his friends as he told the story. Though neither of them would admit it, they were enthralled. Andy was right, the familiar accounts, told multiple times, provided no suspense or surprises. A story, such as this, however, woven out of whole cloth, while flawed and improbable, at least had the benefit of novelty.

No one volunteered to follow Jeff's act, so the boys got to talking about school, sports, and girls. In other words, topics boys have discussed since time immemorial. When the fire dwindled, one of them placed another log in the flames. As the night wore on, Neil walked off into the woods to relieve himself while Andy and Jeff remained, staring into the fire.

"So how late do you wanna stay up?" Andy asked.

"I guess till the fire goes out."

"OK."

Jeff and Andy sat staring at the gyrating shapes formed by the flames, almost hypnotized. Once in a while, a log would burn all the way through and fall on the ground, sending up a shower of sparks and cinders. The boys would then brush themselves off and resume their vigil.

At one point, the fire flared up, catching Jeff's attention such that his line of vision shifted.

There was something there, just beyond the fire's circle of light.

Jeff jumped, startled, and it was gone. He was about to write it off as a trick of the light when he noticed Andy's expression. It was one of surprise, with a bit of shock thrown in.

Andy spoke first. "Did you see it?" he whispered.

Jeff nodded. "You too?"

"What did it look like?"

"What was it wearing?"

"What was it carrying?"

The questioning went back and forth. As if by unspoken agreement, the boys only asked open-ended questions of each other; nothing that could be answered with a simple yes or no. It appeared that they'd each seen the same thing. For a split second, there appeared a gaunt old man dressed in American Revolution clothing, holding an old-fashioned gun with a short barrel and flared muzzle.

11

When Elliot reported to Dr. Pressman the first Monday of November, 1998, the doctor was bent over his examination table. He'd been scrutinizing what looked and smelled like a chunk of spoiled hamburger. On closer inspection, Elliot realized that it had once been a living animal.

Dr. Pressman looked up as Elliot entered the room. "Disgusting, isn't it?"

"Wha—what …" Elliot stammered, a chill descending over him.

"A rabbit. I'm conducting an autopsy on her right now. If you'll hand me …"

But Elliot was gone before Dr. Pressman could finish his request. The sound of footsteps running down the hall, then a wet retching noise coming from the bathroom. Dr. Pressman shook his head, and went back to work. Not that he could blame the kid any. It was pretty gruesome.

#

Elliot was on his knees, head in the toilet.

It wasn't the gruesomeness of the dead rabbit that caused Elliot to lose his lunch. Rather, it was a flashback.

At the first spring thaw after his visit to the cave, Elliot had gone back to the carriage house where he had some stash left. It was a warm spring evening and it had been a while since Elliot had gotten high, and he had a real desire to get high. He'd spend the day fighting with the old man during a transmission job they were doing. Dumb really, but

Elliot was in a dark mood and he had just stormed off. Now he needed something to mellow him out and nothing could accomplish that better than some of Geary's finest.

So he made his way to the carriage house, dislodged his stash, sat on the ground in his accustomed spot, and lit up. A few tokes and he was happy and relieved again.

Then he felt a sort of mental tugging, and he found the walls of the carriage house falling away, replaced by underbrush from another part of the woods. He felt the calm stillness that his own body was experiencing give way to a forward motion that he knew only too well. He felt the contentment he'd experienced seconds ago give way to the icy dread he'd felt the last time he emerged from the cave.

For the first time since he'd discovered that he could see through the eyes of another, Elliot felt no sense of exhilaration. Now, he felt only revulsion. He was in the thrall of something which liked to kill and kill violently, and the knowledge disgusted him. Desperately, he tried to fight it, to break away.

He couldn't. To his horror, he found that he was trapped behind the eyes of this terrible being.

He found himself loping through the woods and numerous scents assailed him, sensations to which he was incapable of responding in his own body. The scents excited him, in spite of himself, and the loping gait turned into a fast and resolute run.

There was movement in the thicket immediately ahead of him and he ran toward that movement. At the last minute, he found himself in mid-air, in mid leap as he came down upon something soft, furry, and squirming. With eyes different from his own that could make out fine details in the dim lightless dusk, he saw the possum, squealing in pain, terrified. He knew that the leap had broken the poor creature's back. Revolted, he tried to break away again; again he was unsuccessful.

To his horror, the predator's head lowered toward the now-screaming marsupial. He felt and he tasted the possum's hair and flesh in his own mouth.

Elliot leaped up in disgust, dry heaving. He was himself again. The gag reflex accomplished what no effort of will was able to do; it broke the link between himself and—whatever. The next thing he knew, the bile was rising from his throat and he was puking his guts out on the stone wall. He was dimly aware that he was still holding the spent joint and he thrust it away. He puked some more, and when he was done puking, he spat, and spat again to rid his mouth of the residual taste that still lingered. Finally, he staggered back to the path and made his way home.

When Elliot had told Parsons that he wasn't doing drugs, he was telling the truth. He never touched another joint after that day.

#

"You OK, son?"

Dr. Pressman found Elliot leaning over the toilet, apparently weakened from his gustatory upheaval. Elliot nodded.

"Good. Take your time. Then come into my office, and we'll talk."

"No, I'm OK now."

Dr. Pressman led Elliot into his office, sat behind his desk, and gestured to the chair in front of it. Elliot appeared only too happy to sit. His color was still off and he was breathing heavily.

"I'm sorry you had to see that, Elliot," Dr. Pressman began. "Unfortunately there's been a lot of this kind of thing happening lately. Maybe you've been hearing about it. A lot of animals are being attacked and mutilated. When someone finds the body of one of these animals, they bring it in to me. I autopsy it and try to find out what killed it." He paused. "So far, I haven't been too successful."

"What do you think it is?"

"What do I think? I think it's some sadistic son of a bitch who gets his jollies out of torturing innocent animals.

"There are people out there who like nothing better than inflicting pain," Dr. Pressman went on, his anger rising. "When they can't do it to people they do it to animals. They make me so goddamn sick …!"

Dr. Pressman stopped. "Sorry. It's a subject I get carried away on. Anyhow, you asked me what I thought it was, and that's what I think. I think it's people doing this. Human scum. Maybe one of those satanic cults that use animal sacrifices. I don't know.

"But there's something that really frightens me about all this. You ever study abnormal psychology?" Elliot shook his head. "Well, they've found that many murderers and serial killers got their start slaughtering animals.

"I'm afraid that eventually, this son of a bitch is going to start killing people."

12

Sometimes it danced, sometimes it floated.

Sometimes it faded from sight only to reappear somewhere else, dancing, floating.

It was formless, yet visible, a creamy white shape materializing and receding in the *stygian* darkness.

Fifteen-year-old Jeff Strickland sat up in bed with a sharp suddenness. The shape was still in the process of becoming clear and familiar with a tantalizing slowness. During this time, Jeff became aware that he was completely naked.

When the shape finally did become recognizable, Jeff became aware of another sensation, not altogether unpleasant (hell, not unpleasant *at all*) between his legs.

Cheryl Conway. The hottest girl in school. A girl who somehow managed to function simultaneously in two opposing camps: the brainy and the popular. Cheryl was in every honors class, including some of his own, where he (and every male classmate of his) lusted after her.

Here she was, in his bedroom, dressed (if you could call it that) in her tight cheerleader's sweater with the low V-neck and short cheerleader's skirt.

Well, not her exactly. Even in this moment of …

Ecstasy? Delight? Anticipation?

... Jeff knew it wasn't *her*, but rather some hallucinatory facsimile thereof, courtesy of his friendly neighborhood *Presence*. It was a gift horse he wasn't about to look in the mouth (although, somewhat lower, definitely).

"Hi, Jeff," she whispered.

"Hi," he whispered back, amazed he could talk without stammering.

The apparition put a very solid hand on his chest and gently pushed him back. She removed the bed covers from his body, her eyes fixed on his wood, her lips smiling. In one impossible motion, she divested herself of skirt and sweater and Jeff was not surprised to see she was wearing nothing underneath.

Her body was as he'd always pictured it. Ample breasts, protruding at just the right angle from her slim torso, tapering down to a slender waist. Below that, a gossamer thatch, on either side of which flowed smooth legs, long and beautifully tapered. There was only one thing Jeff could think of more exciting than seeing those legs emerging from the short hemline of a cheerleader's skirt. That was feeling them wrapped around him.

"I want to go with you to the dance next month," she whispered, moving away from him a quarter turn, so she could caress his thigh.

For the first time, Jeff understood the meaning of the song lyric, "hurts so good."

"But you're with Neil," he whispered, or rather croaked back at her.

Cheryl stopped caressing his thigh, and turned toward him again. She was holding something in both hands and fingering it, but he couldn't see what it was. Lucky something, whatever it was.

"No," she answered. "I like jocks, but there's nothing between Neil and me." He could see that she was holding something yellowish. It was a likeness of a man, or maybe a boy bent forward at the waist, knees bent, arms thrust backward. A swimming trophy.

She leaned forward and somehow, the swimming trophy was gone from her hands, which were now caressing both sides of his face. "I want to go to the dance with you. I like you very much, Jeff, and I want you."

The next thing he knew, she was lying next to him, one hand cupping his scrotum and kneading it gently. He gave a little cry, half of surprise, half of pleasure. With her other hand, she reached for his penis which felt more like steel than flesh. It took her two tries before she was able to hold onto it because it was throbbing so vigorously. Once she got hold of it, she began moving her hand up and down gently, always extra-careful to stroke the hyper-sensitive underside by the tip.

"You like?"

"Me like! Me like!" he almost shouted, as he spasmed upward in a wave of unmitigated rapture.

She giggled. "Shh." She laid her head on his chest where her shoulder-length blond hair ticked his chin. "You're big, Jeff, you're wonderfully, delightfully big. I'm having trouble with the car; I don't trust it; it's making funny noises …. You're the one I want, you're a nice guy, and very good-looking, but I bet you don't know that …. No, don't move, let me pleasure you. I'm by the landing. I want you Jeff, please come …. Oh yes. YES …. close your eyes …. Bring it on home, baby, bring it home!"

He spasmed one more time; he couldn't help it. A spurt of wetness hit him on the chin, then another, working its way down and pooling on his chest. His eyes were closed and he was breathing heavily, certain that the goings-on in his room would surely awaken his parents.

It was several minutes before his breathing returned to normal and he opened his eyes.

He was not surprised to find that Cheryl was gone. There was no cheerleader's uniform, no swimming trophy. There was no evidence that she'd even been there, except for the sticky wetness on his body and a feeling of well-being, both physical and emotional. The moonlight was framed in his window and he could see the outlines of the furniture in the room. After a few moments' listening, he could hear a car pass in front of the house.

Jeff took the sheet and cleaned himself off. Tomorrow, he'd sneak it into the laundry room and wash it himself; no need for his mom to see it.

Jeff was no stranger to wet dreams or beat-offs, but this was something completely new and different. He had no idea what stroke (pun intended) of luck or fate prompted this latest visitation, but he was grateful for it.

"Thank you," he whispered into the semi-darkness.

The Cheryl-vision had asked him to take her to the dance next month. She'd said other stuff, too. Stuff that didn't make sense. Something about a car? Something about a landing? What did that mean anyhow?

Well, he wasn't about to dwell on that. Tomorrow, he was going to ask her to go to the dance with him. Not only that but—why not?—he'd also try out for the swimming team.

Jeff grabbed a clean sheet, lay down, and fell into the deepest, happiest sleep a fifteen-year-old boy could have.

13

At first, he was aware of nothing except a full moon. It hurt his eyes and a low angry growl emerged from a throat that was not his.

Next came movement.

He was running with great speed through a thick wooded area whose familiarity disturbed him. Once again, the momentum snapped low-lying branches with the force of a whiplash on his face, yet with no more pain than a feather brushing against him.

The trees cleared and fifty feet ahead, he could see a drop-off. He expected to be propelled over the drop-off, but at the last minute, he turned aside without slowing. He crashed through more branches, leaping over protruding roots and stumps, maintaining speed on uphill inclines, increasing it on downhill.

Throughout it all was that heady sense of power, supremacy, dominance.

Accompanying those sensations: revulsion, disgust, loathing.

He tried to break free. He could not break free.

All at once, the speed was gone. Movement went from slow to still, then back to slow again. He smelled something. Something not unpleasant, but musty. Somehow, the fragrance stimulated him. Movement continued, toward the source of the odor.

It was then he found his vision shifting, just as it had when he saw the water snake during that first trip years ago. This time it wasn't a snake his vision sought, but a deer, a magnificent deer.

Another shift.

The deer appeared in greater clarity. It appeared close enough to touch, though in reality, it was a good hundred yards away. It wasn't even aware it was being watched.

Not watched, stalked.

The deer was a few feet from the bank of a little stream. Unconcerned, it covered the distance to the water, lowered its head and began a series of dainty sips.

The movement started again. Fast, faster, covering the distance between itself and its prey in fractions of a second.

The deer had no time to react save to raise its head in the direction of the danger, perhaps to bleat in terror, perhaps to …

#

… Scream!

Joe Ryan, wakened by the deafening shriek from Elliot's room, raced down the hall. He burst into Elliot's room, followed by his wife, to find their son sitting upright in bed, eyes bulging, unmoving, save for a faint quivering of the jaw.

Emily Ryan put her arms around her son and stared up at Joe. "My God, Joe, he's not moving!"

"Is he all right?" Joe demanded, rushing to her side.

"I don't know," Emily sobbed, keeping one arm around her son while with the other, she fingered the cross around her neck.

Joe reached forward and grasped his son's arm. His sleep shirt was so wet and the arm was as stiff as a two-by-four. Or a corpse.

"Elliot! Son, are you all right?" Joe began shaking Elliot, gently at first, then a bit more forcefully.

Elliot responded. "Unnhhh."

"What happened? Are you all right?" Joe stopped shaking him as Emily pressed her head against Elliot's shoulder.

"Yeah, I'm OK," Elliot gasped, took a few deep breaths, then added, "Bad dream."

"That's all it was? You sure you're OK?"

"Yeah. It's all good, Dad. I'm OK."

"Let me get you some water."

"That'd be great. Thanks, Mom."

Emily rose and Joe sat next to his son. "Elliot, are you sure it was a bad dream? Is anything bothering you?" Pause. "You're not ..."

"I'm not doing drugs," Elliot said, as he made a cross-your-heart gesture. "It was a bad dream. That's all."

Joe believed him. The kid had really cleaned up his act in the past few years. Whether it was his mother's constant praying, his own constant discipline, or just plain maturity, Joe couldn't say. Not that he could argue with the results. Ever since Elliot started working for that Pressman guy, his son had been like a different person. His attendance and performance in school improved. He graduated with a C+ average and since college was not an option, he joined Joe in the repair business. Their relationship improved over time as well. Elliot proved to be as conscientious as he was skilled. Just two nights ago, it was getting onto 9:00 pm and Joe was ready to call it a day. Elliot insisted that they finish working on that transmission job before they turned in. Joe was amazed, but delighted. They finished the job.

No, Elliot wasn't doing drugs anymore. It was a long time since he'd come home with that sickening sweet smell on his clothes.

Emily returned with a glass of ice water from the fridge. Elliot made quick work of it in long greedy gulps. He assured his parents that he was OK. After saying their final goodnights, Joe and Emily Ryan left the room.

#

Elliot wasn't OK. He hadn't been dreaming. He hadn't even been asleep. Recently, his thoughts had been turning to those nocturnal excursions when the weed was his ticket of admission into the body of another. He remembered how much he enjoyed them at first, but how horrible they became. It was like opening the door of a cage and releasing an active, playful animal, only to have that animal turn vicious on you.

When he'd given up the weed, he'd assumed that he'd put the animal back in its cage, locked the cage, and thrown away the key.

But he hadn't. He now knew that those recent memories that suddenly cropped up weren't memories at all. They were the thing tugging at his brain, trying to get back in. Tonight, it succeeded.

Elliot remembered how nauseated he was on his last trip when he participated in the killing of that possum. Tonight, it was after a deer, an animal infinitely more fragile and graceful than a grungy old possum. It was about to kill that beautiful deer and it wanted Elliot to participate in that killing. Thank God he was able to get out of it before that happened.

For the first time in many years, Elliot Ryan wept. For the first time in many years, Elliot Ryan was terrified.

14

Excerpt from The Taylorville News, November 1, 2004:

Five Deer Slain On Dunbar's Ridge

THE LATEST instance of animal killings occurred last night on Dunbar's Ridge. The mutilated and dismembered bodies of a buck, two does, and two fawns were found within a three-mile radius.

The area has been the site of similar intermittent killings over the last few years.

"This is the first instance of so many animals being attacked in one locale," stated Police Chief Linus Parsons.

"It's also the first instance of such large animals being killed in this manner."

As a result of this latest find, the following recreation areas have been closed until further notice: Dunbar's Lake Campgrounds, Taylor Creek Campgrounds, and the Stockton Pond Recreation Area.

When asked if the police and Animal Control Officials were pursuing any leads, Chief Parsons declined to comment.

The remains of the deer are being brought to Dr. Marvin Pressman of Taylorville for further analysis.

Local police and Animal Control Officials reiterate that residents are to keep their pets indoors, stay out of the woods, and report any instances of dead animals to their local Department of Animal Control.

15

"No way."

"Way."

"Never gonna happen."

"Want to bet?"

"Yeah, what are you betting?"

Jeff paused to think. "Winner buys burgers and Cokes for everyone at Burger Barn. You good with that?"

"I'm good," Neil answered. "'Cause you'll never do it!"

"Jeff, don't," Cheryl beseeched him.

"I can do it, babe. You'll see."

"I don't think it's a good idea." This from Judy Murchison, Neil's girl, a raven-haired long-legged beauty in a very skimpy bikini.

Neil gestured toward the bluff overlooking the quarry. "You really think you can do it?"

"You got it, dude."

Neil blew a raspberry.

"Neil, you're being obnoxious," Judy chided.

"He's being himself," Jeff responded. "Same thing, actually."

"Ooohh, you're both impossible!" groaned Cheryl.

"I'm not being impossible," Jeff protested. "Just truthful. Anyone with brute strength and a walnut-sized brain can be a football star. It takes a real man to take first place in freestyle. Hmmm, now who do we know who'd done that? Oh yeah …" At this point, he struck a pose. The girls giggled.

Neil replied, "Listen, you overgrown water lily, I could make the swim team if I wanted to. I just like football better. You couldn't make the football team if you had the whole starting line of the Patriots standing in for you every step of the way."

"Maybe not, but you couldn't jump from up there, touch the rock, and swim back to the beach, underwater, without coming up for air."

"No and neither can you."

Which was why Jeff made his way to the rim of the cliff and readied himself to jump. He remembered how scared he'd been the first time he'd made this leap, but that was past history.

He backed up to get his usual three long, deliberate strides. He filled his lungs with air, jumped straight up, arched his back, head down, hands poised to hit the water.

He broke the surface.

#

That which had been lying in the cold comfortable darkness sensed something plunging into its watery territory.

Prey. On two legs. Prey on four legs good. Prey on two legs, better.

Barely moving, it undulated upward.

#

Jeff began kicking and stroking with the same ease and power he'd used in the meet against Stockton. He saw the rock coming closer, faster, as he continued his descent with deliberate, unpanicked kick and strokes. His aerobic fitness had served him well in the past. It was not letting him down now.

Keep kicking. Keep stroking.

His hand reached out and he touched the rock.

#

The prey was getting deeper, coming closer, moving quickly, not quickly enough. No matter how fast it moved, it would be overtaken, its flesh shredded.

#

In one fluid motion, Jeff pivoted his body in the direction of the shore, where his friends were standing. It was a good fifty feet from the rock, and now, he was first starting to feel the need for air.

Keep kicking. Keep stroking. Don't panic, don't speed up.

#

The prey changed direction.
It followed, closing the gap.

#

Jeff began to exhale in a slow, controlled manner. He was close. If he got flustered and speeded up, he'd burn up energy quicker. He might even be forced to break the surface to breathe before he reached the shore. The trick was pacing yourself, and Jeff knew how to do that. He was doing it now.

#

Almost there. Almost …
Light! Hated light!
With a guttural snarl, it turned away, making for the bottom, back to the cold comfortable darkness.

#

Jeff's timing was perfect. Just as he exhaled the last bit of air from his lungs, he felt the gravelly surface at the edge of the quarry. He emerged, shook the water out of his eyes, took deep, welcome breaths, and awaited the accolades of his friends.

"All right, out of the water, Aquaman."

That wasn't Neil's voice. It was Chief Parsons. Standing off to the side were Cheryl, Judy, and Neil.

"Just what do you think you were doing there?" Parsons demanded. "How many times do I have to tell you kids to stay away from here? Don't you realize how dangerous it is? There's no lifeguard. What would you do if you got a cramp or got hurt? Huh?"

Jeff lowered his eyes, not out of contrition, but to keep from looking at Neil who was gesturing and making faces in imitation of Parsons, behind his back. Jeff figured he was in enough trouble as it was, so he averted his eyes to keep from laughing in front of the angry lawman.

Judy wasn't so lucky. She was watching Neil and something between a giggle and a snort escaped her. Parsons turned.

"Do you find this funny, young lady?"

"No, sir," she answered, managing to affect a serious voice. Neil was standing off to one side, with a look of exaggerated innocence on his face. As soon as Parsons turned back to Jeff, she smacked Neil on the shoulder.

"I haven't seen you here before. What's your name?" Parsons demanded.

"Jeff Strickland, sir."

"Strickland? You Peter Strickland's boy?"

"Yes, sir."

The lawman's angry features began to soften a little. "I know your father, Jeff. He's a good guy. What do you think he'd say if I told him I'd seen you here?"

"Well, I guess he wouldn't like it."

"Tell you what, Jeff, and the rest of you listen up, too. I'm going to let you all off with a warning this time. But if I catch you here again, any of you, I'll run you in and charge you with criminal trespass. This isn't a safe place to swim and I don't want to catch you kids here again, you got me?"

Four heads nodded in unison.

"Good. Now gather your stuff and get moving."

The four friends walked toward the road. When they got to Crow's Nest Pike, Neil asked, "So how does Parsons come to know your dad?"

"My dad does *pro bono* work for the county. I guess that's how they know each other."

"What? Pro boner? What does that mean?" Neil asked.

"Neil, you're so bad," said Judy as she whacked him on the shoulder again. Cheryl giggled.

"Pro *bono*, Donkey Breath," Jeff answered. "It means 'for the public good.' Dad's a lawyer. Sometimes he defends people who can't afford a lawyer without charging them."

"Whatever you say. Aquaman."

"Right, Superman." Jeff noticed Neil's chest swell, in response to what he no doubt interpreted as a compliment. Jeff then whispered in a tone only Neil could hear, "That's 'cause Judy says you're faster than a speeding bullet."

Jeff took off, running, with Neil in pursuit, yelling, "You are so dead, Strickland!"

The girls lingered behind, with Judy rolling her eyes. "Guys are so *weird*."

Cheryl just nodded.

#

At the bottom of the quarry, that which had stalked its prey lay unmoving, unbreathing, as it had for lengths of time both meaningless and measureless. It hated that its prey escaped, but it hated the light more.

It could wait.

Darkness would come again, and there would be more prey.

Soon.

16

Excerpt from The Taylorville News, feature story, May 23, 2005:

Slain Students Remembered at Graduation Ceremony

GRADUATION IS USUALLY an exhilarating event in a student's life. It marks the culmination of years of stress, effort, and accomplishment. For the 2005 graduating class of Taylorville High School, however, any joy associated with the accomplishment was marred by tears and tragedy.

The graduating class consisted of 512 seniors. There should have been 514.

"Judy Murchison and Neil Coleman will never experience the pride and elation of high school graduation," said Cheryl Conway in her valedictory speech. Conway's voice broke as she requested a moment of silence in respect for the slain classmates. That moment of silence was also punctuated by weeping as these two fine young people were remembered by students, faculty, and parents.

17

"Yeee-HAWWWWW."

A booming thud, a splash, and "Neil, you jerk, I just finished drying my hair."

#

From the cold comfortable darkness, it sensed prey plunging into its watery territory.

It began moving upward through darkness. As it got closer, the darkness lessened. It liked the darkness, preferred the darkness. The light hurt it, made it angry, made its hate grow.

It slowed. There was light, but not as much as the other time. The light was not pleasant, but it was bearable.

How long had it been without prey? Too long.

It quickened its undulations.

Upward. Toward the meager light.

Toward the prey.

#

Judy Murchison stood naked on the strand, clutching a towel which was now as drenched as she was, courtesy of a Coleman cannonball.

Neil emerged from the water, also naked. Judy ran forward and punched him in the shoulder.

"You're such a jerk, sometimes."

Neil's jaw dropped. He brought the back of his hand to his forehead in an exaggerated theatrical gesture and fell to one knee. "Oh, the shame of it! She thinks I'm a jerk! A jerk! King Jerk! The King Of All Jerkdom!"

Despite her anger Judy couldn't help laughing. "Come on, you dope. It's getting dark and we've got a party to go to."

Neil got to his feet and Judy could not help but notice (and be flattered) that he was still big, his plunge into the icy water notwithstanding.

"Just one more," he said, "then we'll get going."

Judy made a "tsk" sound. "OK, but let me move out of the way." She reached for her bikini and flip flops, then made her way to a patch of ground between two large trees, well out of range. She was thinking about the graduation party at Cheryl's, the one they were already late for. It would be a bittersweet event—the old crowd would be together, but for the last time. Some would be staying in the area, but many of them would be going off to college in other parts of the country.

She had just put on her bikini bottom when she looked toward the bluff overlooking the quarry. Sure enough, there was Neil in the midst of his running start toward the edge. One second later, there was Neil in mid-air, clutching his knees and dropping toward the surface. Once second later, there would be an earsplitting "Yeee-HAWWWWW, and a thunderous splash.

Only there wasn't.

Instead, a dark shape loomed upward at headlong speed and enveloped Neil before plunging back into the quarry with barely a disturbance in the surface of the water.

Judy gaped.

It had all happened too fast for her to absorb.

Neil Coleman, the boy she loved, had vanished before her eyes, in the midst of doing something she'd seen him do a thousand times. More than vanished, he'd been taken, snatched, literally out of the air by something, a shape, too fast for her to get a bead on it, but something unnatural.

Judy stood there, too transfixed and terror-stricken even to scream. The only sounds were her gasping breaths, the gentle lapping of ripples against the strand and an occasional birdsong from above.

She found her voice. "Neil?"

Please, God, let this be one of Neil's dumb jokes. Let him be all right. I swear I'll never call him a jerk again. Just let him be all right. Please please please…

Something moved beneath the surface and was making its way toward the shore.

Judy took a tentative step forward, barely aware of the sharp pebbles beneath her bare feet.

As she watched, Neil broke the surface.

She ran to greet him, hug him, then give him hell for scaring her like that when in the dim light she saw …

His mouth was open, not in a jaw-dropping gesture of theatrical silliness, but in pure, unadulterated agony, spewing blood. His eyes were tearing red. As he tried making for the shore, he stumbled and she could see why: his right leg was missing from his mid-calf.

Before she could scream, he disappeared back into the depths with the speed of a dust bunny being sucked into a high-powered vacuum.

Now, she did scream. Over and over. Long, piercing shrieks of terror, grief, and fury, echoing and deafening, taking the place of terrified gasps, drowning out ripples and birdsongs.

Judy fell to her knees when, in the growing darkness, something moved beneath the surface once again.

Her eyes locked upon the shadowy *thing* that emerged from the water, growing larger as it made its way toward her, upon the twin orbs that radiated an unwholesome yellow glow at its uppermost parts.

Judy got to her feet, turned and ran.

The thing lunged for her.

Razorlike shards raked her back.

She almost stumbled, but managed to stay on her feet and keep running.

From behind her, something was growling, its tones animalistic, raucous, coming closer. She felt something hot and caustic blowing on her back, further inflaming her wounds.

She ran faster.

Behind her, amidst the growls, were the sounds of unhurried footsteps, as she pushed herself to a feverish pace. Absurdly, they sounded like someone wearing oversized flip-flops coming down on a wet, sandy surface. Leisurely though they were, they were coming closer, even as she pushed herself, lengthening and quickening her strides.

The narrow path gave way to a slight rise just short of a wider trail when she tripped over a root. She tried to rise, but her limbs, having taken all the punishment they could bear, failed her. She collapsed, gasping, sobbing, a horde of thoughts and impressions flowing through her brain in an impossibly short span of time.

Neil.

Graduation.

The party.

How she and Neil had …

Something leaped on her from behind and clasped her head in a spike-studded vise. A flash of pain, then blackness.

18

If anything good came out of Elliot's vision with the deer, it was this: he learned to recognize when his mind was being violated. Once he was fully immersed in the vision of God-knows-what, he was trapped there indefinitely. If, however, he fought back when he first felt the mental tugging that came before full possession, he could prevent the visions from overcoming him. He came to recognize that recollections of those exciting runs through the Ridge did not come from within himself. Instead, they forced themselves on him from outside, and by turning his thoughts elsewhere, he could forestall any invasion of his mind.

Positive thoughts worked the best, and lately, there was a lot to be positive about.

Sometimes, he thought back to the day he'd first forged a bond with Dr. Marvin "Call Me Doc" Pressman.

#

A few days after his run with Killer, and after a particularly violent summer storm, Elliot noticed Doc inspecting a drain pipe. The pipe had pulled away from the wall and was on the verge of falling away. Seeing an opportunity to get out of cleaning animal pens, Elliot offered to reinforce the pipe. Doc was skeptical, but he figured that any son of Joe Ryan had to know his way around a tool box. Doc decided to give him a shot at it.

Elliot did a good job with the drain pipe. On a whim, Doc asked him to look over the gutters on his office which also took a beating. Looking to have them overhauled, he'd already gotten one estimate on the work. It seemed high, so what could it hurt to have a second pair of eyes give them a once-over?

Elliot checked them out and reported that they were in good shape. Some spots needed a minor overhaul, but that was it. Doc then mentioned the estimate and Elliot's response was, "You're getting ripped off."

Doc's property was large, with a sprawl of land. It therefore occurred to Doc, that there was no reason to limit Elliot to duties related to his veterinary practice. Why not have Elliot help out with the upkeep of the property? Hadn't Chief Parsons told him to "keep this kid busy any way you can"?

So Doc put Elliot to work trimming the lawn, doing simple landscaping, plus minor repairs and maintenance to his house and car. It worked out well. The kid had a genuine talent for working with his hands.

A week after the drain pipe incident, Doc handed the boy a check for $100. Elliot, not used to such generosity, could only stammer, "What's this for?"

"Just a way of saying thank you," Doc answered.

"For what?"

"Remember those gutters you looked at?" Elliot nodded. "You were right, son, I was getting ripped off. I got a local outfit to do it for a fraction of the cost. You saved me a lot of money, Elliot. I figure I could send some of it back your way."

Elliot was dumbfounded. "Thanks."

"Not a problem. There's something else I'd like you to consider. When you're done with your hundred hours, I'd like you to stay on. I'll pay you, of course. There's a lot of work to do around this place and I'm too old and too busy to do it myself. What do you say? Will you think about it?"

It was a no-brainer. Doc was a pretty nice guy. Not only that, but Susan wasn't exactly hard on the eyes.

Elliot stayed on. From there, it was like the old TV commercial where two friends tell two more friends who tell two more friends, and before you know it, everyone's using the product. If someone needed a handyman, Doc mentioned Elliot's name. Soon, two friends told two more friends, and so on. Granted, there was some doubt at first; Elliot *did* have a reputation for wildness. But enough people figured that if a pillar of the community like Doc Pressman vouched for him, Elliot deserved a second chance.

By the time he was twenty-one, Elliot had a respectable clientele. He had even decided to get his contractor's license and go into business for himself. Yes, the future looked good.

His favorite client, of course, was Doc himself. In fact, it was on the day that Elliot was putting the finishing touches on a tool shed he'd built for Doc, that it happened.

Perhaps it was because Elliot had been working so hard, perhaps he was simply caught off-guard. Whichever it was, it happened again.

#

Elliot was kneeling on the grass, putting his tools away when his vision started to go. Too late, he realized what was happening. He tried to turn his thoughts toward other things, but it was too late.

Before he knew it, his vision was gone. It was as if someone had covered his head with a black hood.

Forms and contours took gradual shape. He was back in the cave, but not a part of the cave he'd seen before. It was colder here and the walls looked like something hot had trickled down them and hardened in mid-flow, like the drippings on a candle. The thing whose eyes revealed things to him was making a slow and deliberate circuit. There were no visible passages adjoining the cave walls in any direction.

He was at the bottom of the chasm beyond the boneyard. The chasm whose bottom he could not see when he flashed his light downward. Perhaps miles down.

He was stuck there!

Then the thing began to move. Elliot felt himself being lowered to the ground as if creeping on all fours. He felt himself crawling in the wet mud-clay, his limbs sometimes sinking elbow-deep into holes where rancid water gathered and coagulated. Once, the thing actually lowered the equivalent of its lips to one of the holes and drank.

The taste was putrid and Elliot wanted to break free and retch. He could not. The thing moved on and the taste of that disgusting water lingered in Elliot's mouth.

At last, he came to a wall with an opening about the size of a doggie-door, just large enough to accommodate a beast one-quarter the size of Killer. Elliot found himself scrunching down to the level of the passage, feeling a vague sense of relief. Surely he would not be going in there.

Next thing he knew, he had somehow insinuated himself in this narrowest of passages and was actually *slithering* forward. The limbs were immobile, yet there was a kind of serpentine forward movement: relentless, calculated, and terrible.

The passage twisted and turned in three dimensions. Sometimes it curved or made a hairpin turn to the left; other times to the right. Sometimes, it sloped upward, other times downward, often at impossible angles, yet there was always that unstopping forward motion. Whatever was doing the driving knew where it was going.

Just when Elliot feared that the passage could not go any further or get any more convoluted, it opened into a wider corridor. The passage was about ten feet wide and forty feet high. About thirty feet from the floor, a slab or rock was wedged between the walls. He felt himself stand again and focused on the rock bridging the corridor.

Suddenly, he found himself leaping upward, landing unerringly on the rock. For a moment, the sense of excitement returned, only to be replaced by abhorrence.

On the cave wall, mere inches from his eyes, was a colony of bats, unmoving, yet alive. They rested, unaware of any intruder in their midst, and Elliot realized what was about to happen.

These tiny, exquisite creatures were about to become prey to whatever had taken hold of him.

Sure enough, he felt himself lunge forward with unbelievable speed. Some of the bats flew off, but others, he felt in his mouth. Worse, they were still alive, struggling in agony as his predator host chewed slowly, not allowing its prey the dignity of a quick death.

Elliot wanted to puke. He could not.

He wanted to scream himself out of this unspeakable vision. Again, he could not.

Fortunately, someone else could.

#

"Uncle Marv, come quick!"

When Elliot came to, he was lying on the grass, shivering despite the summer heat. Leaning over him was Doc, his hand beneath Elliot's shoulder, lifting him gently and asking, "Are you all right, son?" Off to the side was Susan, also shaking, her hands to her mouth with a look of terror in her eyes.

"Are you OK, Elliot?" Doc said again, and felt relief when Elliot started gulping air. "Here, take this," he said, handing Elliot a Nalgene water bottle that had been lying next to him. Elliot took it and gulped the water. To Doc's amazement, he spat it out, then repeated the process again and again, as if ridding his mouth of something foul.

"I'm OK, Doc," Elliot wheezed as Doc and Susan helped him to his feet. "Thanks. I'll be all right."

"You sure?"

"Yeah, really."

Doc studied Elliot and felt his head, expecting signs of fever. On the contrary, Elliot's head was cold and moist. What the heck was going on? The boy *seemed* all right. He was standing steady, without wobbling. His color wasn't off and his breathing was returning to normal.

"Tell you what I want you to do," Doc said. "Knock off for the rest of the day. Go into my house and lie down. You rest a while, and we'll get you home."

"No, Doc, it's OK, I'm …"

"I'm not taking 'no' for an answer, son. I want you lying down now. You'll finish the shed another time. After I'm convinced you're really all right." So saying, he took Elliot by one arm, motioned Susan to take the other, and together, they led Elliot to the day bed in Doc's house.

#

In his office, Doc sat behind his desk and said to Susan, sitting in the chair across from him, "Who else do we have today?"

"Ms. Friedman. She's bringing in her dog."

Doc nodded. "That won't take long. All Mickey needs is his shots. They'll be in and out in no time. Once they're done, we'll close up shop.

"Here's what I want you to do." He stood up, reached into his pocket, pulled out the keys to his Caddy, and passed them to Susan.

"Take my car. Drive Elliot home. I'll get the keys to his car and follow you. I don't want that boy driving home by himself."

Susan started to reach for the keys, then stopped, gawking at them. "Uncle Marv, I'm not sure if I should. Maybe you can drive Elliot home and I'll follow …"

"Suze," Doc said, understanding her trepidation at being alone with Elliot, "Don't worry. He's not a bad kid. Besides, something's eating away at him. I don't have a clue as to what it is and he's not about to tell me. He's more likely to open up to a pretty girl like you than an old codger like me." He dangled the keys in from of her.

Susan hesitated a beat longer, and then took them. "Are you sure?"

"About what? Him being a good kid or him opening up to you? Both, I guess."

Susan looked at the keys for a moment without saying anything. Finally, she spoke. "What do you think happened out there?"

"Haven't the foggiest. At first I thought it was heat stroke, but his skin was too clammy. Besides, it's not all that hot out, and I've seen Elliot work. He keeps himself well hydrated. No, it wasn't heat stroke, but darned if I know what it was."

"All right, Uncle Marv. I'll let you know if he says anything."

Doc kissed his niece on the forehead. "Thanks, Suze. You're the best."

19

The line outside the Tremens Brothers Funeral Parlor was long, extending into the parking lot. At its tail end were Jeff and Cheryl, Andy and his girl, Pam. The line was moving slowly. At this rate it would take a good hour before the foursome reached the room which held Neil's casket.

As far as Jeff was concerned, it could take ten times that long.

Giving voice to the fear that had been gnawing at him since they'd arrived together, he asked, "Is it really going to be an open casket?"

Cheryl looked at him, wide eyed. "No way. Where did you hear that?"

"Gary Kovacs said …"

"Gary Kovacs is a brain-dead asshole," Andy said, and Pam nodded in agreement.

"But his uncle works for Tremens …"

"Kovacs is a pathological liar," Andy interrupted. "And his uncle's a lush who probably drinks embalming fluid. You can't believe anything he says. Besides, the way they found …"

At this point, Cheryl's eyes started to tear. Pam put a hand on Andy's shoulder and shook her head. Andy got the message.

The four friends fell silent and Jeff found himself replaying that awful, unforgettable night.

It was the night of Cheryl's graduation party. There was talking, laughing, eating, drinking, planning, reminiscing, and waiting for Neil and Judy. Everyone knew that they had gone up to the quarry earlier that day for a picnic (a euphemism which fooled no one). They probably got so caught up in their "picnicking" that they lost track of the time.

They never showed.

The next day, Jeff heard the news, as did all of Taylorville. Neil and Judy did indeed go up to the quarry earlier that day. Judy was found in the brambles just off the trail leading to the quarry. Her right leg had been hacked, chewed, chopped, or bitten. She had been running. She was wearing only a bikini bottom and her neck was snapped. Behind her was a trail of blood and her body was violated with an abundance of wounds.

As for Neil, there was no trace of him until divers in wet suits began exploring the quarry itself. They found his body, all right, but not in one piece and not in its entirety.

There were theories, of course. Most supported Marv Pressman's belief that psychotic sickies had come upon the kids in the woods and had murdered them in some unholy rite. Others claimed that a rogue bear or mountain lion wreaked such havoc. One rocket scientist swore that a shark must have somehow gotten into the quarry from the sea. Inevitably there were those diehards who claimed that the Backwoods Demon was responsible.

For Jeff, the *how* didn't matter; it was the *what* that devastated him. Neil was more than just a good friend—in an unconscious and unforeseen way, Neil was a role model. Jeff still recalled his shy, uncool, days and how, over the years, his closeness with Neil had helped mold him into someone confident, secure, comfortable in his own skin.

Sometimes Jeff, who had never outgrown his affinity for the horror genre, saw an analogy in the Frankenstein story. Neil was a positive twist on Victor Frankenstein and he was a positive twist on Frankenstein's creation. The day he learned of Neil's killing, he felt that a part of himself had been lost as well. He knew that it was illogical to think that way, but that didn't stop him from grieving. It was a loss deeper than that of just a good friend.

Cheryl nudged him out of his reverie. "The line's moving."

"Oh, right."

Once again, Jeff plunged into a state of contemplation. Andy was right. Gary Kovacs was a prime bullshitter, but what if he was right, this one time?

What if, against all odds and logic, Neil was lying in an open casket?
Jeff didn't think he could stand the sight.

The line shuffled forward.

The mindscenes took over once again.

He was in a dark, unfamiliar room, facing a frightening and unfamiliar future.

Don't be afraid.

He was at the top of a high cliff running at full tilt toward the edge. At the bottom was a lake with a big gigunda rock waiting to impale his plummeting body.

Don't be afraid.

He was walking through the hallway toward the lockers where the hottest girl in school was surrounded by a bunch of other kids, including boys, and he was working up the courage to ask her for a date.

Don't be afraid.

He was moving on a line which was no longer in the parking lot, but had reached the doorway to Tremens and was making its way into the room where his friend was.

Nothing.

He was through the outer doorway, outside the room where the last remains of his closest friend lay.

Nothing.

No familiar reassuring refrain, only the sounds of murmured conversation and muffled sobs.

"Jeff?"

"Huh?"

Cheryl put her arm around him. "Are you OK?"

"Yeah, sure."

"'Cause you looked like you were listening for something."

"No, I'm good," he lied.

They stepped into the chapel, which held Neil's closed casket.

The line shuffled forward and Jeff felt both relieved and abandoned. Relieved because he would not have to look upon Neil's butchered remains, no matter how well old man Tremens did his job. Abandoned because the inner voice he'd come to rely on for comfort would not come. In the past, it could not be forced, it could not be summoned. It was just *there* when it was needed and it had never let him down. Not until today.

117

In that moment, Jeff Strickland came to the inescapable and totally non-rational realization: it was gone. It was gone forever.

They reached the casket. Cheryl knelt and crossed herself. Pam and Andy did likewise.

Jeff stood there, hoping his thoughts would somehow reach his friend in whatever ethereal domain he inhabited.

Good bye, Neil. Sleep well, and thank you.

20

He was back in Florida on the winter vacation he'd taken with his parents two years ago.

They had done the things that Florida visitors are sure to do: visit family then hit Disney World, Epcot, and Universal Studios. They also made a point of seeing the Everglades National Park. Driving through Dade County, they had stopped at one of the many alligator farms that dotted the roadway to the Everglades.

They were at the farm they had visited. Jeff was standing, as he had stood in real life, at the fenced enclosure which held the gators. The enclosure consisted of a grassy stretch and a natural-looking lagoon area. Several smaller gators and a few larger ones were lolling about, luxuriating under a stretch of palm trees. There was one section of lagoon, however, in which a lone humongous alligator lolled. The young Seminole guide described him as the alpha male of the lagoon. If one of the other gators approached his spot, the alpha would turn on the intruder, tail flailing, jaws wide, throat booming.

"His jaws have over 2,000 pounds of pressure," the guide explained, looking straight at Jeff. "He's a mean one and once he gets hold of you, he won't ever let go."

Jeff noticed that the alpha was now facing him, radiating a sense of power that was daunting, even from the enclosure. But what caught Jeff's attention were its eyes. The boy had seen enough nature specials to know that alligators have prominent eyes on the top of their heads with convex pupils. But the alpha's eyes were not simply prominent; they were disproportionately, grotesquely large, and they had no pupils at all. They were a bright but sickly yellow, which somehow gave the creature a look of malevolent intelligence.

The alpha turned its head in Jeff's direction, focusing those horrendous eyes right on him.

Suddenly, Jeff found himself in the lagoon, under the water. He began swimming with frantic strokes; he knew he had to get out of there. If the alpha attacked one of the other gators, what would it do to a human?

For all his effort, Jeff was making no headway. No matter how fast his strokes, no matter how forceful his kicks, he wasn't moving. His efforts became more and more frenzied, but he wasn't going anywhere.

All at once, he became aware of a dark shape in the water with him. He looked up and saw the alpha. It no longer looked like a gator. Somehow, it had morphed into something else. It still had a vague reptilian configuration, covered with hard and bony scales but its limbs had taken on subtle humanoid contours. Its yellow golf-ball eyes while devoid of pupils, seemed focused on him.

"His jaws have over 2,000 pounds of pressure," the guide's voice reverberated. "He's a mean one and once he gets hold of you, he won't ever let go."

Jeff redoubled his struggles without success. In hideous contrast, the alpha, in its new and threatening form, was moving very fast. Toward him.

He jumped back, and found himself in a place of darkness and silence. Initially, he assumed that the sudden jump in his dream caused him to start in his bed, waking him, and that he was back in his room. In a split-second, he realized that this was not the case.

For one thing, he was not lying in bed. Rather, he was standing and when he tried to move his feet, he found he couldn't. He tried again. This time, he found he could take a step, but not without some resistance, as if he was trying to walk on a large piece of flypaper. The realization that this made him the fly was not comforting. After a few more attempts, he found he could only move by channeling more strength to his limbs greater than normal walking called for. When he was able to walk, the silence was broken with a wet, *splooshy* sound.

He was fully dressed in what felt like jeans, a short-sleeved T-shirt, and sneakers.

It was cold. Not the pleasant chill from the central air conditioning, but a wet coldness that was both disagreeable and unfamiliar.

As his ears became more attuned, he heard the faint sound of water trickling, as if someone had left the faucet on in another room. Also, a fainter sound, harder to distinguish. For lack of a better description, it sounded like paper rustling, barely audible.

He didn't like this place. It wasn't safe here.

He was afraid. There was no voice telling him not to be.

You should be afraid, intruded a different voice. *You can't see it, but that doesn't mean it isn't out there. It's mean and won't ever let go. Maybe you can't escape it, and maybe you can't kill it. The best you can do is get rid of where it comes from.*

The voice faded and Jeff tried taking a step back, but his foot held fast. He tried again, to no avail. He tried a third time, exerting all of his strength and found himself falling backward ...

#

... and sitting on his butt on his bed. This time, there was no mistake. He was in his room, observing the contours of his desk, dresser, and bookshelves and the green glow of his digital clock, which read 2:54.

Drowsily, Jeff lay back down.

By 3:05, he was asleep again. He did not dream again that night.

At 7:00, he awoke, excited, happy, and a little nervous. In a few hours, he'd be heading to college on a four-year adventure. His mom had ushered in the day before, using a time-worn cliché: "Tomorrow is the first day of the rest of your life." His dad had groaned, but Jeff could see the validity to the statement and it heightened his excitement a little.

He felt no regret over leaving Taylorville; the place would never be the same.

Besides, there was still stuff to do and much to look forward to. He had some last-minute packing to do. He wanted to give Cheryl one more good-by call. He had to haul his trunk out to the car.

Still, he could not shake the idea that there was something else he had forgotten. Something he had to get rid of.

But for the life of him, Jeff Strickland could not figure out what it was.

PRESENT DAY

1

"Jeff, watch it!"

His wife's cry roused Jeff from his reverie. He saw the headlights of a car coming directly at him in time to realize that he was veering over the double yellow line on Route 29. He jerked the wheel back in time. He'd managed to avoid a Saturn coming the other way, but not a blast from the Saturn's horn and an angry shout from its driver.

"You OK, honey?"

"Yeah, sure. Just daydreaming. Sorry about that."

"You sure? You've been acting weird since you got that call from your mom."

"No. She was just telling me that Dad's doing better."

"Yeah, but's that's not all she said." When Jeff didn't answer, she went on, "So how do you feel about your folks staying out there?"

"It makes sense," he answered. "New Mexico really agrees with Dad. Since he's been out there, his lungs have cleared and they've both fallen in love with the place.

"I mean how do you feel about selling your parent's house?"

"It's the logical thing to do, I guess."

"Because, you know, we don't have to," Cheryl went on. "Your mom and I talked about it. She said that she and Dad would be willing to sign over the house to us as a gift." When Jeff didn't say anything, she went on, "I suppose we could give them something for it. I doubt that they'd take our money, but it would make me feel better if we offered them something. We could …"

"No."

His abruptness startled her.

"Why not?"

Jeff drove another quarter of a mile without answering. Finally, he said, "I just don't want to live there. I don't want to live in the past."

"How would that be living in the past?" Cheryl asked, hurt that the idea she thought was such a good one was rebuffed so quickly.

Jeff continued to drive without responding.

"Jeff, I asked you …"

"It's where I grew up," Jeff interrupted, "and it'll always be my parent's house to me. I want us to have something that's ours. I don't know. It just feels like a hand-me-down, I don't want that."

It was Cheryl's turn to pause. "You know, Jeff, we've been wanting to buy something for a while now and we've agreed that we're ready. No, let me finish. It makes a lot of sense. You work in Stockton. It'll shorten your commute by half an hour …"

" … and lengthen yours by just as much."

"No, it won't. Ten, twenty minutes, maybe."

"Half an hour. You know I'm right, Cheryl."

Cheryl was silent again. He *was* right. They currently lived in a two-bedroom apartment in Dandridge, about an hour from Stockton Prep where Jeff worked. She worked outside of Dandridge as a Programmer/Analyst. Both were happy in their work and switching jobs was not an option.

Still, why was he being so damn stubborn?

"I don't mind the commute," Cheryl said, choosing her next words carefully. "But there's another reason. We've talked about starting a family Jeff, and we're both ready. The place we live in is just too small."

"Then we'll buy something. You yourself said we're ready to do that. We've got money put away."

"OK, how about this? We take your mom up on her offer, just for a few years. That way, we'll have more money put away and we'll be able to afford something nicer. We can …"

"Cheryl, *I don't want to live in my parent's house.*"

"I still think it's silly," Cheryl went on with a bit of an edge in her voice. "After all, it's an empty house …"

"It's not empty. My mom rented it to someone. Guy with a kid. Widower. Rented it for a song in return for him keeping the place up."

Cheryl was surprised. This was something Anne hadn't mentioned to her. "Who's living there now?"

"Guy named Elliot Ryan. You know him?"

2

"Daddy?"

"Yeah, pal, what is it?"

Six-year old EJ Ryan hoisted himself onto his father's lap on the back deck of the Strickland house. "I saw the man there."

"What man?"

"The man who sometimes comes into our yard."

Elliot was immediately attentive. "Where did you see him?"

EJ pointed to a fence surrounding the property approximately two o'clock from where they were sitting. "There."

Elliot squinted in the direction his son was pointing. It was a summer night, and darkness came late to Taylorville. Even in the semi-darkness, Elliot could see the fence and the woods beyond, but nothing else.

"There's no man there now, pal."

"There was. I saw him."

Elliot put his arm around his son's waist. "OK, OK. What did he look like?"

"He was tall and he was skinny and he was real old."

"Older than Grandpa?"

"Yeah."

Elliot let out a low whistle. "He must have been really, really *old* then."

"No, Daddy. Grandpa's not old. Grandpa's *cool*."

Elliot couldn't help chuckling. "OK. You're right. Grandpa's not old. But tell me more about the man. What did he look like? What was he wearing?"

EJ scrunched up his eyes and nose, the way he did when he was thinking about something. "I don't know. Funny clothes."

"Funny how?"

"I don't know. Just funny." A pause. "And he looked *mad*."

"Were you scared?"

Another pause. "A little."

"Well, I tell you what. You go on upstairs and get ready for bed. I'll stay out here and keep an eye out for him and I'll chase him away if he comes back."

"OK, Daddy. Daddy?"

"Yeah?"

"Can I watch my Big Bird DVD?"

"OK, but only for a little while. When I come up, you have to go to bed."

"OK, Daddy. 'Night."

"Good night, pal."

EJ kissed his father and trotted upstairs. Elliot sat on the deck for a few minutes, listening to the sounds of his son washing up, and then turning on his favorite video. He sat a bit longer, then got up for a beer.

Elliot didn't know what to make of his son's story about the man. No could anyone have come onto the property without him knowing about it. The high fence that separated the yard from the woods ran all around the property, with a gate whose latch stuck. If you fiddled with it to get it open, it rattled loud enough to be heard anywhere in the house. Even, by some chance, if he did sneak into the yard, how did he sneak out without being seen?

Elliot took a swig of Heineken, and walked back out onto the deck. His eyes surveyed the fence, to assure himself that what EJ had seen was just imagination, or possibly a game of pretend. If there was one thing EJ was blessed with, it was a healthy imagination. Elliot recalled how he and Susan were watching the *The Phantom Menace* when EJ came into the room during the pod race. The scene had fascinated the little boy. For days afterwards he would be twirling around his room like a ballerina on uppers with his Bert and Ernie dolls, recreating the pod race.

Susan. Not a day by went that he didn't miss her.

Not a day went by that he didn't replay in his mind the all-too-brief time they'd had together.

The way she'd ignored him at first, and the way he'd dismissed her as a prep school snob.

How that changed that day she'd given him a ride home after that alarming episode at her uncle's and how he'd opened up to her.

How, from that point on, casual conversation begat frequent conversation. Frequent conversation begat friendship. Friendship begat dating. Dating begat courtship. Courtship begat marriage. Marriage begat a blond-haired blue-eyed son, Elliot, Jr., better known as EJ.

And how, every so often, he'd feel an awful tugging, that warning rattle telling him he was about to experience something through eyes other than his own. He was able to fight it, by thinking about Susan. Later, he thought about EJ. The tuggings became less frequent, less severe, and finally they stopped.

And how, on that terrible night after EJ's fourth birthday, something burst in Susan's head as she was on the Massachusetts Turnpike. She'd lost control and smashed into a divider. By the time the emergency vehicle reached her, she was dead.

A *skritch-skritch* noise behind him interrupted Elliot's musings. He turned and saw Garfield scratching at the screen door.

Elliot got up and opened the screen enough for Garfield to squeeze his way through and join him on the deck. No sooner did Elliot lower himself onto the deck chair than his royal fatness leaped onto his lap, purring and nuzzling Elliot's fingers as Elliot chucked him under the chin.

He took another swig of beer. He was sure that EJ hadn't really seen anyone out there. Still, he figured he'd sit out there for a little while, just to be able to tell EJ that he kept watch, as he'd promised.

Another swig, and the beer was almost done. Elliot contemplated getting up for another, but the cat looked so serene, that Elliot didn't have the heart to disturb him. Instead, he leaned back, and found his thoughts wandering to his agenda for the following day.

He'd be meeting with the Stricklands, or rather, with their son and daughter-in-law. He and EJ were living there on a month-to-month basis, with the understanding that the Stricklands might move back or decide to sell the property. That's what was happening now and Elliot was not a happy camper. It was his busy season and looking for a new place to live was not high on his things-I-want-to-do-in-my-spare-time list.

Elliot was pondering the repairs that these pains in the butt would want made when Garfield let out a loud and sudden hiss, jumped off Elliot's lap and ran back into the house.

"OW." Elliot jumped up. He noticed in the dim porch light that Garfield's claws had punctured his jeans and spots of blood were oozing onto the denim.

"What's the matter with you, you dumbass cat?"

Elliot rubbed his leg. As he did, his eye happened to fall on a certain point on the fence. For a split-second, Elliot was sure he saw *something*. It could have been a trick of the moonlight. Or it could have been his own imagination, stemming from his conversation with EJ about a tall, skinny, old, angry-looking man in funny clothes.

He was ready to write the whole thing off to imagination but not *quite* ready.

Because Garfield had responded to something out there, and Garfield was no one's wussy pussy.

Because Elliot knew from experience that there were *things* in Dunbar's woods.

Just what was it you saw out there, EJ?

3

While Elliot Ryan was daubing Neosporin on the puncture wounds in his leg, Jeff and Cheryl were entering the Top Hat Restaurant.

"Yo, Jeff, right here!"

Jeff strained his eyes in the direction of the call and saw a hand waving over the heads of the crowd in the bar. The owner of the hand had a shock of curly red hair, toward which Jeff guided his wife. Andy and Pam were at the bar, nursing their respective Manhattans and white wine spritzer.

"Hey, how are you guys doing?"

"OK. Good to see you, Andy. What's that, a new addition?" Jeff said, pointing to the growth of red foliage adorning his friend's chin.

"Yeah, Pam says it makes me look *professorial*, right sweetie?"

"It makes you look grungy," Pam laughed, tweaking his beard.

"See, what did I tell you?"

At that moment, a voice announced, "Strickland—Buchanan party. Table for four." Andy responded, "They're playing our song. Shall we?"

From the outside, the Top Hat looked like a huge log cabin, with a spacious rear deck for those who preferred dining *al fresco*. Inside, it had wooden beams going up the walls and across the ceiling. Wagon wheel chandeliers were appropriately spaced to give adequate lighting without negating the romantic atmosphere that some of its patrons craved. The menu was mostly continental; high-priced but worth the cost. Each table held a basket of homemade sour cream and herb biscuits. Paintings were hung on the walls, some of which depicted New England landscapes. Others were portraits, contributions from prominent local families of their ancestors, including one of the town's founder and namesake, John Taylor. Jeff noticed that there weren't any pictures of Isaac Dunbar, but before he could say anything, Pam said:

"Did we tell you the news?"

"What news?" Cheryl asked.

"You want to tell them, honey?"

A foolish grin began creeping across Andy's face; in the half-dim light, it looked as if he were blushing. "You're gonna like this one, Jeff. It looks like I'll be getting that assistant professorship at the university next semester."

"Oh, Andy, that's wonderful," Cheryl exclaimed as she leaned over and kissed him.

"Congratulations, man, that's super." Jeff extolled. Andy had been teaching film courses at the local university. Andy had done his graduate work there and was offered a job as an instructor in the media department. Jeff remembered how enthused Andy had been about getting the position, so this professorship was a big thing in his friend's life.

"Tell them the best part," Pam prodded.

"Oh, yeah. My chairman okayed my idea for this course I want to teach in the fall semester. The name of the course is ..." Andy began rapping his fingers on the table in an imitation of a drum roll, " ... Theories and Structures of Horror in Cinema."

"You're kidding."

"Uh-uh. I'm starting off with the work of Méliès and Murnau, working my way up to Whale, Browning ..."

"What about Wegener?"

"Sure."

"Dreyer?"

"Absolutely."

For the next few minutes, it was as if there was no table with four young adults in a secluded corner of the Top Hat. It seemed, rather, like a campfire blazing on a dark October night, as it had so many years ago. Two young boys tried to out-scare each other, with spook tales, one more ghastly than the one before, but in reality, only more hackneyed, but no less.

Pam rolled her eyes. "He's at it again, Cheryl. Would you believe that whenever there's a horror movie on cable, my husband has to watch it. It could be three am, and there he is, at the edge of his seat, eyes glued to the screen."

"Couldn't he just record it?" asked Cheryl.

"He does," answered Pam, "but he gets up to watch it anyway, pad in hand, taking notes ..."

"But honey," Andy cajoled, breaking off his conversation with Jeff, "that's research for my course. Besides, you know that if it ever came down to a choice between you and the Frankenstein monster, I'd take you in a heartbeat."

"Gee, thanks. My Romeo."

"Well, maybe two heartbeats," at which Pam aimed a mock punch at her husband's shoulder.

"I don't know what you see in those flicks," Pam said, in a kind of pseudo-put-down.

"You never will, "Cheryl answered. "It's a guy thing."

"Like us never knowing why you women always go to the bathroom in pairs," Andy retorted. "It's a girl thing."

"On that note," said Pam, rising. "You coming, Cheryl?"

"Right with you, girlfriend."

After the women had departed, Andy took on a more serious mien. "Listen, Jeff, how long do you plan to be in town?"

"I don't know. Tomorrow and the day after, maybe. I want to check on the house, find out what needs to be done with it." He paused, contemplating whether or not to mention the discussion he and Cheryl had had earlier that day, then deciding against it. If Andy knew that Cheryl was even thinking of living there, he would have tried persuading Jeff to do so as well. That kind of double-barreled pressure, Jeff didn't need. "I think we're going to sell it."

"Reason I ask," Andy went on, "is I'm working on this project and I could really use your help for it. Do you think —"

"Jeff? Jeff Strickland? I thought that was you."

Jeff turned around to see the imposing form of a large, formidable-looking black man towering behind him. It took him a few seconds to recognize Chief Parsons. After all, Jeff had seldom seen him wearing anything other than a police uniform. Nor could he recall ever having seen the man with an attractive statuesque woman by his side.

"Chief," Jeff said, standing, and shaking the man's hand. "How are you?"

"Just fine, just fine. I'd like for you to meet my wife, Renee. Renee, this is Jeff Strickland, Peter Strickland's boy."

"Pleased to meet you, Jeff."

"Good to meet you, Mrs. Parsons."

"Renee."

"Renee. This is my friend, Andy Buchanan."

"Andy."

"Chief Parsons. Mrs. Parsons."

"Come on, now," chided Parsons, "we don't need to be formal here. It's Linus and Renee. What have you been up to?"

"Not much. I'm married now. Working at Stockton Prep as a phys. ed. instructor and swim coach.

"Fine, fine. How's your father doing?"

"Much better," Jeff answered. "He and my Mom spent the winter in New Mexico and they just fell in love with the place. They're looking to buy something …"

At that moment, Parsons' cell phone trilled.

"Parsons here." The chief's demeanor went from jovial to somber within a few seconds. When Parsons was finished, he turned to Jeff and Andy and said, "Sorry I have to run, Jeff. But give your father my best."

"Is everything OK?" Jeff asked.

"No. I'm afraid not."

4

Chuck Bascom was a happy man, and why not? His work was just about done. He was soon to be heading home. Tomorrow at this time, he and Linda would be down in Falls Church, Virginia, playing with their new grandkid. He wouldn't be thinking about work for a whole week.

Chuck was the foreman at the North Rim Circle Development construction site. A huge, multi-acre chunk had been torn from the Ridge. Where there was once a forest, there was a plain of reddish-brown dirt, adorned with bulldozers, cranes, backhoes, and pits. These would soon be the foundations for a new housing development. At the easternmost end of the development was a bank of prefabricated mobile-type structures, one of which served as Chuck Bascom's office.

Linda Bascom often called her husband a workaholic, and Chuck had to admit she was right. He could still remember the lean years in the construction industry, and he felt fortunate to have this job. It was a damn lucrative one, and more importantly, a secure one. There was a lot of development going up around Taylorville, Stockton, Dunbar's Crossing, and all of the outlying areas. Malls, housing developments, industrial centers, you name it—they were going up all over. The company Chuck worked for was getting all of the major contracts, and Chuck was glad to be on board at a time like this. So what if he worked a few extra hours each night and a few extra weekends each month?

It was a small offering to make at the altar of Lady Luck. Besides, it bought him a week off to visit Chuck, Jr., Marilyn, and the new grandkid.

The last of the daylight had faded behind the Ridge as Chuck checked the final invoice on his PC. Everything seemed in order. There was little left to do. Log off. Leave a final note for his assistant. Give Linda a quick call to tell her he was on his way home (and wouldn't she be surprised?). Kill the lights. Lock up. Just forget about everything until this time next week. Yes sir, all was right with the world.

He was about to phone Linda, when he heard the sound.

He had the receiver halfway to his ear when the heard the something scraping against metal. He replaced the phone and listened intently. When he didn't hear anything for about a minute, he decided it was nothing, and reached for the phone again.

Then he heard it a second time.

There was no mistake. Someone was on the site and had scraped something against one of the prefabs.

Chuck felt anger welling up inside of him. Someone who had no business being here was in the site. *His* site. He knew that the project wasn't popular with everyone in the area. Some residents resented the environmental damage done to the Ridge. They had tried to shut down the project using every means from legal action to organized protest. In the end, their efforts all came to nil. Still, some of the more vocal and vehement ones threatened acts of eco-terrorism, which Chuck shrugged off as the self-righteous mouthings of a few malcontents. Besides, these were people he'd known for years. They might speak in anger, but Chuck doubted that any of them would resort to vandalism.

Still …

Chuck reached behind the file cabinet by the door and pulled out a baseball bat. Sometimes during breaks, the guys would toss around a baseball. Chuck, an avid Red Sox fan, would join in to get some batting practice.

He opened the door of his office and stood there, holding the bat in front of him. "Who's there?" he boomed. Chuck was a big man, and he hoped that by showing himself holding the bat, he would scare away the intruder. By nature, he was a gentle man who had no desire to crack skulls, but this was *his* watch and if push came to shove …

"Who's there?" he shouted again.

For a moment there was silence. Just as Chuck was ready to assume that the intruder had sneaked off, he heard it again. This time, it was footsteps along with that scraping sound coming from behind the prefab directly across from him.

The footsteps were slow and measured, and coming closer.

"Get out of here, you son of a bitch!"

In answer, another sound emanated from behind the prefab. A cross between a cough and a growl. An animalistic sound.

Did the son of a bitch have a dog with him?

Chuck came out of the office, gripping the bat.

"This is your last warning, pal! You better get off this property and I mean now!"

Another sound. There was movement behind the prefab plus a hissing sound, as if steam were escaping from a very large radiator.

Ordinarily, Chuck would have gone back in the office and phoned Chief Parsons' office, but a mixture of anger and curiosity was overwhelming him. Any ordinary vandal would have waited till after hours, when the site was deserted, to do any dirty work. Yet this bastard, who couldn't miss seeing the lights in the office, chose now to come onto the site. Not only that, but he was raising enough hell to make his presence known, unmistakably. This display of arrogance only served to heighten Chuck's ire.

He walked closer to the prefab, beyond the light from the office, and noticed something else. A smell. The fetid odor of something that died and had long lain dead. He gagged.

The noise of footsteps began again, and to Chuck's relief, they seemed to be moving away from him. This relief was short-lived, however. The sound of retreat gave way to a faster sound of footsteps approaching. This sound gave way to no sound. This silence, in turn, gave way to the clunk of something heavy being dropped on metal.

Chuck turned in the direction of this last sound, and realized what it was.

The intruder had backed up for a running start, and then run forward so it could leap onto the roof of the prefab!

Chuck, a good thirty feet from the prefab and with the light at his back, could only see the structure dimly. Squinting, he could make out a hunched-over shape moving on its roof.

Chuck froze, still brandishing the bat. He wasn't sure what he was looking at, but this was no disgruntled environmentalist. It was some kind of animal. There was that horrid smell, the growling, and the sound it made against the roof as it moved—*tap-tap* that could only come from claws on metal.

Brandishing the bat, Chuck backed up. Perhaps this would be a good time to call Chief Parsons after all.

He never got the chance.

Whatever was on the roof leaped, covering the distance effortlessly, landing upon Chuck's chest, knocking him to the ground. Chuck's head snapped back, hitting a rock, and amidst the painful pinwheels of light, something else registered. Two huge unblinking yellow orbs.

Chuck pushed against his attacker and drew back his hand with a cry of pain. His hand was all bloody as if he'd rammed his palm full strength into a porcupine. It also burned, as if the quills were doused in acid.

Miraculously, Chuck's other hand still clung to the bat and he swung it like a billy club. To his relief, he felt something give. After the first blow, the attacker shifted its weight so that Chuck was able to strike a few more hits. With each one, the attacker backed off a little more.

Just as Chuck was starting to feel jubilant, he realized what was really happening. The attacker wasn't retreating, merely changing position. This became excruciatingly clear when Chuck leveled his next blow, only to find his hand immersed in something wet and sticky. Suddenly, something snapped with the force of a bear trap, and Chuck found himself looking at blood-gushing stump which no longer held a baseball bat, or even a hand, for that matter.

Even before the pain could register, Chuck found himself upended and off the ground. The bear trap snapped shut again on Chuck's upper leg and this time, the pain did register. He screamed as the bear trap came down again and again on his other leg, his torso, his torso again, his head.

The screams died when the man did. On the heels of those screams sounded a shrill keening ululation that never came from a human throat. It might have been a sound of triumph.

5

Freakin' tightass.

Elliot had just concluded his meeting with the Stricklands and there was something *off* about them. The wife was nice enough, but the husband was a freakin' tightass. It was he who informed Elliot, quite adamantly, that the decision had been made to sell the house. But from that point on, it was the wife who did most of the talking. It was she who asked about the repairs, the landscaping, the logistics of the upcoming sale, and very hesitantly at that. It was she who took charge of the transactions, not because she wanted to, (it was clear that she didn't) but because the husband suddenly clammed up. It was also she who asked about Elliot's son; they understood that Elliot had a little boy—could they meet him? Elliot explained that EJ was up in his room getting over a hissy fit. Just before the couple left, the husband found his voice again and told Elliot that he'd be in touch.

Yeah, definitely *off.*

Well, there was no point in pondering the oddities of the Stricklands. Elliot had something more pressing to attend to. He had to make peace with EJ.

Elliot tried to be a good father to his active and energetic boychild. He'd often come home drained and exhausted, but never so much so that he wouldn't muster up some vigor on his son's behalf. And as for discipline, he was a total mush. All EJ would have to do, after some major mischief, was put on a tearful, scrunched up face and his father would melt and all would be forgiven.

Until today.

That morning, before the Stricklands showed, EJ returned from a visit with his best friend, Jamie McAlister. When EJ got home, he told his dad about this "really neat place" he and Jamie went to: a certain ruined stone structure alongside the carriage road on the Ridge.

Elliot lost it. Without thinking, he grabbed his son's arm, spun him around and smacked EJ's butt, not hard, but emphatically and yelled, "Don't you ever go up there again, you hear me? YOU STAY OUT OF THOSE WOODS." Elliot's sudden anger coupled with fact of the blow, rather its force, caused EJ to burst into tears. He ran up to his room, and slammed the door, but not before giving his father a combined look of hurt, surprise, anger, and fear.

It was now time to begin the slow walk upstairs to EJ's room. The door was still closed and when Elliot turned the doorknob, he was relieved to find that it hadn't been locked. He walked in and found EJ lying on his stomach on the bed. At the sound of Elliot entering the room, EJ turned, and the look of reproach made Elliot feel one inch tall.

Elliot spoke first. "Hi, pal."

EJ turned away.

"EJ, I need for you to look at me," Elliot persisted.

With exaggerated slowness, EJ turned around and faced Elliot, that terrible look of reproach still frozen on his face.

Elliot took a deep breath and began. "I'm sorry I hit you, but you have to understand something. Those woods, and especially those ruins you were at, are very dangerous. When I heard you went there, I guess I just lost it and I'm sorry." He stopped, attempting to gauge EJ's response.

The look of censure on EJ's face remained, but it melted, just a little. "But, Jamie goes there all the time, Daddy. It's not a bad place."

Elliot leaned forward, and put his hand on his son's shoulder. "You have to listen to me, Elliot. It *is* a bad place, and you have to stay away from there." Elliot paused. He'd heard about the death of that foreman at the North Rim Circle Development construction site. For maybe a nano-second, he was tempted to tell his son about it to bolster his argument, but decided against it. No reason to lay that on the kid. Still, he had to get his point across. "You remember the story of *Peter and the Wolf?*"

"Sure, Daddy," EJ answered, wide-eyed, no longer sullen. It was serious business when his father called him "Elliot." "Are there wolves up there?"

"Yeah, I think maybe there are," Elliot answered, figuring that this type of white lie was OK under the circumstances. "That's why I want you to stay out of those woods. So if Jamie or any of your other friends tries to get you to go up there, you tell them that your father said that you can't go. Do you understand?"

"OK, Daddy, I'm sorry."

"I'm sorry too, pal. Friends?"

"Sure."

Father and son hugged each other and things *were* cool between them.

For the time being.

6

Chief Linus Parsons was sitting in his office, cursing himself for a damn fool.

On the one hand, his common sense was telling him that his latest course of action was foolish, far-fetched, ridiculous. On the other hand, the objects on his desk in front of him were telling him the exact opposite. He was doing the right thing, the logical thing, the *only* thing he could do.

Chief Linus Parsons was still a firm believer in a sixth sense. Not the John Edwards variety; but the kind that a man develops after being a cop for thirty-plus years. Linus Parsons *was* a cop for thirty-plus years. He hoped his sixth sense would break the deadlock between his common sense and the objects in front of him.

His sixth sense remained uncooperative and silent.

Linus Parsons sighed and reached for his coffee cup. Usually, he preferred decaf, but now, he opted for the heavy-duty stuff. His brain had been working overtime for the last twelve hours and he wanted to keep it working in that mode until he had some answers. Maybe not conclusive ones; he'd settle for interim answers if they led him to conclusive ones.

It would be inaccurate to say that Linus Parsons' crisis began with the Bascom killing. It began way before then, but it was the Bascom killing that bumped things into high gear. It began, Linus supposed, with the animal killings that started back in the nineties. They were more Animal Control's problem than they were his, but he got involved when residents' pets and livestock began turning up dead. The animal killings were alarming, but sporadic, not enough to galvanize the community into an overwhelming sense of outrage. Then, there were the deaths of those two kids just before graduation back in 2005. This got people really up in arms and Linus had barely held onto his job. That killing was still unsolved as were the countless others involving dead deer, possums, dogs, cats, and in one case, a young foal. And the disappearance of the MacAuley woman had never been solved.

But the killing of Chuck Bascom brought community outrage to a new high. Chuck was a longtime resident of Taylorville, well-known and well-loved. Add to that the fact that the construction company which employed Chuck Bascom was one of the area's main employers. They were now making noises about curtailing future projects. That meant less development, fewer jobs, and less money coming into the area. All of this in the face of a long chain of unsolved crimes resulted in some heavy pressure on the broad shoulders of Linus Parsons.

Of all the theories propounded, the one that made the most sense to him was Doc Pressman's. Doc held to his oft-stated conviction that these killings were the work of a group of sickos. Linus had applied his well-honed instinct to that perfectly valid belief. Unfortunately, he found it didn't quite ring true even to his own way of thinking. Trouble was, he couldn't come up with an alternative explanation that *did* ring true.

Linus knew that as a cop, he was expected to be hard-nosed, rational. He was expected to deal in facts. Talk of a sixth sense would negate that expectation, so he generally kept his own counsel on the subject. He'd only discuss it with his wife.

Renee had given voice to that particular belief even before he did. She was a teacher for as long as Linus was a cop and the way she put it was, "Baby, when you've been doing something for as long as I have, you know how something's going to play out even before it does." She swore that when she met a class on the first day of school, she could tell who the devils and angels were. More often than not, she was right.

The more time Linus spent on the job, the more he pondered his wife's statement. She *was* right. Even back in Hackensack, New Jersey, and here in Taylorville, if he saw a group of kids on the street at odd hours, he'd start talking to them. Just innocuous conversation, but within seconds, he knew if they were up to no good. If so, he knew just how hard or how little to lean on them. More often than not, he was right.

Approximately twelve hours ago, Linus Parsons got a call from a man with a funny accent. The man identified himself as Henrik Baumann.

Baumann offered his help in the Bascom slaying. Parsons asked what Baumann's connection was to Chuck Bascom. Baumann replied, "I have never met any member of the Bascom family."

"Then how do you know what happened?"

Pause. "I realize that you will be skeptical upon hearing this, Chief, but sometimes I can see things." A longer pause. "I understand that you are skeptical," Baumann went on, "but I have assisted many police organizations throughout the country in various investigations. Let me give you the names and phone numbers. Do you have email?"

Parsons was in no mood to prolong the conversation, or to humor this nut, so he declined as politely as he could, and hung up. A few minutes later, he checked his email and discovered a message in his inbox from a Henrik Baumann. An email containing a list of contact names, email addresses, and phone numbers of various police officials throughout the country.

What the *fuck*?

Parsons was flabbergasted. He didn't give his email address to this nut, yet—wait a minute. Baumann was no psychic, just a computer geek who knew how to track down an email address. Parsons was about to delete the email when his eye fell upon a familiar name among the contacts.

Anselmo Irrizarry. An old friend of his from the Hackensack days.

He called Anselmo, now a chief like himself. Anselmo was surprised and delighted to hear from his old friend and after much catching up, Linus posed the inevitable question.

"Say, buddy. Does the name Henrik Baumann mean anything to you?"

"Baumann called you?"

"Yeah, I've got this case I'm working on ..."

"He's for real, Linus."

"Say, *what*?"

Anselmo Irrizarry launched into a full description of the Machlan case. How little Kathie Machlan had disappeared for three days and no one knew where she was. How suspect number one was the mother's volatile and uncooperative boyfriend. How suspect number two was the little girl's estranged and unreachable father. How the police were following both threads and coming up with nothing.

Then this guy with a foreign accent calls and tells Anselmo that Kathie Machlan is safe and "in a place where there are many small horses."

"What the hell did that mean?" asked Parsons.

"Craziest thing," Anselmo answered. "I remember it like it was yesterday. Kathie ran away because she was scared of her mom's boyfriend. She'd hid in the basement of a neighbor lady."

"How'd she manage that?"

"Apparently, Kathie knew where the neighbor hid her back door key. She let herself in, and hid for three days. The woman was an elderly widow, hard of hearing, and frequently out of the house, at the local senior center. Kathie would sneak upstairs, take food and water, then head back to the basement."

"So where does this Baumann come in?"

"That's the crazy part, Linus. Baumann told me that Kathie was in a place where there were many small horses. Turns out this neighbor lady had a hobby of collecting small, ceramic figurines of horses she kept in the basement.

"Turned out the boyfriend had nothing to do with Kathie's disappearance," Anselmo went on. "Neither did the father. He was away on a religious retreat, as I remember."

"You gotta be kidding me."

"No joke, Linus. First time I spoke to this guy, I wasn't any more convinced than you are, but I tell you, he's on the level. He's not out for the glory. He's not out for the bucks. He's just out to help out where he can. What do you say?"

Linus said nothing. Talking about it so matter-of-factly with level-headed Anselmo Irrizarry, it seemed so believable. Of course, if it were coming from anyone other than Anselmo …

"OK, I'll talk to him."

Baumann's phone number was on the email and Parsons called him. He listened politely as Baumann stated his credentials and past experiences, followed by an offer to come to Taylorville. Parsons remained skeptical until Henrik Baumann asked him something that changed his mind.

"What did you determine from the scratches on the roof?"

"What scratches? What roof? What are you talking about?"

"Check the roof of the trailer nearest to where Mr. Bascom was found. You will see scratches there which are not on the other roofs of any of the other trailers in the area. Then call me back at this number. If you think I can help you, call me any time of day."

Linus Parsons had taken Henrik Baumann's advice. On his desk, laid out in front of him were a number of Polaroids taken on the roof of the prefab. Polaroids showing scratches which looked like claw marks.

Goddamn, how did he know? Linus Parsons kept asking himself, knowing there was only one way to answer that question.

Chief Linus Parsons reached for the phone.

7

EXTERIOR. The ruins by the carriage road.

CAMERA pans the perimeter of the ruins.

ANDY (voice-over): These ruins date back to Revolutionary times. There's been a good deal of debate as to what their original purpose was. Some say it was a carriage house, others say it was a farmhouse, still others believe it was a way station for colonial troops. One thing is certain, however. These now-crumbling ramparts stand on a tract of land which at one time belonged to Isaac Dunbar ...

CAMERA switches to a close-up of an eighteenth-century style engraving of a man, thin-faced and of uncertain age, but probably in his late forties or early fifties, piercing black eyes, and a stern, forbidding expression.

ANDY (voice-over): ... reputed to be the prime mover behind the event known as Dunbar's Massacre in which thirty-three untrained locals, armed with farming implements and muskets ambushed a contingent of armed British troops numbering one hundred and ten, in these very woods ...

CAMERA switches to a close-up of a Gilbert Stuart-style profile portrait. The subject is a paunchy man in a powdered wig dressed in a red military uniform. His bearing is stiff and rigid, totally military, with the serene expression of one accustomed to easy victories. There is a trace of arrogance in his expression.

ANDY (voice-over): … commanded by General Lowell Burgess, reputed to be King George's top military strategist. All of Burgess' men, including Burgess himself, were killed. (Pause)

CAMERA pans back to the Dunbar engraving.

ANDY (voice-over): None of Dunbar's followers was killed. According to some accounts, the spirit of Isaac Dunbar still patrols these woods. Over the years, people have actually claimed to see an old man walking through these woods carrying an old-fashioned musket or blunderbuss.

EXTERIOR. Cape Cod House. The area between the house and the road is lawn except for a stone walkway from the street to the front door. On the lawn there are toys strewn, a skateboard and a tricycle, indicating that there are kids living here. To the left of the house is a driveway where there is a Chevy Blazer parked. There is also a side door from the house to the driveway from which a pony-tailed blonde woman emerges. She is Wendy Amundsen, in her mid-thirties, a bit on the plump side, but not unattractive. She walks toward the driver's side door of the Blazer.

CAMERA zooms in on Wendy slowly.

ANDY (voice-over): Superstition? Imagination? Mass hysteria? Wendy Amundsen would disagree with you on that.

CLOSE UP on Wendy.

WENDY: It was on a Friday night, last March 26, about 3:30 am. I was coming home from work—I do the books for Haven House, you know, the restaurant down Route 29 in Fardale—you know the place? Anyhow, they stay open late on Friday nights, so sometimes I don't get home till …

ANDY (off-screen): What did you see that night, Wendy?

WENDY: Yeah. Well, I'm driving, and of course it's dark, so I have my brights on …

WENDY DRIVING POINT OF VIEW of car, driving along Route 29.

WENDY (voice-over): … when all of sudden, I see a man just standing in the road.

WENDY CLOSE UP.

ANDY (off-screen): *In* the road?

WENDY (nodding): Yeah. Not off to the side or anything. Right smack-dab in the middle of the road.

ANDY (off-screen): What did you do?

WENDY POINT OF VIEW driving along Route 29, but this time, showing the motion of a car swerving quickly. Screeching tires can be heard.

WENDY (voice-over): Hell, I swerved. I didn't want to hit him, or anything.

CLOSE UP on Wendy.

ANDY (off-screen): Then what?

WENDY (nodding): Well, I stopped the car. I'm just shaken you know?

CAMERA zooms in to CLOSE-UP of Wendy in her car, clearly agitated.

WENDY (voice-over): I figured it was some old guy who wasn't quite right in the head, you know? I mean what's an old guy doing out in the middle of the street at 3 am, you know? So, I started to get out of the car, you know, to see if he's ok. I mean, I know I didn't hit him or anything …

CAMERA zooms out as WENDY starts to open the car door.

WENDY (voice-over): … but then I figure, maybe I should get the hell out of there.

ANDY (voice-over): Why?

WENDY (voice-over): Because it didn't register on me at first, I was so shook, but then I realized the guy was carrying a gun.

CAMERA zooms in to CLOSE-UP of Wendy. As she gets further into the story, reliving the experience, she becomes progressively less composed and more tense as she recollects the experience.

ANDY (off-screen): What kind of gun?

WENDY: I don't know. It all happened so fast. But not the kind my husband has. He's got rifles. It wasn't a shotgun either. It was … uh, I don't know.

Andy's hand passes a piece of paper to Wendy. She's perplexed and uncertain as she looks at it, but if you look carefully, you can see she's nodding, just barely.

ANDY (voice-over): I showed Wendy Amundsen the picture you saw earlier of Isaac Dunbar and asked her if this was the man she'd seen.

WENDY: I don't know. It happened so fast. But you know, the old guy … now that I think of it, he didn't look like he was just wandering there. I mean, he didn't look confused or anything. It was like … well, he looked like he knew where he was and he meant to be there. Oh, yeah, he looked pissed off.

ANDY (off-screen): How do you mean?

WENDY: You know …

CLOSE UP on Wendy scrunching up her face in a scowl.

WENDY: Mad. Kind of mean. (Pause) Scary.

Andy hit the Pause button on the remote. Wendy Amundsen's scrunched-up face froze on the widescreen. "Well, what do you think?"

Jeff leaned back, took a swig of his beer, and answered, "I don't know. That woman? Is she for real?"

"If by that you mean 'Is she an actress?' the answer is no. She's a real person who claimed to see a thin old dude one night on a country road which just happens to run alongside Dunbar's Ridge, where over the last two hundred plus years, other real people have also claimed to have seen the same thing, or some facsimile thereof. That what you're asking?"

Jeff downed the last of his beer. They were sitting on the couch in Andy's rec room exactly one week after the Stricklands' and Buchanans' dinner at Top Hat. Cheryl had been surprised that Jeff wanted to return to Taylorville so soon, particularly after he'd seemed so discomfited after their last visit. Jeff explained that Andy wanted his help on a film project that he was working on. Besides, he'd gotten a call from Elliot Ryan, telling him that he'd gotten estimates on repairs to the plumbing and walkway to the Strickland house. Elliot offered to go over them with him that Sunday, so it made sense to head back into town. Andy had offered to put them up for the night and Cheryl didn't need her arm twisted. She genuinely liked the Buchanans, particularly Pam, and was delighted for the opportunity to engage in some "girl time." She and Pam were currently out shopping while the men viewed Andy's video.

"Jeff?"

"Huh?"

"Earth to Jeff. Earth to Jeff. I asked you what you thought."

"Of the film?"

"No, of having wild, orgiastic sex with farm animals. Yeah, the film, what do you think I meant?"

"When did you decide to become a filmmaker?"

Andy reached for another beer, offered one to Jeff, who declined, then popped the cap himself, and took a swig. "You know I've always been a film buff. I've been teaching film at the university for the past few years. But I've never actually *made* a film, and I've always wanted to. *Capisce?*"

"Yeah, I guess," Jeff responded, having an inkling where this was going, and not liking it.

"Well, you know how I've always been into ghosties and ghoulies and long-legged beasties and things that go bump in the night—from which, may the Good Lord deliver us. I figured it would be a good subject for a film about the area. You know, Dunbar's Massacre. The Backwoods Demon. The various and sundry legends about the Ridge." When Jeff didn't answer, Andy went on, "I'd like you to be a part of it."

"Why?"

Andy's joviality gave way to pure seriousness, something Jeff seldom saw in his friend. "Come on, Jeff, do you really have to ask? Don't you remember what happened that night we were camping at Taylor Creek?"

Jeff did. It was something of which they'd never spoken, for reasons which now seemed obscure to him. "Yeah, I remember."

"Well, I'd like to interview you on tape and kind of re-create that night. Like I did with the Amundsen woman. What do you think?"

"You're not going to stick a video camera up my nose and expect me to tell you how scared I am, are you?" Jeff asked, jokingly.

Andy shook his head, but did not laugh. "No, Jeff. I'm not going to Blair Witch you. This is on the level. I've got a few names of people who live in the area who claim to have had Isaac Dunbar sightings and my best friend just happens to be one of them."

"Where did you get these names from?"

"Well, as you may or may not know, the Psychology Department at the university has the second biggest Paranormal Phenomena research facility in the country. Did you know there's actually a Parapsychology Laboratory at Duke University? It does extensive research in telepathy, extrasensory awareness, precognition, out-of-body experiences, hauntings, you name it. Well, we do too. We've got documentation from all over the country from people who've had weird things like this happen to them. Yeah, a lot of them are cranks, and the resources are limited, but when the staff gets a lot of the same kind of experiences, particularly from the same area, they follow up on them as best they can. When they can't shake the peoples' stories, they take them seriously. One thing they haven't been able to shake are the Dunbar sightings."

"Come on, Andy, you spoke to that woman. She's a whacko."

"She's not, Jeff. Wendy Amundsen may come off as a bit of a flibbertigibbet, but she's not stupid. The documentation she forwarded to the university was articulate and thorough. She's got an extensive bookkeeping business; she's going part-time for her BA with a major in accounting, and pulling a 3.5 index in the process. She's no dope and she believes that she saw something that doesn't quite belong in the normal, everyday world of debits, credits, and ledgers.

"Besides, you and I saw the same thing. Are we whackos?"

"Well," Jeff answered, and then broke into a cockney accent in imitation of the comic-relief sanatorium attendant from the original Tod Browning/Bela Lugosi *Dracula.* "I ain't croizey, but sometimes, I 'ave me doubts about *you.*"

This time, Andy did smile. "OK, I walked into that one. But seriously, Jeff, I'd like your help on this. What do you say?"

"How did you get onto the Amundsen woman?"

"I told you. The university has records of people who've had these types of experience."

"Yeah, I know, but, I mean, aren't they confidential?"

"I've got an in with members of the Psych Department. They contacted the people who wrote them, explaining what I was doing, and asking them if they'd be willing to speak to me. About a third agreed. Believe me, Jeff, no one's confidentiality is being violated. Now quit stalling, huh? Will you help me out on this or not?"

Jeff sighed. It was time to stand and deliver. On the one hand, Andy was his best friend and he wanted to help him out. Besides, the project was interesting and Jeff would be lying if he said that the supernatural lore that clung to the Ridge area hadn't always fascinated him. He was also enough of a ham to relish the idea of being in a film.

On the other hand, though, Jeff was no stranger to the paranormal. He'd grown up in what he believed to be a genuine haunted house, one whose associations were no longer pleasant to him. Participation in this project reawakened those feelings of unpleasantness that he wanted to put behind him. Yet …

"OK, Andy," Jeff answered, "I'll do it. But I still don't understand why you need me for this. You've got other names; you said so yourself. Don't forget, you saw Dunbar yourself, or whatever that thing was. Why don't you go on tape yourself and describe what you saw?"

"To answer your second question first," replied Andy, "if I got on film and told what I saw, it'd look like I was making the film just to put my own experience out for the world to see. It'll have more credibility if I let others describe what they saw, yourself included. As to why I'm so anxious to get you, specifically, on film, do you remember what else happened that night?"

"Sure, we sat around the fire trying to scare the piss out of each other."

"Yeah, but do you remember the story *you* told?" Jeff shook his head. "Well, I do. You called it 'the true story about Isaac Dunbar and Dunbar's Massacre.'"

"Right, now I remember. But so what?"

"The basis of your story was that Isaac Dunbar was a warlock. That he'd been cast out of Salem during the time of the witch trials and that he summoned something dark and evil from out of the earth. How there was lightning and thunder and how the thing that Dunlap summoned not only killed, but utterly *slaughtered* Burgess and his army."

Jeff started to interrupt, Andy held up his hand. "No wait, let me finish. Remember how I asked you where you got that story from? You said it just came to you, remember?"

"Yeah, but …"

"Remember how you said that Dunlap summoned the Demon, not because he wanted to defeat the British, but because he was just flat out evil? That the story we all knew was just a watered-down version?"

"Yeah, but wait a second. You called him Dunlap twice. You mean Dunbar."

"Yes and no." Andy reached for a spiral notebook resting on the end table. He flipped through a series of pages with handwritten notes. "Yeah, here it is.

"Remember how I pointed out to you that the Salem witch trials started in 1692 and that Dunbar's Massacre was in 1771, which would have made Dunbar ancient? You said that because he was a warlock, he might actually have been over a hundred. You remember?"

"Vaguely."

"Well, check this out. There was a Joseph Dunlap living in Salem at the time who was accused of 'trafficking with the devil'. Get it. Joseph Dunlap? Isaac Dunbar? Biblical first name? Similar sounding last name?"

"You're shitting me."

"No, have a look." Andy reached into the notebook and pulled out some photocopies of original documents he'd found in the course of his research. Sure enough, there was the name, Joseph Dunlap, along with other names Jeff knew from his own extensive readings on the era: Sarah and Mary Bishop, Dorcas and Sarah Good, George Jacobs Senior and Junior, the Proctor family.

"Yeah, but wait a minute. These other people were hung or died in prison. What happened to Dunlap?"

"No one knows. One version of the story says that when they came to get him, he was gone. No Dunlap, no servants, no nothing. Another version has it that he was captured, but escaped during a fire in the Meeting House where he was being tried. Whole place burned down. Everyone died. Everyone except Dunlap.

"Now get this. I have some scattered descriptions of this Dunlap. Listen to the words used to describe him: hoary, gaunt, sallow, formidable-looking. Sound familiar? Like the descriptions of the Dunbar sightings I showed you?"

"Come on, Andy," Jeff persisted, exerting every possible effort not to believe, "it's probably some ancestor of Dunbar's. Do you really think Dunbar and Dunlap are the same person?"

Andy shrugged. "It's your story, buddy. I always thought it was something you made up until I started doing some digging. There's a whole body of information about Dunbar which never made it into our high school history books, really obscure shit. Yet, here you are, some kid who isn't even from around here, spinning this story out of nowhere, and you don't even know where you got it from, but it has a basis in fact. Doesn't that sound kind of 'Twilight Zone' to you?"

Yes, it did. And Jeff didn't want to go there. "You're creepin' me out, Andy."

"You think that's bad? You should hear some of the stuff I dug up on Dunlap. Man, if half of what they say about him is true, the guy was a real psychopath. He was accused of killing and torturing people, some of them kids. A real Ted Bundy type. And supposedly, when he confessed, he was *enjoying* himself, getting off on telling what he'd done, stuff he hadn't even been accused of."

"And you're saying that Dunlap and Dunbar were the same person?"

"No, you said it, Jeff. Which begs the question: what was his real purpose in conjuring up the Backwoods Demon?"

"You're talking as if the guy really did summon up a demon from hell. Come on, Andy. It's just a legend."

Andy sighed. "OK, OK, you're right. I guess I'm letting my imagination run away with itself. Let's just wait for the wives. They should be back soon. I could use a cup of coffee right about now. How about you?"

What Jeff could use right about then was a double shot of scotch. Legend or not, the thought of a psychopathic mass murderer invoking a demonic being to do his bidding was just too disturbing.

He settled for coffee.

8

"Daddy, DAD-EEE!"

Elliot leaped out of bed and nearly tripped over Garfield in a mad rush to get to his son's room. Negotiating his way through the darkened house, not taking the time to turn on a light, Elliot made it to EJ's bedside. He flicked on the overhead light, horror-stricken to see EJ sitting up in bed, rigid. The little boy's eyes were wrenched open, locked on some imaginary pinpoint straight ahead, but unfocused and unseeing, like those of a blind person. Tears were streaming down his face and his mouth was pulled back in terror. Elliot practically leaped from the door to his son's bed. He encircled the boy in a fierce embrace, horror-stricken to feel his son's unyielding, unresponsive body in his arms, like a two-by-four. Or a corpse.

"EJ, you OK? Come on, pal, snap out of it!"

Gradually, EJ's stiffness gave way to a series of shakes, and finally, his body went limp, its only motion a series of hysterical sobs. Elliot held on tighter, and kissed the top of his son's head, over and over, until EJ responded by putting his arms around his father's torso in a veritable death grip.

"It's all right, pal. I'm here. I'm here."

EJ continued sobbing and Elliot continued holding him. Obviously, the child had had a bad dream. He'd had them often after Susan died. Thankfully, they declined in frequency since that dreadful day, but EJ occasionally awoke in the middle of the night, weepy and tearful.

At such times, Elliot would sit up with him until he fell asleep again. Often, it was all he could do to keep from crying himself.

But this wasn't just weepiness. EJ was hysterical.

"EJ, you OK? Talk to me, pal. What's happening?"

Finally, EJ responded to the sound of his father's voice. "Daddy, can I sleep in your room with you tonight? Please?"

"Sure, pal. Bad dream?" EJ slowly released the death grip on his father and Elliot loosened his hold as well. Father and son faced each other and there was a look of fear on the little boy's face, such as Elliot had never seen on anyone.

"I saw the man again, Daddy. You were right. It is a bad place. I wish I never went there."

"What man? What place?" It was clear Elliot wasn't going to get any answers right then. The worst of EJ's sobs had given way to a set of rapid-fire hiccups, which, mixed with EJ's dwindling sobs made the boy incapable of answering. Elliot took his son by the hand, walked him into the bathroom and poured him a glass of water.

"Here you go, pal. Drink it up. Slowly now. That's it. Slowly."

EJ downed the water, after which sobs and hiccups subsisted to the point where he could talk again. Elliot led him to his own bed, lay EJ down and sat beside him. "You feel up to telling me what happened?" he whispered.

"I saw the man," EJ said again.

"The same one you told me about before?" EJ nodded. "The one who comes into our yard? The real skinny, old one?" EJ kept nodding. "The man with the funny clothes? Was he still mad?"

EJ nodded vigorously. "He's mean, I don't like him!"

"I don't like him either. What did you dream, pal?"

"You know the place I went to with Jamie?"

Elliot stiffened.

"Yeah. I know the place you mean. What about it?"

"Well, I went there, and there was something there. An animal."

"What kind of animal?"

"I don't know. I didn't see it good, but it was standing on the rocks there."

"What did the animal look like?"

"I don't know. I couldn't see it too good."

155

"Well, what could you see?"

"It was big and black and it had these big yellow eyes and it kept looking at me."

"Then what happened?"

"Then I was inside the animal."

"What do you mean inside the animal? Did it eat you?"

"No, I was looking out, but it wasn't me. I was looking out from inside the animal. OW, Daddy, you're hurting me!"

"Sorry." Elliot became aware of the tight grip he had on his son's shoulder, and gently started to rub it, to comfort EJ. "Is that what scared you?"

"No, Daddy, I wasn't scared then. It was kind of fun. The animal started running really fast and I couldn't see the man anymore. It was like being on a roller coaster."

"Yeah," Elliot answered, listening with only half an ear. He remembered only too well the sensation that his son was describing. He remembered the elation, the feeling of supremacy within him when he was seeing the world through this other set of eyes. The exhilaration he felt in that state, when he pondered what he could do to the Coreys and anyone else who messed with him. Now EJ's dream had just had the same feel to it. But this was just a dream, wasn't it?

"It sounds exciting."

"It *wasn't* exciting, Daddy, it was *bad*," EJ shouted and started crying again. Elliot reached out to comfort him. He was at a loss as to how to get him to tell the rest of the dream. He wondered if he should even try, given that the boy seemed so traumatized. It turned out to be a moot question; the words just poured out of EJ's mouth. Apparently the experience was so toxic, that he just had to get rid of it.

"There was a man in the woods, and the animal started chasing the man. It caught the man and started eating him and tearing him apart with its teeth. The man was screaming and telling it to stop, but it wouldn't. I tried to make it stop, but it wouldn't, it just kept biting and hurting the man."

"Was this the man you told me about seeing in our yard, EJ?"

EJ shook his head. "He was there, though. He was standing there watching and laughing. I hate him, Daddy, he's *mean*!"

"Yeah, I hate him too. What happened to the other man?"

EJ broke into a fresh round of sobs. "It was *you*, Daddy. The animal killed you with me inside it!

"And Mommy was there too, Daddy!"

9

Demons and specters were the last thing on Jeff's mind as he sat at the kitchen table, reviewing the quotes Elliot had obtained for him. There were three for the plumbing and four for the walkway, two of which were within $100 of each other. One was way up there, and eliminated at once. Elliot, who had done business with all of them, was describing the type and quality of work they did. Jeff was processing the information, anxious to conclude all house-related business and get the place on the market as soon as possible.

Elliot seemed preoccupied as well, going over the information with a brusqueness he hadn't exhibited in their previous meeting.

The other distraction was Elliot's young son, a towheaded six-year-old who looked as his father must have looked at that age. The little boy, who Elliot sometimes called "EJ," sometimes "pal," was indifferent to Jeff, but clingy to his father in the extreme. If Elliot was sitting in a chair, EJ was in his lap with an arm around his father. Once, when Elliot got up to get a Coke, EJ clung to his father's leg with both hands and wouldn't let go, even as his dad was walking. It looked like a comedy routine, and even if this degree of attention didn't amuse Elliot, he was certainly tolerant about it. The only time EJ let go of his father was when a car horn sounded outside the house, and Elliot said "That's Grandma, pal. Come on, let's go," and led the child out to the waiting car.

"You'll have to excuse my son," Elliot said as he returned after escorting EJ outside. "We both had a real bad night last night."

"Sorry. Is everything OK?"

"I hope so. He dreamed about this old guy that he says he keeps seeing around the house and it really spooked him …" Elliot stopped in mid-sentence.

"What's wrong?" Jeff asked.

"You OK?"

"Yeah, why?"

"There's this look on your face. You look …"

"I look what?"

"You look like my son did when he was telling me this bad dream he had."

"Bad dream?"

"Yeah, something about an old man hanging around the house …"

"Wait a minute. Your son said he saw an old man hanging around the house?"

"Yeah, why …"

"Did he say anything else?"

"Look, Jeff. I'm not sure that's any of your business."

"Please," Jeff prodded. "I'm not being nosy here. I have a reason for asking. Your son saw an old man hanging around the house?"

"Yeah," Elliot began, choosing his words with care. "He said that the guy was real old and wearing funny clothes and he looked mean."

"Did you see this man?"

No, but my cat did, Elliot almost said, remembering the puncture marks Garfield left on his thigh, that had gone from throbbing to itching. Instead, he answered, "No."

After a long pause, Jeff spoke. "You got some time? There's something I think you need to see."

#

WENDY: I don't know. It happened so fast. But you know, the old guy … now that I think of it, he didn't look like he was just wandering there. I mean, he didn't look confused or anything. It was like … well, he looked like he knew where he was and he meant to be there. Oh, yeah, he looked pissed off.

ANDY (off-screen): How do you mean?

WENDY: You know …

CLOSE UP on Wendy scrunching up her face in a scowl.

WENDY: Mad. Kind of mean. (Pause) Scary.

Jeff stopped the video and turned to Elliot, who sat there, transfixed. The two men were sitting in the living room watching a copy of Andy's film that Andy had lent to Jeff. Jeff had intended to take it home and watch the rest of it (*sans* Cheryl—she didn't share his enthusiasm for "ghosties and ghoulies and long-legged beasties," etc.). He agreed to let Andy interview him for the film, but he wasn't comfortable with that commitment. He wanted to see the rest of the video before deciding whether he wanted to go ahead with it or make some excuse to back out.

He didn't expect to view it again so soon, and certainly not with Elliot Ryan.

The two men sat in silence for what seemed like a long time, after which, all Elliot could say was "Far out," in a dry whisper. Just "Far out." No comments about how Wendy Amundsen was some kind of whacko. No criticism of how outlandish her story seemed. No accusation as to how dare Jeff show him this travesty of aborted science fiction and make light of his son's discomfort. None of that, just, "Far out."

Far out indeed.

Elliot stood up. "I'm getting a beer. You want one?"

"Sure, thanks."

Elliot returned with two Heinekens, passed one to Jeff and resumed his seat on the couch. "Turn that back on again. I want to see the rest."

HAND HELD POINT OF VIEW SHOT OF CARRIAGE ROAD

ANDY (voice-over): This is a carriage road also dating from the Revolutionary War. It was used to transport goods by the resisting continental army as well as by British troops. It was on this road that General Lowell Burgess and his men were ambushed by, what many have believed to be a group of local area residents, led by Isaac Dunbar, in resistance to the British incursion. But there are people who might debate that version of the facts.

CAMERA switches to a barrel-chested man in a cambric shirt, blue jeans and calf-high Timberland boots, walking along the carriage road. Despite his white hair, his walk is sure and robust; this man is no frail and feeble senior citizen stereotype.

ANDY (voice-over): One of these is Roy Matthews, lifelong resident of the area, ex-Marine colonel, former mortgage banker, now retired.

ROY (voice-over): I've been hunting, camping, and hiking in these woods, man and boy ...

MONTAGE effect of old photographs showing several versions of a much younger Roy Matthews in the woods, sometimes with friends, sometimes holding a brace of ducks.

ROY (voice-over): ... and I've been listening to stories of the Backwoods Demon all my life and as far as I was concerned, it was all a load of hooey.

ANDY (voice-over): But something happened two years ago to change Roy Matthews' mind.

CARRIAGE ROAD, Roy walking, only now, it's dark and Roy's wearing hunting togs and carrying a rifle.

ROY (voice-over): I was just about winding up the day when I heard something ...

TREES AND BRUSH alongside the road. RUSTLING SOUNDS, not the kind from an errant breeze, but something moving with a sense of deliberation and intent. CAMERA PANS the vegetation and the rustling continues.

ROY (voice-over): ... moving in the trees. I stopped and the movement stopped too.

CAMERA switches back to Roy who has stopped walking and is holding his rifle in a position of semi-readiness. After a few seconds, Roy begins walking again, but he's now more alert and cautious.

ROY (voice-over): I don't know what it was. I don't think of myself as a man who lets his imagination run away with him. But there was something about that noise gave me the willies. When I'm hunting, I'm very attuned to what I can't see. You have to be. What you don't see can be one of your buddies or it can be game. But there was something out there that was trying to keep from being seen. I didn't like that.

TREES AND BRUSH, ROY'S POINT OF VIEW. The sound heard earlier continues, then changes. It is no longer some abstract rustling; now it sounds like footsteps and it's coming closer.

CAMERA switches back to Roy who is bringing the rifle up to aim.

ROY (voice-over as the footsteps get louder): Whatever it was, was getting closer and soon, I figured it would be out of the woods and onto the path.

ANDY (voice-over): Did it cross your mind that it could be a fellow hunter?

ROY (voice-over): No, sir. No hunter worth his spit is going to sneak up on another hunter in the dark. That's stupid. Childish. Like I told you, I was getting a bad feeling about this.

POINT OF VIEW OF SOMETHING IN THE WOODS, Camera shakes as something emerges onto the carriage road, facing Roy.

CLOSE UP ON ROY. What he sees clearly surprises him. Perhaps he is even a little afraid, but he isn't about to break position and run. He's holding the rifle in firing position.

ROY'S POINT OF VIEW on a spot about thirty feet from where he is standing. It is dark and there are sounds of footsteps, not rapid, but measured and calculated. There is a suggestion of something there, but it is unclear and indistinct. Then, there is another sound, a GUTTURAL SOUND.

ANDY (voice-over): Did you see anything?

ROY (voice-over): Can't be sure. Like I said, it was dark and whatever it was, was standing a ways from where I was. But there *was* something there. All I can tell you is that it was dark and it was big.

ANDY (voice-over): How could you tell it was big?

ROY (voice-over): For maybe a split-second, I saw its eyes. They were a bright orange, or maybe yellow, but they were at my eye level, so I know that it was big. It made this noise, kind of like … (imitates a cat hissing at high volume).

ANDY (voice-over): What did you do?

ROY (voice-over): I fired at the son of a bitch. (Pauses) I never fired at anything I couldn't see before then or since, but, so help me, I fired.

SOUND OF RIFLE SHOTS.

POINT OF VIEW OF SOMETHING IN THE WOODS, only this time, the movement races back into the woods away from the carriage road.

ROY (voice-over): It made that (imitates cat sound) and high-tailed it out of there. I don't know whether I hit it or not, but it ran like a son of a bitch. (Pause) I high-tailed it out of there too.

CAMERA switches to daylight shot of Roy on the carriage road, dressed again in his cambric shirt, jeans and Timberlands.

ANDY (voice-over): What did you think it was?

ROY (shaking his head): No idea. I want to say it was some kind of cat, a cougar, what with that noise it made, but a cougar doesn't stand on its hind legs. Those eyes were on a level with mine, sure as I'm here talking to you.

ANDY (voice-over): Do you think it might have been the Backwoods Demon?

ROY: (long pause): I don't know. (Pause, shorter this time) No comment.

There were several more interview segments. Some were with people who had sighted an ethereal old man answering to Isaac Dunbar's description. Some described something black and threatening that they couldn't identify somewhere on the Ridge. Both Jeff and Elliot were transfixed, but it was the final segment that really hit home to Elliot.

EXTERIOR: Downtown street in Stockton.

ANDY (voice-over): It's something that's common in dreams. You see not only the world conjured up by your sleeping mind, but your own body, from the outside. But not many people have one while awake, and not many people have one that takes them to Dunbar's Ridge. It's called an out-of-body experience, or OBE.

CAMERA TRACKS, finally focusing on one of the storefronts. This one has a funky logo which reads "Which Craft."

ANDY (voice-over): One person who's had such an OBE, is Carrie-Ann Bell, owner of a shop in Stockton that buys works made by local crafts people and artisans, and sells them.

CAMERA TRACKS the interior of Which Craft. What's revealed is a mélange of organized clutter including (but not limited to) sculptures, jewelry, stained glass lights and *objets d'art*, paintings, and macramé. It rests on Carrie-Ann, leaning against an antique desk toward the rear of the store. Carrie-Ann is an attractive woman in her mid-forties. She's an aging hippie wearing a peasant blouse and skirt with a shawl around her shoulders, Wonder Woman-style sandals with straps that coil upward along the calves. No socks or stockings. Her voice is bell-like and her words spoken with meticulous enunciation.

CLOSE-UP on Carrie-Ann.

CARRIE-ANN: My first time was in eighth grade. Saint James Academy for girls. It was a typical Catholic school. I hated it. I used to zone out all the time. One day, Sister was going on about something—I don't even remember what—when I started focusing on the cover of my loose-leaf. I'd written my boyfriend's name on it. Sister hated when we did stuff like that, but I didn't care; I did it anyway. Anyway, I'm looking at his name. Joey DiBartolo. I still remember it. Anyway, I'm looking at it and I'm thinking things about Joey that would give Sister a heart attack. (Giggles) Then I notice that Joey's name is getting smaller and smaller, and so is my loose-leaf, my desk, everything. Then I see the top of this girl's head and I notice this pink headband she's wearing and I realize it's me. I'm looking down and I'm seeing myself. It's not everything getting smaller, it's me moving up. I'm having—what did you call it before?

ANDY (off-screen): OBE.

CARRIE-ANN: That's right. OBE. And I just freaked. I started screaming and all of a sudden, I'm back in my own body, sitting at my own desk, and all of my friends are starting at me, just as scared as I am. Sister's trying to hold me down. I guess she figured I had the devil inside of me.

ANDY (off-screen): What happened then?

CARRIE-ANN: I don't remember it too well; I guess I calmed down and they called my mother and she took me to the doctor. They thought I might have had an epileptic fit, but after they performed a battery of tests on me, they said I was OK, told my mother to keep me home for a few days and keep an eye on me. Anyway, I was OK, and they sent me back to school the next week.

ANDY (off-screen): Did it happen again?

CARRIE-ANN: One of those … OBEs? Yes. Several years later.

POINT OF VIEW typical dorm with two beds at either side of the room, two desks across from each bed, and two dressers along the wall perpendicular to the beds. Between the desks is a large window overlooking a college campus.

CARRIE-ANN (voice-over): It was the end of my sophomore year in college and I'd just finished the last of my finals. I had to pull an all-nighter to cram for it and I was really wasted, so you can imagine how I felt now that it was all over. I was sitting on my bed with a bottle of wine and all I wanted to do was just drink it down and sleep for a million years.

164

POINT OF VIEW shot continues, a wine bottle is brought up to the viewer's eye level, to simulate the act of drinking. This is repeated several times during Carrie-Ann's speech.

CARRIE-ANN (voice-over): It was a cheap wine, but I didn't care. I'd been so stressed the last few days and I just felt so mellow getting it over with, and the wine just warmed me all over. I just felt so *good* …

POINT OF VIEW subtly changes as CAMERA cranes upward, showing the room from above. As it does so, a girl resembling Carrie-Ann, but obviously much younger, becomes visible. She is wearing raggedy jean shorts, a T-shirt, and the same kind of sandals we saw Carrie-Ann wearing earlier. She is holding a bottle of wine to her side. CAMERA continues to crane.

CARRIE-ANN (voice-over): … and the next thing I knew was it happened again. I saw myself looking down at my own body, my room, everything.

ANDY (voice-over): The first time this happened to you, you were terrified. How did you feel this time?

CARRIE-ANN (voice-over): A little scared at first, I guess. I don't know. Maybe it was the wine. Maybe because I was older, more mature. Anyhow, it felt kind of *nice*. I'd done meditation and it made me feel all warm and peaceful. I felt the same way looking down at myself. I just went with it for about—I don't know, a couple of minutes, maybe. Then it was over. I was sitting on my bed again, holding a bottle of wine.

ANDY (voice-over): What did you do then?

CAMERA returns to close-up of Carrie-Ann in the Which Craft.

CARRIE-ANN: I finished the bottle of wine and slept for a million years.

MEDIUM SHOT of Carrie-Ann, this one taken at a different time. She's no longer wearing the peasant blouse, dress, and shawl, but a cable-knit sweater and jeans.

ANDY (voice-over): You've had numerous OBEs since that last one, but tell us about your most recent one.

CARRIE-ANN (after a long pause): It happened about three years ago when I first moved into the area. I'd just broken up with this man I'd been living with …

ANDY (voice-over): Not Joey DiBartolo?

CARRIE-ANN (laughing): Oh, good Lord, no. Anyway, I'd just taken an apartment and it was just me and my two cats. I was smoking a joint when I felt—I don't know how to describe it; it was kind of a gentle tugging on my mind. Like something going on out of the corner of your eye and you find your attention being drawn to it. Know what I mean?

ANDY (voice-over): I think so. Go on.

CARRIE-ANN: Anyway, I find myself …

CAMERA cuts to the quarry where Jeff first met Andy and Neil, only now, it is dusk. The CAMERA is static.

CARRIE-ANN (continues as voice-over): … at this mountain lake. It's absolutely beautiful. Then, I realize something.

CAMERA begins to move toward the water and we realize that this is a POINT OF VIEW shot.

CARRIE-ANN (voice-over): I'm not floating above my own body. I'm not even *seeing* my own body, the way I did the other times. I'm totally away from it. That's when I realize something else. I'm in someone else's body. I'm seeing this lake and these woods through someone else's eyes.

ANDY (voice-over): How did you feel?

CARRIE-ANN (voice-over): Marvelous. Absolutely ecstatic. The feeling was like nothing I'd ever felt before. The next thing I know, I'm in the water and it feels *wonderful* …

POINT OF VIEW shot to the edge of the lake, then rapid movement through the forest along one of the trails.

CARRIE-ANN (voice-over): … then I'm running through the forest faster than I ever ran before. You know what a runner's high is? It has something to do with increased endorphin levels during physical activity. Anyway, I run, but I've never experienced a high like that. I don't know. I was going so *fast*. I must have covered about ten miles. Then it was over.

CAMERA switches back to close-up of Carrie-Ann.

ANDY (off-screen): What do you mean "it was over?"

CARRIE-ANN (sadly): It just was. Next thing I know, the cat jumps on my stomach, and I'm back lying on my couch in my apartment. (Pause) You know how it is when you're having a really nice dream, then you wake up, and you try to fall back asleep to finish your dream, but you can't? That's how I felt.

ANDY (off-screen): Are you sure it wasn't a dream?

CARRIE-ANN: It wasn't a dream.

Tape ends.

Both men sat silent, absorbing what they'd seen.

For Elliot, the Bell segment was a validation of the horror he'd experienced years ago. The fact that it had happened to his own son was like something foul and putrid thrust into his face. Something he tried to bury when he gave up weed and started working for Doc, but couldn't, not completely, until years later. What did the video call them, OBEs? Now they were back, still out there. EJ's dream and the video proved it.

For Jeff, who had never seen the entire video, it was a negation of what he'd experienced growing up in this house. Nearly every visitation he'd had had a positive effect on him. That external voice, in time internalized, telling him not to be afraid helped forge him from an awkward pre-teen to a confident fully-actualized man. He hadn't been afraid when he took the initiative and made new friends at the quarry. When he jumped off a cliff into a bracingly cold mountain lake. When he tried out for the swimming team. When he asked out the prettiest girl in school, and later when he asked her to marry him.

Elliot had heard of the Backwoods Demon, of course; it was impossible *not to* while living within twenty miles of Taylorville. He'd never taken such talk seriously. Even when he'd had his OBEs, he didn't associate it with the legends and old wives' tales so common in the area.

Jeff was familiar with the term, "paranormal," and up to now, it held no terrors for him. But suddenly, it was like learning that a beloved family member had a dark side. Learning that there was a putrefying, festering skeleton in a closet. Once that closet door was opened, it could never be shut again.

Elliot's response was anger. His son had been threatened by something that lived on the Ridge, and he as well, based on the tail end of EJ's dream. Perhaps it even had something to do with Susan's death. The doctors believed she died of a cerebral aneurism, but now Elliot wasn't so sure.

Jeff's response was denial. His comfortable world view—or, to be more precise, *otherworld* view—had been threatened.

Elliot wanted to take action as effectively and as quickly as possible.

Jeff wanted to walk away from the whole thing as soon and as quickly as possible.

Elliot spoke first. "It's true. I've had one—several—of those OBEs." He told Jeff about how he'd been both transformed and transported into something else when he was an angry and hate-filled teenager. He related how he'd determined the veracity of the experience when he saw the burnt McSweeney barn. He described the surge of power he'd felt, running, jumping, swimming through the woods at impossible speeds. He told of the time he'd seen through the eyes of the other, the stone ruins where a boy was smoking a joint seeing through the eyes of the other. How he returned to awareness in his own body with the sense that something was watching him. How vulnerable that experience left him feeling.

Jeff listened and when Elliot was done, he said the words that Elliot had never heard from an adult (excluding Andy's film). They froze him to the core. "I saw the man."

Jeff went on to tell how he and Andy were sitting at a campfire at the Taylor Creek Campgrounds. An old man dressed in garments from the American Revolution materialized holding a strange-looking gun which Jeff now knew was called a blunderbuss. He also remembered another night, back at the house on Crow's Nest Pike. How he woke up to find himself in his parka on the back deck of his house. How the wooden fence surrounding the back yard was gone. How he thought he detected movement and sound of breathing and the certainty that someone was in the woods behind his house. How he put his hands in his pockets for warmth and felt his Swiss Army knife with the initials JSS taped to the handle. How after that night, he'd never seen the knife again. How he called out to the man in the woods and got no answer, but the man *did* go away. How he now believed that what was out there that night was the revenant of Isaac Dunbar. He said as much to Elliot.

Elliot let out a low whistle. "OK, what do you think we should do about this?"

"We?"

"Yeah. Seems to me you have a stake in this, too."

"Well, maybe we should talk to the people at the university. Or my friend."

"NO WAY." Elliot shouted with a vehemence that startled Jeff. "Listen, anything said in this room goes no further, you got that?"

Jeff nodded.

"OK. Here's how it plays out." Elliot paused. "I've lived in this town all my life and—how do I put this?—I've fucked up a time or two. I've gotten my shit together, everything's cool now, but if I go to your friend and tell him about what I've seen and people get wind of it, they're going to start looking at me as the old fucked-up Elliot Ryan. That is *not* going to happen. Not to me, and certainly not to EJ."

"Then what did you mean when you said 'what are *we* going to do about it'?"

Elliot paused again and looked out the window. The sun was starting to go down, and for what he had in mind, he wanted daylight. Bright, cheerful daylight. "Can you be back here tomorrow morning?"

Jeff thought a minute. "Tuesday's better. Why?"

"There's something I want to show you."

10

The more time Linus Parsons spent with Henrik Baumann, the less he knew what to make of him.

Baumann had come up to Taylorville Sunday night. He'd checked into the Comfort Inn, and presented himself at Police Headquarters first thing Monday morning. Baumann was short and slender, with a pencil moustache and a shock of unruly gray hair. He wore a long-sleeved white shirt, one that looked like it had never seen an iron. His thin black tie was loosened and his gray suit was shiny in more places than it was not. Despite the summer heat, he wore a mousy-colored trench coat. When Parsons saw him, he wasn't sure whether he should laugh, groan, or tell him to forget the whole thing.

What he did was grit his teeth, and play the good host. Cup of coffee? Perhaps a buttered roll? No? Toasted English, maybe? All of these amenities, Baumann waved aside.

Parsons showed Baumann the Polaroids and said, "Let me ask you something, Mr. Baumann. How did you know about these—marks? I mean ..."

"I sometimes see things. Yes, that is true."

"But how? I mean—everything you said—it's just ...."

A slight smile made its way onto Henrik Baumann's solemn face. "I don't quite understand it myself, Chief. If I did, I doubt that I could explain it. Do you know how some people have certain skills, certain abilities? One may have a natural aptitude for music. Another for mathematics. Another has an instinct for cooking. Do you follow me?"

"I'm not sure."

Baumann's smile widened a little. "To be honest, neither am I. But if you asked the musician, the mathematician, or the chef how he came by his particular ability, I doubt that he could tell you either. It's just something that's there. Do you understand?"

Parsons began to, a little. If not actually convinced, he was alternately intrigued and amused by this man with the funny Dutch accent (not German as he'd first assumed). As Anselmo had intimated, there was something very sincere about Henrik Baumann. He was no grandstander, no con artist, just a regular good citizen who saw opportunities to help the police.

Sure, an ordinary citizen who could see things others couldn't.

Baumann asked, "May I see the files on the Bascom killing?"

"There's a lot of them."

"That is all right. You do understand, of course that I cannot guarantee that I will be able to tell you anything, do you not? Your friend, Chief Irrizarry might have been a bit effusive, but it is important that you understand that my efforts are not always successful. In fact, more often than not. "

"Yeah. I understand."

"Is there someplace where I can view them undisturbed?"

"Sure." Chief Parsons marveled that he could provide these assurances with a straight face, while thinking, *Anselmo, old buddy, what have you gotten me into?*

Parsons found an empty office, more of a cubicle really. It had a chair and a desk, and an air conditioner that blew air only a little cooler than the outside temperature. This didn't bother Baumann; he was perfectly content to ensconce himself there and go over the materials left to him. Watching Baumann reminded Parsons of that old TV show, *The Six Million Dollar Man.* where Lee Majors performed feats of derring-do in slow motion. That was how Baumann seemed to work. Each page he turned, each file he opened, each note he perused, he did with the same meticulous slowness. Finally, Parsons shrugged his shoulders, and went about his daily routine, leaving Baumann to his business. More than once, Parsons vowed he'd kick Anselmo Irrizarry's butt if ever he saw him again.

It was not until noon that Baumann emerged from the cubicle and approached Parsons' desk. Despite the heat, Baumann had neither removed his jacket nor loosened his tie. He was still carrying the trench coat.

"Anything?" Parsons asked.

Baumann shook his head, and just as Parsons was reaffirming his vow to kick Anselmo's butt (the fantasy now included steel-toed boots), Baumann spoke. "I wonder if it would be possible to visit some of the sites I read about in your reports."

"Sure, why not?"

It looked to be a slow day, anyhow.

#

The first stop was where several deer had been killed. It was over ten years ago, but Parsons remembered the night well. A ranger patrolling the trail in his jeep had come across the body of a doe, eviscerated, and called it into Animal Control. By the time the investigation was completed, the disemboweled remains of another doe plus a buck and two fawns were found. One of Parsons' men had responded to the carnage by tossing his dinner by the side of the road. Every outdoor recreational area within five miles of the killing radius was shut down.

Parsons parked the car at the side of the road where the ranger had noted the first killing. Baumann walked to the spot unerringly and stood there, one hand clutching the ever-present trench coat, the other held limply at his side. He appeared to be perplexed. Parsons walked up to him. "What's wrong?"

Baumann didn't answer right away. "There was something killed at this spot, yes?"

Parsons double-checked his memory before answering. It was a long time ago, but yes, he was pretty sure that this was the spot where the doe had been killed. He said as much to Baumann.

The quizzical look left Baumann's face. In its place appeared one of absolute assurance. "No. I'm sorry. You are mistaken. There were *two* killings here."

"No. There was—" He stopped. Come to think of it, there was something about that first killing. If he could only ...

Yes. Now he remembered. It was days later when Marv Pressman's report came out. Parsons had only perused it, but now he remembered. The doe had been pregnant.

Two killings.

"Yes, you're right."

Baumann was no longer listening. The little man had found a path and was walking into the woods. Parsons followed. He was starting to have second thoughts.

Baumann stopped, gingerly stepped off the trail and walked to a little brook that was flowing through the woods. "It stopped to drink here," he said. "The buck. It was thirsty and stopped to drink. It was killed here, yes?"

"Yes," Parsons said, almost in a whisper. It was true. All of these facts were documented, but Parsons couldn't see how this little caricature of a man could have been privy to the information. Even if he were, how did he know about the scratch marks on top of the prefab?

This guy's for real, Anselmo had insisted.

Yeah, maybe he was.

Baumann stood by the brook a little longer, then returned to the trail and started walking toward the road.

"Wait a minute," Parsons called. "Don't you want to see any more while we're here?"

"No, that is not necessary," Baumann replied, continuing to walk back toward the road, but Parsons was sure he was saying more than that.

From Baumann's tone and demeanor, he got the unspoken message: *I think now you believe.*

#

The next stop was the quarry where Neil Coleman and Judy Murchison met their ends. Parsons led, but he got the feeling that even if he held back, Baumann would find the spot without any help from him.

They stood on the shore for about five minutes, Baumann staring out at the center of the quarry. Then without speaking, he followed the shoreline until he came to a narrow path, nearly hidden between two large trees. He continued up the path to a small incline, after which it fed into a wider trail.

Baumann stopped at the incline. "The girl died here," he said in a monotone, as if he were describing the weather. "The boy died first; he died in the water. The girl saw it. It was dark, but she saw the boy killed, and she began to run. She ran this far, then she ..." He stopped, then continued. "She was only partially clothed. They had come here to ..." He stopped again, his Old World modesty preventing him from continuing. "The boy went in the water one last time. That was where he died."

Parsons listened and realized he was nodding. He wasn't there when it happened, of course, but that was pretty much how the investigating team put it together. The kids went there to have sex. Neil was in the nude, Judy had on nothing but a bikini bottom. They had gone skinny dipping and were preparing to leave. Suddenly, someone got hold of Neil and killed him in a most terrible way with his girlfriend watching. Judy fled in hysterics, but had only gotten as far as the path when she too was attacked and her neck snapped. The coroner had said he thought her death was instantaneous. *Thank God for small favors*, Parsons thought.

Both men stood in silence a little longer, then began walking back to the road again.

#

Henrik Baumann stood outside Chuck Bascom's office and the prefab whose roof had a strange series of scratch marks etched onto it. Occasionally, he walked from one spot between the two structures to another, but mostly he stood in one place—the spot where Chuck Bascom was murdered.

Brutal though the killing had been, there were no signs of it now. Heavy summer rains had doused the entire tri-county area. The ground at the North Rim Circle Development construction site now consisted of a sticky red mud. It squished every time Henrik Baumann took a step.

Baumann had never been so frustrated. He had hoped that this site, the scene of the most recent killing, would be far more rich in impressions than the others he'd visited. The violence by the brook and at the quarry had taken place years, almost a decade ago. Yet, for some unfathomable reason the readings were clearer there. He had no idea why.

Over the years, Baumann had assisted in hundreds of police investigations and his success record, while not overwhelming, was significant. When he was successful, people never failed to ask him how he came by the insight. When they did, Baumann never failed to answer the same way he answered Linus Parsons. He didn't quite understand it himself; if he did, he doubted that he could explain it. While he didn't know how to explain it, years of honing taught him how to invoke it.

The secret was patience. Intense, scrupulous patience. You had to concentrate on an event but without actually concentrating. In other words, you had to have an event as the last thing in your mind before you made your mind a complete blank. Once you cleared your mind, you had to try to keep it blank, knowing that you couldn't do it indefinitely. The last thing you were thinking about would affix itself to that part of your brain which housed this extraordinary ability. It would manifest itself as a vague, hypnagogic impression or image. Something you might see when you were just on the verge of falling into a deep dream, but just awake enough to be aware of that fact.

This was where the patience came in. If you tried to focus on the image, it would disintegrate like dandelion fuzz in a heavy wind. The trick was to let it dance on the outer edges of your consciousness as long as it wanted to, before coming clearer.

It was like coaxing a shy animal to eat out of your hand. Be absolutely still, and the animal will come to you in its own time. Move, even twitch a little, and the animal will run.

It was like looking through a pair of precision binoculars at a distant object. You had to make adjustments with painstaking slowness and watch the object clarify, with equal slowness, into recognizability. It you got impatient and adjusted the lenses too quickly, the image would be clear for a second, then rush out of focus again. It would revert to an indistinct blurriness and you'd have to start the process from scratch.

Henrik Baumann could visualize such an image. What was so maddening was that the image made no sense.

Standing there, as he did at the other sites, Baumann had hoped to get a sense of the killer. His identity. How he looked. Something about him that might give Chief Parsons something to work with. Instead, something so *non sequitur*, so incongruous, appeared that

Baumann doubted its relevance.

There were four shapes. Two were immaterial. One was identifiable, but its presence in this context was inexplicable. The fourth was crucial and Baumann fought the temptation to focus intently. (Don't move or the animal will run away; don't adjust the binoculars too quickly or the image will fade). Gradually, an association materialized which only made things more perplexing than ever.

A crash of thunder disrupted Baumann's near trance. Anything he could see or sense disintegrated like dandelion fuzz in a heavy wind. Baumann looked up and saw that the sky, which throughout the day had been festooned with fast-moving white clouds, had turned an ugly shade of gray. Drops of rain were beginning to fall, the kind of rain that becomes very severe with very little warning.

Baumann sighed and began walking back to the car where Chief Parsons was waiting for him.

From the look on Baumann's face, Parsons could see that there would be no miraculous insights coming out of this visit.

Baumann shrugged. "I am sorry."

"It's OK. Come on, let's call it a day."

11

"You've got to be shitting me."

"I'm not shittin' you."

This was the second such interchange between Jeff Strickland and Elliot Ryan.

The first was when Elliot told Jeff that they'd be going into a cave.

They had just driven to a trail head not far from the McSweeney farm. Across the road was an ill-fated seafood restaurant called Dunbar's Wharf. This place had opened under a different name years ago, and due to mismanagement, had reopened and closed several times over the years. In fact, during one of those few periods when it was open, Jeff had taken Cheryl here for their high school prom. Now it was closed, boarded up, but with an ample parking lot in back, strewn with broken bottles, rotting wooden boxes, discarded furniture, an old mattress. A cautious driver could find a clear spot to park his vehicle, and many did, before embarking on the trail head. This was where Elliot steered his pickup just as he informed Jeff as to the exact nature of their excursion.

"We can take this trail for a couple of miles, then we go through the woods a little ways in before we get there," Elliot said.

"Where's 'there'?"

"The cave."

That was when Jeff expressed his incredulity, and Elliot explained how he came to discover the cave. Jeff continued to stare open-mouthed before asking, "You sure this is safe?" Elliot undid his rucksack and displayed its contents. There were three flashlights, two skeins of clothesline, a bag of trail mix, a plastic water bottle and a large handgun.

For the second time, Jeff asked, "Are you shitting me?"

"Look, Jeff," Elliot went on with the patience he'd use in explaining something to EJ, "I don't think we're in any danger. I was in this cave once before and nothing happened. But I'm bringing it for insurance. I don't think we'll need it, but I'd rather have it with me, OK?"

"No, not really. Look, I know a lot of people around here own guns, but my family never did and I'm not comfortable around them."

Elliot sighed. "I can understand that. Look, if you'd rather sit this out …"

"What aren't you telling me, Elliot?"

"What?"

"First you tell me that there's something you want me to see. You're pretty vague about it, but OK, I go along with you. Then you tell me it's in a frickin' cave. Next you tell me there's no danger, but you pull a piece, but then you tell me don't worry—there's no danger. Come on, what's going on?"

Elliot sighed. "OK, Jeff. Maybe I wasn't being all the way straight with you. Maybe it was because I was afraid you'd back out on me. But here it is. Something bad's been going down in this town for a lot of years, and now it's messing with my son, and I'm not going to allow that. Besides, from what you've told me, it's been messing with you too. I think that this cave is its starting point and I need to check it out one more time."

"Why?"

"I don't know. I just do. Now if you're scared, I can dig it. Be honest with you, I'm scared too. Shit, maybe it had something to do with my wife's death. If so, I'm going after it and putting an end to it once and for all. You want to stay here, that's cool, but I'm heading out. What are you going to do?"

Jeff surprised himself by answering, "I'm going with you." It wasn't so much that his curiosity was stronger than his trepidation; it was something he felt he had to do.

Why?

He didn't know. He just did.

#

Elliot led them along the trail, past a stream, into the woods to an outcropping of rocks. Without pausing, he led them through a crevice in the face of the rock. They came to the rocky blockage and proceeded beneath the crawlspace. From there, Jeff could see a gap between the floor and the left-hand wall of the crevice.

"This is it. We'd better move. I don't like the looks of that sky."

Jeff looked upward. Through the cleft he could see somber gray clouds.

Elliot proceeded to take a length of rope from the ruck and tied one of the straps to the end of the rope. He then handed one of the flashlights to Jeff.

"You aim the light down," Elliot instructed. "I'm going to climb down. When I yell, you put the flash back in the ruck and lower the whole thing down to me. When I yell again, you start down. I'll hold the light for you so you can see what you're doing. You OK with that?"

Jeff wasn't, but he nodded, without hesitation.

"OK, here goes."

Elliot lowered himself down through the opening. Jeff held the light steady and watched Elliot make his way to the cave floor quickly.

"OK, Jeff," he called up, "lower it."

Jeff cut the power to the flash, and lowered the ruck.

"Got it."

A few seconds later, Jeff saw a light shine upward and heard Elliot shout.

"OK, Jeff! Come on down."

Jeff hesitated, then wormed his way into the cave opening. Having noted the handholds and footholds Elliot used, he embarked upon the down-climb with caution, but without wavering.

"How's that, not so bad, huh?" Elliot asked when Jeff had made his way down.

"No, not bad. But you're going first."

Elliot led them down the passage, following the clothesline, then got down on all fours. Jeff did likewise.

"OW."

"What's the matter?"

"Bumped my head."

"You OK?"

"'Yeah. I'll live."

"Sorry. Should have warned you. Keep your head down. Some of these passages are pretty low.

"And stay alert. If anything happens, backtrack and get the hell of here!"

Elliot's words and his tone made Jeff remember the gun and snippets of their earlier conversation.

"Something bad's been going down … messing with my son … messing with you too … cave is its starting point … something to do with my wife's death …"

Keeping his light aimed forward, Jeff could only see Elliot's back, butt, or the soles of his feet, but he knew Elliot was holding onto the gun. He knew that this had nothing in common with the touristy-type caves, like Howe's Cavern, which he and his parents had visited years ago. Howe's Cavern didn't hide something shadowy and malevolent which might jump out at you and "mess with you." You didn't need a big ugly gun in Howe's Cavern. And you didn't have to crawl where it was wet, narrow, messy, and chilly.

What was he doing here? Why had he agreed to accompany Elliot to this place? Why had he crawled through that narrow cave opening, climbed down that cave wall, followed Elliot through these winding twisting passages where they might meet—what? Why didn't he just tell Elliot to forget the whole thing?

He didn't know. All he knew was he was if he had to do it over, he'd do the exact same thing. He would enter the cave, make the climb, and crawl, crawl, crawl his way to wherever Elliot was taking him. Backing out was not an option.

"Watch it, Jeff. We're coming to a puddle. Keep your light dry."

"Shit!"

"What's the matter?"

"I'm up to my elbows. This isn't a puddle, it's a goddamn lake!"

Despite the gravity of their expedition, Jeff found himself fascinated by this irregular world where you might walk, scuttle, or slither for a few feet. As you moved, the view was nothing like the one you were looking at only a few feet back. Bare featureless walls gave way to vistas of smooth, shiny flowstone formations. Sometimes, there were stalactites that looked like inverted soda straws, which gave way once again to walls that looked like they were plastered in mud. For a moment, Jeff completely forgot about the grim purpose of this excursion. He found himself entranced with the beauty and majesty of this environment.

Elliot led them to where they could stand again, but after a few steps they found themselves before a wide lateral gash bisecting the passage. The passage was wide enough for both men to stand side by side. When Jeff aimed his light down the cleft, he couldn't see where it ended.

"How do we get across?" he asked.

Elliot gestured with his light and Jeff could now see a short side tunnel he'd missed before. In this tunnel, the chasm tapered, and on the other side was a ledge which was easily reachable. The two men continued along a passage through which it was possible to walk upright, Elliot leading, Jeff following close behind.

They came to a tiny slot, at which point, Elliot said, "This part's a little tricky. You hold the light and I'll go through. Once I'm through, hand me the ruck and the lights, then I'll hold the light and talk you through it."

"OK."

Elliot handed his light and the ruck to Jeff. He got on his back and eased his way through the slot, past the four-foot drop, and disappeared into the spacious chamber beyond. He called out to Jeff, who passed him the ruck and the lights, then did likewise.

Jeff landed on a surface which was incredibly sticky and reminded him of flypaper. He found he could move his feet but not without exerting a certain amount of effort. Elliot was standing a few feet away from him, pointing his light upward.

"Check this out."

Jeff pointed his light in the same direction, and saw some movement and heard a papery rustling sound. In the aureole of light, aimed toward the high ceiling of this passage, a couple of bats were flying.

"Wow."

"Cool, isn't it?"

Jeff aimed his light along the sides of the chamber and saw another passage, or rather two passages. He and Elliot made their way toward the fork, struggled, actually. The stickiness made their progress difficult.

"It wasn't this bad the first time I was here," Elliot noted. "Must be from all the rain."

Jeff strained his ears and heard the sound of water trickling.

Elliot led them to the mouth of the passage on the right, then stopped. He reached into the ruck and pulled out the gun. "This is it."

For the first time since this excursion began, Jeff paused. Elliot continued into that passage. Jeff followed warily into the tunnel, which ended in a rounded chamber where Jeff made the same grisly discovery that Elliot had, years ago.

Against the far wall was a large pile of bones. Some of the bones still looked too big to have come from small animals like squirrels and woodchucks.

Jeff walked toward the gruesome heap. He knelt and sifted through the pile with his hands. He came to a familiar object and froze, unaware that Elliot had moved closer. The only movement was in his hands, which were fingering something which wasn't a bone, something perfectly preserved in the chamber's damp coolness.

A dog collar.

#

It was not until they returned to the truck and the storm broke that Jeff made his toneless pronouncement.

"We've got to destroy that place."

Elliot sat silent. Monotone though Jeff's statement was, its tone carried a conviction that would tolerate no argument. Not that Elliot wanted to argue. He remembered the revulsion he'd felt the first time he was in that chamber, but he'd attributed it to the fact that it was where some predatory animal did its killing. Today, however, he'd seen another person react to it more viscerally than he himself had, way back when. When they were in that chamber, he sensed something positively *organic* about it.

He knew, from his years of association with Doc Pressman, that animals had senses more finely attuned than those of humans. They knew when another animal, a natural enemy, was near, and prepared to do harm. Pheromones, Doc called them, those chemicals in the body which sent out those signals. Was it possible, that a *place* might do the same thing? Emit a different kind of pheromones indicating danger?

Elliot looked across at Jeff in the passenger's seat. Jeff was staring straight ahead, as if transfixed, his mouth a straight edge, embedded in a clenched jaw.

"You really think that'll get rid of that—whatever it is?" Elliot asked.

"It feels right," Jeff answered, still unmoving. "Besides, what else is there to do? Stand guard outside the cave and shoot it when it comes out?"

Actually, that idea did flit across Elliot's mind, and he rejected it immediately. It seemed ridiculous when he first thought of it, doubly so, when someone else verbalized it. As he found himself nodding, he noticed Jeff turn to face him.

"You have any idea how we're going to do it?"

Elliot shook his head.

"You're in the construction business," Jeff prodded. "Don't you know anyone who has access to explosives?"

Elliot shook his head again. Sure, he knew a couple of demolition contractors in the area. They were scrupulous businessmen who wouldn't just turn over explosive materials to him for the asking. They'd want to know what he wanted them for, and what was he supposed to tell them? *I'm using the stuff to blow a monster off the face of the earth, guys.* Oh yeah, they'd really turn it over to him after hearing that, right? More likely they'd think Elliot Ryan was back to toking the old weed once again. The high octane shit.

Jeff sighed, and Elliot could hear the exasperation. "So what are we going to do?"

Elliot sat silent. Jeff sat silent. The only sound was the staccato tattoo of the rain hammering the truck and the ground.

Finally Elliot spoke. "I may have an idea. Let me check it out and get back to you in a couple of days."

12

When Baumann first set foot in Chief Parsons' office, he couldn't help but notice how small an office it was for such a big man. That impression was reinforced as the Chief paced in an area hard pressed to accommodate a desk, a chair, two file cabinets, and a credenza. Outside, the sky rumbled and heavy drops of rain fell on the roof. Fitting sounds, Baumann thought. Perfect complement to the storm that must be raging inside Chief Parsons since Baumann gave him his feedback regarding the Bascom killing.

After his unsuccessful attempt at insight the day before at the construction site, Baumann returned with Chief Parsons to Police Headquarters.

"May I see the materials from the files from the other killings?"

"Man, you're talking a few hundred pages," Parson replied.

"Well, why don't you give me the most important ones? I will study those."

"Yeah, I can do that. Sit tight, and I'll make copies for you."

"Thank you, Chief."

An hour later, Baumann took the copies and returned to his motel room where, isolated from the effects of inclement weather, he tried again.

Once again, he concentrated without actually concentrating. He cleared his mind, waiting for the shadows of a past event to re-cast themselves. After a few minutes of nothing, he turned on the radio and found a classical music station, turned the volume to low. Sometimes that helped.

Still nothing.

Baumann would not let himself be frustrated. Patience was the key. Patience was always the key.

As the time passed things did seem to come clearer. Random images, tumbling one on top of another. Images of violence and fear and terror. Reliving the last moments of Chuck Bascom's life. Unendurable pain. Blackness. Then the cycle of violence and fear and terror began again, which Baumann found utterly repulsive. Yet, while he could have shut them out completely by breaking concentration, he dared not do so. Eventually, they would recede, like a song that goes through the mind over and over again, but finally fades into mental oblivion. He hoped that would happen soon and that something clearer and more palpable would take their place.

It wasn't until close to 2:00 a.m. that this finally happened. That same image that tantalized Baumann reasserted itself. As before, even as it took on a clarity that it lacked earlier, it made no sense.

#

"Tell me again." Chief Parsons had stopped pacing. He was behind his desk, leaning on it with both hands in front of him. He wasn't looking at Baumann, rather he was looking straight down, but Baumann could see that his expression was one of sheer concentration.

"There is a man," Baumann began, choosing his words carefully. This was not because the redoubtable officer intimidated him, but because the image was still so elusive in his own mind. "A man in this town who is crucial to this case. I do not know what his role is."

He paused, thought for a moment, and finding no other words, just came out with it. "He is a man who is known to you. He is a man you have spoken to." Another pause, more thought, again no success in finding words to express an absurd piece of information. "Somehow this man is associated with water."

Parsons looked up, not at Baumann, but *through* him. As thwarted as Baumann had felt, Parsons felt even more so. Anselmo had warned him that anything Baumann might say would seem oblique, but it would be on target. Well, Anselmo, not now. This time, your man's prediction is stone-cold *crazy*.

"Let me get this straight," Parsons said, trying to reign in his vexation, "you're saying I know the man who's been doing all this killing?"

"NO," Baumann replied, almost shouting. "That is *not* what I am saying. I do not believe that this man is a killer. What I am saying is that he is the *key* to all of this. Perhaps he is—what is the word?—a material witness? I do not know. But things will not come to a conclusion without him. I am sorry that is all I can tell you."

"Wait, wait, wait a minute," Parsons went on, trying to clear his head. "You said something else before. Something to the effect that there were other people around? You remember?"

"Yes, I remember."

"What about them? Who were they?"

Baumann brought his hand to his forehead. "I am not certain. I gather that it was a public place. There was this man and two others. You and he are speaking. The others are on the side. They are not important."

Parsons sighed and began to pace again. Someone he'd spoken to. In the presence of other people. A public place. Around the time Chuck Bascom died.

He began to reconstruct events leading up to the moment he first heard about Bascom. He and Renee had gone out to dinner at the Top Hat the night of the killing. He remembered having second thoughts about going there. His was a high-profile job in a small town. He knew that if he went out to some local place, people would be coming up to him all night. While he wasn't misanthropic, he did want some undisturbed private time with his wife. On the other hand, it had been a long week and he didn't feel like driving any distance, so they'd settled on the Top Hat.

Sure enough, they'd been spotted and approached several times that night. First, it was that couple in the bar area that recognized Renee, two of her former students.

Then, they made small talk with the bartender. Renee ordered her usual white wine spritzer; he ordered whatever was on tap.

After that, they were greeted by a host of others, before they ran into Peter Strickland's boy with his friend, Andy Something.

They were exchanging pleasantries when he got that call on his cell. Suddenly it clicked.

Four people. Renee. Jeff. Andy. Himself.

Obviously it couldn't be Renee. It couldn't be Andy, since Baumann said that it was someone he knew. He hadn't recalled ever meeting Andy until that night.

He did know Jeff Strickland. A respectful, straight-up kind of kid. A kid who never hung at the quarry after that time Parsons had read him and his friends the Riot Act.

He is associated with water.

Working at Stockton Prep as a phys. ed. instructor and swim coach.

"Jeff Strickland? Not possible."

"I beg your pardon?"

Parsons stopped pacing. He didn't realize that he'd spoken aloud.

"The man you described. I think it's Jeff Strickland. Does that name mean anything to you?" Baumann shook his head.

No, it couldn't be. Jeff was just a kid when these killings started. He couldn't be responsible. Besides, he was at the Top Hat when Chuck Bascom was killed.

But wait a minute. What was it Baumann had said? That "this man" wasn't the killer? That he might be a material witness? Was *that* possible? Did Jeff Strickland know something relevant to this case? Did he perhaps see something, without understanding that what he saw might have some bearing on the case?

"Is there anything else I can do?" Baumann asked.

"No, no. I just gotta work this out on my own."

"Will you be talking to this—Jeff Strickland, is it?"

Parsons returned to his desk and sat down, drained and exhausted. "I don't know," he said almost in a whisper. "I don't know."

Jeff Strickland? How could it be possible?

13

The first thing that struck Elliot was how little the place had changed. It was still there, of course, a piece of property with absolutely no curb appeal and, for that matter, no curb. You got to it by going down a rutted dirt road with holes that looked like craters. After last night's rain, they looked more like lakes. There were still trees on either side and the Ridge in back. In the middle of this mess was a one-story clapboard house. Certainly no testament to conspicuous consumption. Ironically, though, it housed a man who may well have been one of the wealthiest men in the tri-county area. Still, living in a showplace would only call attention to him. Given this man's line of work, attention was not a desirable commodity.

The yard looked the same too. There was still the old Plymouth Duster, or Roster would have been more like it. There was still unrecognizable junk and even more old tires, trashed appliances, and car parts, than ever. There was still the fenced-in area, but the mean old junkyard dog was gone. In its place was a waddling *thing* that moved more like a walrus than a canine. It had one rheumy eye, and all the energy of a blob of Jell-O. It raised its head when Elliot drove onto the property, chuffed once, and laid its head back on its paws. Presumably it was dreaming of its glory days, shredding stray cats and squirrels with its once redoubtable set of fangs.

Geary had changed but little. He still looked like Bluto, only a little grayer and with longer hair, now tied in a ponytail. But he still weighed three hundred-plus pounds and Elliot surmised, as he did years ago, that not all of it was fat.

"Well, well, look who we've got here," Geary exclaimed, lumbering out of the house, upon seeing Elliot's truck pulling into the yard. "Ain't seen you for a while, kid. What's the matter? Become a straight citizen on me or something?"

"Hello, Geary," Elliot greeted the other man. "Still in business?"

"What do you think? So what can I do ya?"

Elliot told him. Geary's jaw dropped. "What do you want something like that for?"

Elliot stepped forward and gave Geary a playful (though not painless) punch in the shoulder. "Come on, Geary. I always figured you for the original 'Don't ask. Don't tell' kind of guy."

"Yeah, sure," Geary answered, rubbing his shoulder, "I am. But for something like this?" His eyes suddenly narrowed, the way they did when he wanted to intimidate a younger Elliot Ryan. "I don't think so, kid. This ain't an ounce or two of ..." lifting his thumb and index finger to his lips as if toking on a joint, " ... this is heavy shit." He stopped, and noticed that this Elliot Ryan wasn't intimidated. "I never figured you for this kind of action."

"Well, I'm into it now. Come on, Geary. Can you handle it or not?"

"Yeah, I know a guy," Geary said, looking in Elliot's direction, but not looking him in the eye. "Ex-army ordnance. Total whack-a-doo, but he'll do it for me. Cost you, though."

"How much?"

Geary named a price, a very high price, figuring that it would be out of Elliot's reach. "Cash. Up front."

"Half now. Balance on delivery."

"HELL NO, you got ..."

"Half now. Balance on delivery." So saying, Elliot reached into his jeans and pulled out a wad of cash and thrust it into Geary's greasy palm.

Very slowly, Geary's hands closed on the bills. "How soon do you want 'me?"

"Soon as possible."

Geary pondered. "I'm guessing a week. Maybe sooner."

"I can live with that." Elliot started to leave, then turned around again. "Don't fuck with me on this, Geary. I mean it, now."

"No sweat, bro. I'll take care of you." He would, too.

Kid had the look of a rabid rat.

14

If you asked Chief Linus Parsons what it was that made a good cop, he'd have told you. Dedication. Integrity. Knowing when and how to lean. Toughness and compassion, coexisting. People skills. Street smarts. Above all, humanity. If you asked Chief Linus Parsons if he were a good cop, he wouldn't give you a straight yes or no; he'd tell you he hoped so. He'd tell you that he'd always tried to adhere to the qualities he'd mentioned, particularly the last one.

The only down side to humanity is that being human, good cops, like mere mortals, make mistakes. Linus Parsons was sure he'd made his share, but none, to his knowledge were unduly glaring.

He had no way of knowing he was about to make his second worst such mistake.

His first, his biggest and most glaring, was for another day, not long in coming.

#

Linus Parsons took two nights and a day of soul-searching after Henrik Baumann identified Jeff Strickland as a major player in the Bascom case. On the second day, he decided to question Jeff. It was late afternoon when he drove to 1604 Crow's Nest Pike and got a surprise. When he rang the doorbell, he expected to see a member of the Strickland family, not Elliot Ryan.

"Chief Parsons. What a surprise."

"Hello, Ryan." Elliot's salutation was polite enough, but old enmities die hard. "Where can I find Jeff Strickland?"

"Jeff doesn't live here," Elliot answered, and explained the circumstances under which he was renting the Strickland house.

"I see. You must have a number where I can reach him?"

It was spoken as a question, but meant as a statement. He nodded, not without a little concern. His first thought was that Parsons had somehow learned that he'd been to see Geary the day before. Somehow, Parsons had pieced together what he and Jeff were planning to do. But if that were so, why was Parsons interested in Jeff rather than in him? After all, it was he, not Jeff, who'd dealt with Geary.

"What do you want Jeff's number for?"

"I'm afraid I'm not at liberty to go into that, Ryan. But I need to get in touch with Jeff Strickland. Give me that information. *Now*."

After Parsons left, Elliot phoned Jeff.

"Hi. You've reached the Stricklands. No one's here to take your call right now, but if you leave your name and number, we'll get back to you as soon as we can. Please wait for the beep."

Elliot started to speak, then decided against it and hung up. He wanted to warn Jeff about Parsons, but he didn't want to entrust that bit of news to an answering machine. He'd try again later, when Jeff was home.

#

Jeff was home when the phone rang, but he and Cheryl were otherwise engaged.

Cheryl had just come in from her mid-afternoon run. She caught the look Jeff was giving her, and realized that she was wearing a particularly abbreviated pair of running shorts. She smiled and asked her husband if he wanted to try making a baby. He responded by kissing her, telling her to wait there till he called, and went into the bedroom.

About two minutes later, he did call. She went into the bedroom, she found that he'd drawn the shades, and lit candles throughout the room. Although there was still daylight seeping in, the effect was exotic and romantic. They kissed, languorously at first, then with increasing ardor. They savored undressing each other, and fell into bed together.

They touched each other in those wonderful secret places that only lovers can know, prolonging the pleasure until it could no longer be denied.

He slipped into her welcoming body and she caressed all she could reach. She marveled at how years of aquatics had given his body definition that was at once hard and supple, plus a beyond-extraordinary endurance. When the intensity became too much for her, she reached between his legs and caressed his flesh. She did so with a gentleness and delicacy that never failed to drive him wild. His hardness dissipated and she felt the warmth of his love erupt inside of her. Gradually, their bodies relaxed; exhausted, spent, and delighted.

Somewhere, a telephone was ringing, but neither one of them saw fit to spoil the moment.

When Cheryl opened her eyes, the candles had burned down, and the room was dark. Upon looking at the clock, she realized that she'd actually fallen asleep. She reached over and nudged her husband.

"Honey?" He responded with a twitch and a grunt. She smiled. After years of sleeping next to Jeff, she'd learned that the more fatiguing the effort, the deeper the sleep. The deeper the sleep, the more inarticulate the grunt. This one was positively incoherent. She smiled with pride and pleasure.

"Honey, it's getting late and I have to start dinner. You want to shower?"

Jeff reached up and found his wife's shoulder. He pulled her down to him. When they came up for air, Cheryl asked him again, "Do you want to use the shower?"

"Not alone, I don't."

#

They had just finished dinner when the doorbell rang.

"Chief Parsons, what are you doing here?"

"Good evening, Jeff. Mrs. Strickland. May I come in?"

"Uh, sure, come on in."

"Aren't you a bit far afield, Chief?"

"Well, yes and no. Jeff, I wonder if we can have a moment or two in private. Will you excuse us, please, Mrs. Strickland?"

"Oh. Of course."

Jeff led Chief Parsons into the spare bedroom he used as a den for preparing training schedules and lesson plans over the school year. It consisted of the desk and chair he'd had as a boy in the house on Crow's Nest Pike as well an easy chair. There were several shelves with swimming trophies, a day bed, and several pictures on the wall showing Jeff and the various winning teams he'd coached.

"Jeff," Parsons began as he lowered himself onto the edge of the easy chair. "I'm sure you heard about the murder that took place about a week ago on the North Rim." Jeff nodded and the Chief went on, "I know you're aware that there have been a series of incidents over the years regarding farm animals, pets, and even animals in the woods surrounding the Ridge." Jeff nodded again. "Also," Parsons paused, "the deaths of Judy Murchison and Neil Coleman."

Jeff reacted with a violent start. "What?"

The Chief waited for a beat or two, then spoke the words he'd rehearsed countless times on his way here. "Jeff, please understand something. We know you had nothing to do with these killings. But we have reason to believe that you may know something that can help us get to the bottom of them."

A look of incredulity crossed Jeff's face. "What makes you think that?"

"I'm sorry, but I can't go into …"

"Excuse me, but if someone's throwing my name around in connection with a murder, I think I have a right to know."

Parsons studied the young man before him. He understood Jeff's response, particularly in view of the fact that Jeff was the son of a lawyer. He'd have a better knowledge than most what his rights were. If he felt they were being compromised, he'd know better than most how to protect them.

"I think I need to reiterate to you," Parsons said in what he hoped was a conciliatory tone, "that you're not being accused of anything. I've known you and your family long enough to know you wouldn't be involved in anything like this. But I want you to think very carefully before you answer this. Is it possible that over the years, you might have heard something or seen something that could help us? Something out of the ordinary? It could have been something you might not have thought important at the time. Anything at all?"

"No."

"Don't be so quick to answer, Jeff. We're talking about stuff that's been going on for a lot of years. Maybe if you …"

"No. There's nothing. I'm sorry. I can't help you and I'd like you to leave."

"Now look, son …"

"Don't 'Now look, son' me, Chief. With all due respect, you're out of your jurisdiction here and if, as you say, I'm not being accused, I'm well within my rights not to answer your questions and to ask you to leave, and that's what I'm doing. Please go."

The lawyer's son, Parsons thought. *Well, Jeff, technically you may have a point in asking me to leave, and you may have a point in being so indignant. But you're not just indignant, are you, Jeff? You're downright* hostile, *and my cop's instinct tells me you're hiding something. Just what is it you are hiding, Jeff?*

Parsons stood. "OK, Jeff, I'll leave but I want you to think very carefully about what I said. If you remember anything or change your mind, please give me a call. In fact," he added as he took his card and a pen out of his breast pocket, "I want you to call me at this number …" writing a phone number on the back of my card "… if you can't get me at headquarters. Any time of day. Will you do that?"

Jeff stood glowering at the big officer and for a few moments, it seemed that he would not even take the card. Finally he reached for it and mumbled "Yeah" and led the way out of the den.

"Just a second," said Parsons, holding up his hand. "Does the name, 'Henrik Baumann,' mean anything to you?"

As soon as he blurted out the name, Chief Parsons realized he was guilty of a considerable *faux pas.* Rule of police work: never reveal the name of an informant. True, Baumann wasn't an informant in the actual sense of the word. Even so, playing this particular card (actually, grasping at this particular straw), was a major breach. Parsons was both embarrassed and angry with himself for being guilty of it.

"No, who's that?"

"Just another name that cropped up during the investigation," Parsons replied, hoping to evade further discussion. "Sorry to trouble you, I'll let myself out."

Jeff heard Parsons take his leave of Cheryl, then let himself out. He sat on the day bed, pondering what had just gone on.

He did know something that might very well be related to the North Rim incident. He had been sucked into it, via a combination of things. Andy's film. Elliot Ryan's expedition to the cave. His own experiences in the house at Crow's Nest Pike. Rusty's disappearance. Maybe even the deaths of Neil and Judy.

Jeff felt that he was in the center of a vortex, not of violent and capricious winds, but of occurrences that transpired over the years. They were now pelting him, driving him toward an end he could not guess at, did not *want* to guess at. He did not even want to be in this position, yet he felt a compulsion to see it through, no matter what.

But how could he talk about it? What could he say to a man like Chief Parsons who dealt in the darker side of reality? That was the point; Parsons dealt in *reality*. There was no room for a Backwoods Demon. No room for this familiar of a long-dead practitioner of the dark arts, who killed dogs and people. Not in Chief Parsons' brand of reality. Sure, he could tell Parsons what he thought. But he'd never be believed and might end up in the modern equivalent of a rubber room for his troubles. Besides, did he dare verbalize what he and Elliot Ryan were planning to do? If he did, he'd end up somewhere a hell of a lot worse. No, he'd have to keep this between Elliot and himself and hope for the best. What was the best? That it would all go away after he and Elliot did what they'd set out to do? Worst case, if Parsons actually charged him with anything, he'd simply refuse to answer without an attorney present. But what good was that? At some point, he'd have to tell the attorney what he wasn't willing to tell Parsons, and then he'd be back at square one.

"Knock, knock."

Jeff looked up and saw Cheryl standing in the doorway, with a quizzical look on her face. "Everything OK?"

"Yeah, come on in, babe."

She sat next to him on the day bed, kissed him, and put her hand in his. "I heard a lot of yelling in here. What's going on?"

"Can you believe it? Parsons thinks I know something about that thing that happened at the North Rim last week."

It was Cheryl's turn to look incredulous. "You're kidding. What made him think that?"

"How the hell should I know?"

"Take it easy, honey. Did he say anything? Didn't you ask him …?"

"Yeah, I asked him. He said ..." and here, Jeff began speaking with a mellifluous baritone, in imitation of Parsons, "I can't tell you that."

"That's crazy!"

"Damn right it's crazy!" Jeff stood, and began pacing the length of the den. "He even said that I should think back about these animal killings that have been going on since God-knows-when! That I know something about those as well!"

"But what makes him think ..."

"*I told you, I don't know, Cheryl*!" Jeff shouted.

"Cool, it Jeff," said Cheryl, getting angry. "You don't have to snap at me. I just asked you—"

"You asked. He asked. I'm tired of being interrogated. Let's just drop it, Cheryl, OK?"

"Fine." Cheryl stood up and left the room. Jeff started to follow, but decided against it. He sat on the day bed again and remained there.

#

Cheryl Strickland was totally nonplussed. Ever since they met Andy and Pam at the Top Hat, there were times when Jeff had been unreadable, even to her, and she'd known his every mood since they were fifteen. For someone who didn't seem to want to have anything to do with Taylorville, he'd been spending a lot of time there lately. He said he had business with Elliot Ryan regarding the condition of the house, but somehow, that didn't ring true. Also, what about that day he had come home with mud and clay caked on his jeans? When she asked him about it, he'd claimed that he went for a walk in the woods and took a spill on a muddy stretch. That didn't ring true either.

Now, there was this irrational display of anger directed at her for no discernible reason.

For the first time, Cheryl Strickland began to wonder just how well she knew her husband.

15

In his motel room, Henrik Baumann's frustration increased. His session with Parsons earlier that day bore no new fruit and the Chief's own frustration was mingled with ill-concealed irritation.

Parsons mentioned that he'd spoken to Jeff Strickland. He expected Strickland to be a bit bewildered and perhaps a little resentful, but he did not expect such defensiveness. Certainly not from someone he remembered as a respectful, even-tempered sort; not given to emotional outbursts or fits of pique.

Given this latest development, did Baumann have any new insights into the situation, particularly regarding Jeff Strickland?

Baumann did not.

The rest of the day remained unrewarding. They'd gone over old ground again, reviewed old files and case notes, even driven back to the North Rim site. Under pressure from Parsons, Baumann attempted a more aggressive mode of concentration. Baumann could have predicted the results: the harder he tried, the less successful he was. By the end of the day, both men were thoroughly dispirited and disgusted.

When Parsons drove Baumann back to his motel, the weather, true to its pattern over the past few days, had changed again. By 5:00 pm, the sky had darkened, almost to the point of nightfall. Predictions over the next few days were not optimistic. Thunder boomers were expected into the weekend, which plunged Chief Parsons' mood into a deeper level of gloom. He had hoped to conclude his business with Baumann by Friday and dedicate the weekend to fly fishing. That wasn't going to happen.

Baumann took his leave of Parsons at the Comfort Inn entrance. Both men agreed to meet again the next day and try again.

At 11:15 pm, Baumann was sitting at the desk in his motel room where he'd been sitting since he'd returned. His frustration had not dwindled a bit. For hours, he'd tried the various mind exercises he'd always used to incur insights, but to no avail. He tried the classical music station, but the storm outside kept playing havoc with the reception. At last, he gave up and turned the radio off. Hours earlier, he'd called down for room service, ordered a turkey sandwich and a bottle of beer. Now, the turkey sandwich was barely touched and the beer was warm, but Baumann wasn't ready to pack it in just yet.

Baumann was used to long meditative sessions, sometimes lasting up to eighteen hours before anything came. Sometimes nothing came, and Baumann was used to this as well. He had trained himself to withstand hunger, thirst, and exhaustion. Sometimes, just when he was on the verge of succumbing to one of those stressors, something would materialize, making the entire ordeal worthwhile. He hoped this would happen tonight. Finally, the cloudburst ended, and with the lightning and thunder no longer distracting him, he decided to try again.

On an impulse, Baumann reached for the telephone directory. He looked up *Strickland* and found an inch worth of listings under that name. There were two J. Stricklands, one right here in Taylorville, one in Stockton, and a Jeffrey Strickland in Dandridge. Baumann wrote down Jeffrey Strickland's name and phone number on a piece of motel stationery and contemplated it.

Nothing.

Sighing, Baumann placed it in his breast pocket. Perhaps he'd suggest to Chief Parsons that they visit this Strickland together. He even pondered contacting the man himself. In the past, Baumann's only contacts had been with the local authorities who'd sought his help or to whom he'd volunteered his services. He'd never taken it upon himself to look up a suspect or a witness. He had never spoken to one, even in the presence of the police. Still, he thought that maybe it was time he made an exception. Perhaps a face-to-face meeting with this Jeff Strickland might yield something meaningful.

That was a decision he'd make tomorrow. In the meantime, he decided to try again.

He took a deep breath, and cleared his mind. Let the thoughts come as they will. Gradually, the facts and aspects of the situation began their flow. Random patterns of thought congregating, confluent, merging into a clear cohesive impression.

Random patterns of thought ....

Dead woodchucks, squirrels, snakes, raccoons, and even a skunk ... dismembered deer ... missing pets ... a disemboweled cat ... two dead kids ... missing dogs ... farm animals, throats cut ... dead construction foreman, North Rim ... what kind of mind? ...

... congregating, confluent ...

Jeff Strickland ... a place of total darkness ... two other men, distant, coming closer, linked somehow ... another man, a little boy, also linked, the little boy crying ... a woman ... a place of total silence ... the woods ... another place of total darkness, total silence ... an old man ... something else ...

... merging into a clear cohesive impression.

... all of these images carried by swirling eddies ... currents flowing into one another ... becoming indistinct ... still flowing ... another image ... a man, struggling ... still swirling eddies ... no, the man was struggling to keep from drowning ... something else ... a dark shape in the water with the man ... ... big yellow eyes ... big and dark and fast ... conscienceless ... vicious ... sharp ... ancient ... Yog-Sothoth ... Dunbar ...

... IT KNEW!

Baumann's body rocketed back from the desk, as if hit by a heavyweight's haymaker. The chair tipped over, spilling the little man onto the floor. His head snapped back, hitting the floor with a violent thud. But this pain was nothing to the pain that racked his whole being, like a giant migraine pervading his whole body.

Instinctively, Baumann put his hands to his face and found them wet in blood. He was aware of a wailing sound assailing his ears, coming from his own throat.

It knew! Somehow, the thing that had been perpetrating all this violence had picked up on Baumann's psychic probings and was fighting back!

Upon this realization, Baumann found himself in thrall to something that was in control of his nerve endings, his muscles, his very brain itself. His body was in the throes of what could only be described as a seizure in its most violent form. Unable to control the thrashing of his limbs and torso he propelled himself into a wall-length mirror, face first. The mirror shattered. Shards of glass pierced his right eye.

His right arm convulsed with such force that it was pulled from his socket, with a pain so intense, it rendered the body-migraine all but forgotten. The same thing happened to his left arm. To his horror, he realized that all of his limbs were being dislocated, with all of the excruciating torment that accompanied such injuries. His left leg followed then his right, then a new round of thrashing, which exacerbated the torment.

He could not muster enough air in his lungs even to scream.

There was nothing he could do to break the link between himself and the unknown entity to which he had become subjected. When he was finally able to suck air down into his lungs, he began to scream once again.

He was aware of sounds in the background. Someone was yelling to keep the noise down. Someone else was shouting, "Are you all right?" Someone else was shouting for the manager. Running footsteps in the hall. Someone rattling the door.

#

They decided not to wait for the manager and broke down the door. What they found was the room in a shambles, but that was not the worst: a harmless little man lay on the floor, his limbs all askew. He was not moving save for an occasional spastic twitch, the kind that sometimes occurs even after death. A fast steady stream of blood spewed from his mouth.

He had bitten through his tongue.

16

"It was a dark and stormy night ..."

It would strike none of the people involved in the final horror that it ended as it had begun so many years ago. Of those participating in the experience, only Jeff Strickland might be in a position to appreciate the irony, had it occurred to him. None of the others were in any position to make that association.

Not the four victims of four assaults, one of whom would never again walk unaided.

Certainly not the two who died, one that very night, the other within a few days' time.

#

The day began as did most of the days preceding it for the last two weeks. There was patchy sun in the morning interspersed with clouds of varying darkness and thickness throughout the afternoon. By evening, there would be a particularly powerful thunderstorm.

The weather was the last thing on Elliot Ryan's mind that afternoon as he drove up the dirt road leading to Geary's place. It was nearly four days since he'd placed his order and Geary was his usual paranoid self. He'd insisted that Elliot not contact him by phone, but in person after a few days. No, there was no problem, Geary assured him; his friend would do the job. It's just that this particular job was not to be discussed in even the most general or innocuous terms over the telephone or via email.

"You're in luck, kid," Geary told him. "I've got your stuff." He reached into the trunk of the old Duster/Roster and pulled out a burlap sack and handed it to Elliot. Elliot reached into the sack and saw three identical objects. They were nondescript metal boxes, featureless save for a black button in the center of each. Each one weighed about a pound.

"Don't let the size fool you," Geary was saying. "These babies each pack enough shit to blow up a mountain."

Elliot chuckled to himself. Geary was closer to the truth than he realized.

"So," Geary went on, "you got the cash?"

"Hold it a second," Elliot said. "I told you I wanted these things on a timing device. I want to be able to set each one at a different time before it goes off."

"Yeah, and you also told me you wanted something quick," Geary replied. "Quick and dirty. You press these little doohickeys and you've got an hour to get out of Dodge. You want something more state-of-the-art, I need another week. Maybe two. That and more cash."

For a moment, Elliot was tempted to give the devices back to the fat bastard, but decided against it. Two nights ago, EJ'd had another nightmare, one he couldn't remember, but he'd wakened, crying in terror, and Elliot let him sleep in his bed. He was able to persuade his son to sleep in his own room the next night, but EJ's sleep had been fitful at best. Also, Elliot kept contemplating the true circumstances behind Susan's death. Had the thing been pissed off at him for breaking the connection between them years ago? Had it tried to get back at him first through his wife and now through his son? Did Susan have one of those OBE's before she died? If so, what had she seen in the last few seconds of her life? Is this why it was coming after EJ? No, Elliot opted to go ahead with things as they were. He couldn't stand the thought of the Backwoods Demon or whatever it was surviving another night.

"OK, I'll take them as is."

"Cool. Don't worry. My friend says you don't have to baby 'me. You can knock 'me around all you want as long as long you don't push them little black buttons. Once you do though, you just want to hightail your ass out of there. You sure you know what you're doing with these?"

203

"Don't worry."

"Yeah, right. Got my cash?"

"Right here."

Elliot counted off the balance and stuck the bills in Geary's T shirt pocket. "Thanks, kid. Come again."

Not bloody likely, Elliot thought. He transferred the devices into an extra-large rucksack, and drove off, thinking of nothing but the business at hand.

His son's anguish and discomfort over the past few nights was fresh in his mind. Thoughts of that anguish and discomfort congealed in a cold and concentrated anger in Elliot's breast. It was not the kind of anger that drives a man to an act of impulsive violence or a crime of passion. True, Elliot was contemplating a violent act, but it was a calculated undertaking. It was not the result of some hotheaded fit of temper, but of cool planning, careful preparations, and extreme focus.

It was an act of love, for one gone and one remaining.

Now that he had the explosives, there were other items on his list he had to obtain before re-entering the cave. He'd duct-taped a powerful flashlight to an old bike helmet for use in the cave. He wanted both hands free to navigate the passages and push the ruck through some of the narrower ones. He also decided to stop off at the hardware store at Taylor Square. There, he'd pick up one of those Maglight sets which consisted of one large flashlight, two smaller ones, plus extra batteries.

Of course he had the gun, fully loaded, plus extra ammo.

He would not, could not afford to fail.

A Bronco passed him going the other way as he left Geary's. Elliot was oblivious when the Bronco made a U-turn and proceeded to follow him.

17

Cheryl Strickland was happier than she'd been in days.

Ever since Chief Parsons' appearance, Jeff had been on edge and uneasy. He'd apologized for snapping at her. Unable to stay mad at him, she'd accepted and gently tried to draw him out. Jeff remained obstinate. He didn't feel like talking, and Cheryl had backed off.

This behavior was not like Jeff. He was, she supposed, like most men, prone to keeping things that bothered them inside, at least initially. Over the years, she'd learned that with a little prodding, he could be brought to confide in her. Not this time, and it pained her. Here he was, carrying something so painful, but so deep, that he'd rather let it eat away at him from inside than share it with her.

Apologies and forgiveness aside, the days since the Parsons confrontation were tense and stressful.

But today, Cheryl had news that would surely reverse that trend. She'd just come from Dr. McKenna, who'd given her news she was certain would delight Jeff out of his doldrums.

She decided not to drive straight home. Rather, she'd stop at the liquor store at Taylor Square and pick up a bottle of Merlot, no, on second thought, make that champagne. Brut for him, the non-alcoholic stuff for her. She hoped that he wouldn't be home when she got there. That way, she could surprise him by having a couple of chilled glasses of the bubbly ready for when he walked in. He'd ask what this was all about. She'd tell him and he would break into one of those ear-to-ear smiles she hadn't seen for days. They would kiss, drink, and perhaps re-live the happiness they'd shared only hours before Parsons' visit shot everything to hell.

She pulled into the parking lot at Taylor Square. After she'd made her purchase in the wine shop, she walked into the *chocolatier* to pick up a sampler. Hell, they might as well go all the way when it came to being decadent tonight.

Her mind was filled with thoughts of the joyful night she'd be spending with her husband. At least it was, until the moment she unlocked the door to her Honda and felt something hard pressed against her ribs.

"Get in the car, bitch. Scream and you're dead."

18

Shortly after Cheryl left for her doctor's appointment, the phone rang in the Strickland residence. Jeff picked up.

"Hello?"

"Good afternoon. May I speak to Jeff Strickland, please?"

"Speaking."

"Mr. Strickland. This is Dr. Guthrie from Mercy Hospital. Tell me, do you know a Mr. Henrik Baumann?"

"No, I ..."

Wait a second. Baumann? Wasn't that the name Parsons threw at him a few days ago?

"Mr. Strickland?"

"Yes, I'm here. I'm sorry, did you say Baumann?"

"Yes. We're trying to locate Mr. Baumann's next of kin. There was no contact information in his wallet, but we found your name and number in a shirt pocket. Do you know the gentleman, sir?"

"Uh, yes," Jeff lied, at a loss for words "that is ... yes, I know him."

"Are you a family member, sir?"

"Uh, well, no, just a friend," Jeff floundered. Of course, he didn't know Henrik Baumann from a hole in the wall. But he knew that Henrik Baumann had something to do with Parsons' interrogation. Now, somehow, an opportunity was plopped in his lap to find out more about this Baumann character. It was an opportunity and he wasn't about to let it pass by. "Um, what's he in for?"

"I'm afraid I can't give out patient information to anyone who's not a member of the immediate family, sir," Dr. Guthrie replied. "Tell me, do you know anyone associated with Mr. Baumann?"

For a moment, Jeff was tempted to compound the lie and tell Dr. Guthrie that yes, he really was a family member. If he did that, though, his previous answer might arouse the doctor's suspicions, thereby cutting him off from learning more about Henrik Baumann. So instead, he said, "It's more of a casual acquaintance. Mr. Baumann was to have looked me up; we'd left it very open-ended. Tell me, is he allowed visitors?"

"Yes, he is. Our visiting hours are from 9:00 am to noon, then 1:00 pm to 9:30. Will you be stopping in?"

"Oh, absolutely. Thank you, doctor."

"Thank you, Mr. Strickland."

Jeff hung up the phone, seething, grabbed his car keys and made for his Camry. Oh yeah, you bet, I'll be stopping in, doctor. I have a feeling that Henrik Baumann knows exactly why the Chief of Police thinks I have something to do with a shitload of killings. You're going to answer some questions for me, Mr. Baumann. Oh, yes indeed.

19

Hi. You've reached the Stricklands ...

No answer. Damn!

Elliot contemplated putting off his plans until Jeff could participate in them, but decided against it, almost immediately. He wanted to get this business done and over with as soon as possible. He was uncomfortable holding onto the items he had purchased off Geary. He wanted to put them to use and get them out of his possession quickly. The possibility that Susan had been murdered by the thing in the cave haunted him. Allowing that death to go unavenged was not acceptable. The thought of another restless night for EJ was even more so. No, he'd go it on his own.

Elliot pulled out of the parking lot and made his way to the trail head.

When he got to the crevice, the sky was beginning to darken, and the horizon was turning an angry shade of gray. Elliot knew that from this point, he'd have to walk a line between caution and speed. Caution because he was handling explosive material and a firearm. Speed because it was getting on to late afternoon and a storm was coming. Put those two facts together and you had an early darkness, and Elliot knew from his OBEs that the being he was looking to eradicate craved darkness.

Elliot squeezed through the crevice, gently easing the rucksack ahead of him until the passage opened up. He made his way to the crawlspace under the rock, where he opened the ruck and began to organize its contents.

He removed the helmet with the flash and put it on. He then removed the gun from the ruck's main compartment and transferred it to his fanny pack, positioned in front, just over his belt buckle. He figured he'd carry the gun with him wherever he could. Where he could not, where the passages narrowed or where he needed to climb, it would still be accessible. Finally, he took a flannel shirt and put it on over the T-shirt he wore bearing his business logo. The outside air was hot and stultifying, but the deeper one went in the cave, the cooler it got. The long-sleeved shirt would provide an additional layer of comfort.

Elliot's original plan had been to leave the three devices in different parts of the cave. The first, he would place just past the slot-like opening to the boneyard. The second, by the crevice inside the cave itself. The third, on the cave floor, right at the base of the wall which he had to climb to exit. He had told Geary he wanted timing mechanisms attached to the devices. That way, he'd be able to stagger the explosions so that they'd occur at approximately the same time, but Geary skunked him on that part of the plan. So instead, he'd make his way through the cave, plant the first two devices at their respective chosen points, not activated. When he got to the mail slot, he'd leave the final device there and press the button. He'd then make his way back through the cave, activating the other devices as he went. He'd then get to what he thought would be a safe distance and wait for the resulting explosions.

Elliot had no illusions about what he was doing. He knew it was dangerous, he knew it was chancy, he knew it might not work. Tenuous though it was, however, he felt driven to do it, not only for his own sake, but for his son's as well. It had occurred to him that the thing he was trying to destroy might not even be in the cave, but he did not think that likely. He recalled from his first weed-induced encounter how it hated the lightning. This, plus the recollection that the killings had all taken place at night, told him that it was averse to light. No, chances were that it was down there in some remote, unexplored reach of the cave. Even if it was not in the cave, he'd be depriving it of its den. That meant it would be trapped out in the open, in daylight, and would surely be seen, hunted down, and destroyed.

A greater possibility existed that he might actually encounter it while in the cave. Granted, that hadn't happened the two previous times he'd been there, but that didn't mean his luck would hold out indefinitely. Which made him all the more glad to have the gun positioned where it was. Of course, he'd have to be extra careful when making his way through some of those low-slung passages on his belly.

These preparations having been completed, Elliot lowered himself down and carefully wormed his way under the rocky barrier as he'd done twice before. Geary's assurances that "You can knock 'me around all you want" provided scant comfort. He didn't intend knocking them around at all. As far as he was concerned, they were as delicate as eggshells filled with nitroglycerine. Therefore, he was going to baby them from start to finish.

When he saw that the ruck had reached the cave floor, Elliot began to climb down. Once he was down there, he opened the ruck and pulled out one of Geary's devices. He found a spot on the cave floor, near the protrusion where he'd tied the length of clothesline years ago. With great care, he worked the device into the moist sticky clay where it would remain until he was ready to activate it.

Elliot's senses were on red alert. Since his discovery of the boneyard, he'd begun to understand the enormity of the danger that skulked down here. It was able to reach out to him from great distances and force him to see things he didn't want to see, do things which sickened him. It could do the same thing to EJ, and maybe had done those things to Susan.

Now, he was in *its* territory, It could spring from the darkness at any time, risking the meager beams of the light it hated to fasten itself upon something it hated even more.

When he got to the chasm, he took the second device from the ruck, and placed it in the same manner as he did the first. He then made his way to the other side of the chasm, down the passage, and to the tiny opening leading to the boneyard. Once again, removing his ruck, Elliot put it to the side, and lowered himself through, this time on his back, feet first.

That's when found himself knee-deep in a pool of water.

Unprepared for this unexpected turn of events, Elliot found himself falling forward. He had enough presence of mind to keep the hand holding the gun elevated and out of the wet, but just barely. He had landed in such a way that his clothes were drenched up to his chest in the cold, dirty water. He stood, and when he got his bearings, he looked around him and realized with a thrill of horror that this wasn't the boneyard. He had stumbled into an unfamiliar part of the cave.

It was a passage where the floor was covered with water as far as his light would reach. He dared not move forward. It was possible that the water throughout the rest of the chamber might be even deeper than where he was now standing. In some parts, the chamber might even be bottomless.

Elliot was wearing cotton, which absorbed the water. He shivered in these wet, clammy clothes. In the cool cave air, hypothermia was a real danger. He had to get out of here and find the right passage. He turned to locate the slot through which he'd dropped. Cold and discomfort lent haste to his actions and in his first scrutiny of the cave wall, he missed seeing the opening. Only by a conscious effort of will was he able to keep from panicking, and the second time around, he was able to spot it.

That's when his light began to flicker.

20

The sky was beginning to darken to an angry shade of gray when Jeff pulled his car into the parking lot of Mercy Hospital.

During the drive, Jeff's anger had cooled a little. It dissipated further when he stopped at the nurses' station to inquire where Henrik Baumann's room was. The nurse asked if Jeff was family and he hedged by saying he was a "family friend." The nurse then asked if Jeff knew whether or not there was a history of epilepsy in Baumann's family. To this, Jeff could be truthful and say that to the best of his knowledge, there was not. The nurse related how Baumann had been brought into the Intensive Care Unit after being severely battered, apparently as the result of an unusual and violent fit. He was no longer in ICU, but he was in great pain, his tongue had to be stitched, he was on painkillers, and his speech was garbled. The doctors were doing their best for him, but they were puzzled. Any information Jeff might have regarding the man and his family would be most welcome. Jeff expressed his regrets; he was only a casual family friend, and could offer no further assistance.

When he actually saw Baumann, any remaining vestiges of his anger vanished. It was impossible to feel anything but pity for the pathetic inhabitant of that room.

Baumann was the sole occupant of the room, a thin old man with wispy white hair, a tiny moustache, skin stretched taut on his face, toothpick-like arms, resting alongside his body on a hospital bed, with an IV coming out of the left one. The left eye showed signs of life, the right was bandaged. His good eye fixed on Jeff as soon as he walked into the room and tracked him as he walked to the foot of the bed. The nurse had said that Mr. Baumann would be groggy from the meds. That grogginess, however, did not disguise the consciousness and intelligence behind that eye, which not even strong medication could suppress.

Jeff stopped at the foot of the bed and spoke in a near whisper. "Mr. Baumann?"

Baumann answered him. It was the voice of a stroke victim, attempting to relearn how to speak. Distorted, but Jeff was able to make it out.

You're Jeff Strickland.

Jeff nodded, amazed. "Do you know me?"

The old man shook his head, and then began to speak once more. Again, his speech was incoherent, but Jeff was able to make out most of the gist of it.

A room without light or sound. Then: *Stygian.*

Jeff could only nod. "Mr. Baumann. How do you know about that?"

For the third time, Baumann tried to speak, but this time, his voice was only a dry croak. He turned toward the night table next to the bed and gestured toward it with his head. Jeff looked and saw a Styrofoam pitcher with some Dixie cups.

"Can I get you some water?"

Baumann nodded. Jeff walked over to the night table, poured some water into a cup, and held it to the old man's lips, tilting it gently. Baumann emptied the cup after several tentative sips. Then he gestured at the night table again.

"Some more water?"

Baumann shook his head and tilted his chin in the direction of the night table with a series of short jerks. Jeff looked again and noticed a pad and pen. Apparently, this was how Baumann communicated with the staff when he was unable to speak. Jeff held them up. "Is this what you want?" In answer, Baumann reached for the pad with his left hand and made a writing gesture with his right. Jeff handed him the pad and pen.

Baumann began to write. His motions were erratic, but deliberate. He handed the pad to Jeff, and when Jeff saw what he had written, he was chilled.

Help Cheryl Help Friend Don't Be Afraid

Help Cheryl was underlined.

"What do you mean, 'Help Cheryl'? Mr. Baumann, you've got to tell me!"

Baumann made a "give me" motion with his hands, and Jeff handed him back the pad and paper. He watched as Baumann underlined Cheryl's name again, then crossed out *Don't Be Afraid* and in its place wrote *Eye*.

Jeff was trying to control a fear that was starting to cross over into hysteria. This man knew who Jeff was, without being told. He knew about the dark, silent *stygian* room. He was implying that his wife was in danger. Jeff no longer cared about any connection between Chief Parsons and Henrik Baumann. Over the years, his interest in the paranormal led him to various readings about people with second sight. He was dubious about such people, but he never fully disbelieved, either. He was now convinced that he was in the presence of such a person and the only thing that mattered at this moment was *Help Cheryl.*

"Mr. Baumann, please. You've got to tell me. What do you mean by 'Help Cheryl?' Is my wife in danger? Come on, you've got to …"

"Sir, is there some problem in here?" Jeff turned and saw two of the nurses he'd spoken to earlier coming into the room. He realized that he had spoken louder than he'd intended, and his voice had carried.

"No, I'm sorry. I'm just a little upset. I …"

"Sir, I think you'd better leave. We can't have this patient disturbed. You can come back later if you like."

Jeff was about to protest further when Baumann tried to speak again. Apparently, the meds were kicking in and he was finding it harder to articulate. What he said sounded like "Maw wah."

"What's that, Mr. Baumann?" one of the nurses asked.

"I think he's asking for more water," the other replied.

"Mr. Baumann," Jeff began to speak but the other nurse interrupted him.

"Sir, I think it's best that you leave now. This patient needs his rest."

"But I …"

"Would you prefer that I call Security?"

Jeff bolted out of the room, reached for his cell phone, and turned it on. The *Searching for Signal* prompt appeared and remained displayed.

215

Cursing under his breath, Jeff ran to the elevators. He pressed the *Down* button and after waiting a long five seconds, sought the nearest stairwell and raced down to the ground floor. He rushed through the lobby, out the main entrance and tried again. This time, he got a signal, and autodialed his home phone.

Hi. You've reached the Stricklands ...

Shit! He'd hoped to speak to her directly, to reassure himself she was OK. Instead, he left a message.

"Babe, it's me. Call me on my cell soon as you get this. It's important."

Then he remembered. She'd had a doctor's appointment that day. He tried again, autodialing her cell phone. It rang and rang until he heard: *Hi, it's Cheryl. Can't take your call right now, but if you leave a message, I'll get back to you soon as I can.*

Double shit! He left the same message, and ran for his car. Right now, he wanted nothing more than to get back to their apartment in Dandridge, to assure himself his wife was safe. Once he had that assurance, he planned to hold her close for a very long time.

21

The darkness was unyielding. The only sound was that sloshy noise Elliot made by walking in place in the sticky mud, trying to keep warm.

If his senses were on red alert before, they were now a flaming, glowing crimson. Here he was in total darkness, in an unfamiliar part of the cave, unarmed. If the thing he was seeking was in this chamber, his life could be measured in seconds. He would die here, violently. His body would never be found. EJ and his parents would spend the rest of their lives mourning, wondering.

And *it* would still be out there, preying on his son.

Forcing himself to remain calm, Elliot had reached up and tapped the back of the wavering flashlight gently, hoping to nudge it into a consistent brightness. It dimmed even further and Elliot, afraid of losing it altogether, turned it off. His plan was to get out of this chamber and get back to the rucksack he'd left back on the cave floor. Using one of the spare Maglights he'd purchased, he'd replenish the batteries on his main light, and complete his mission.

It wasn't until he'd turned off his headlight than he realized that he hadn't memorized the location of the opening to this chamber. He stood, continuing to walk in place, waiting for his eyes to grow accustomed to the dark. When he'd begun to see enough of the details of the cave wall he was facing, he would relocate the opening. With no ambient lighting, however, and the seconds turning to minutes, his eyes became no more used to the blackness than before.

He tried turning on his helmet light again, but the light did not respond at all. Whether the batteries had died or the bulb had blown was a moot point.

He was blind, and blind, he would have to get out of this.

Still walking in place, he leaned into the cave wall and began to run his hand across it. He recalled that the opening was approximately chin level, so he started running his hand across the hard moist clay. Contact between his torso and the clammy cave wall heightened the cold. Despite that, he dared not move too quickly, even though faster motions generated more warmth to his body. Quickness might cause him to miss the opening, which would only prolong the hypothermia.

On his third pass, he discovered the opening, just above chin level. It was narrow, and given its height, it would be tricky to get through, impossible without the use of both hands. He was reluctant to relinquish the gun, but did so anyway, placing it as far into the opening as his reach would permit. He then braced himself by grabbing the opening at both sides and jumping up.

He found himself falling back into the wetness, both hands ending up beneath the surface. He was now glad he was not holding the gun.

Elliot picked himself up and, disoriented, colder than ever, began the painstaking task of relocating the opening. Once again, he lucked out. He took a firm grip on the sides, sought footholds in the wall and began to pull his way up.

He began to slide back, and for a moment, feared he would fall back into the watery chamber. By grabbing at the walls, he was able to arrest his backslide.

Making progress was gradual, painstaking, but Elliot managed to pull his upper body and thighs out of the hole. Once he was able to stand, he ran in place for a few seconds, then got down on his knees to feel for the ruck. Undoing the straps, he found one of the Mags and powered it on. In seconds, the passage was flooded with refreshing light, and Elliot, after locating a fresh pack of D batteries, removed his jerry-rigged helmet and placed the new batteries in the flash. Holding his breath, he powered it on and almost cheered aloud when a fresh source of illumination filled the passage.

Elliot could now see where he'd gone wrong. Several yards ahead was a second small opening. This was the one to the boneyard Elliot had sought. He'd never noticed that there were two small entrances to two separate passages along this route. He'd simply chosen the wrong one, but this time, there was no mistake. He could even see the clothesline he'd placed years ago along the passage leading to the second opening.

Locating the gun, Elliot took it in hand. The fanny pack was drenched and he was loath to replace the gun in it. Holding onto it, he worked his way to the second opening. There was no need to go through it. He'd just place the final charge at its mouth, set it, then head back, setting the other charges as he went. He took the charge from the ruck and placed it just outside the opening to the bone-filled chamber. He paused, long enough to offer a silent prayer of hope that Geary had been correct about the timing of the charges. If he was, they wouldn't go off until he was back outside, a safe distance from the escarpment.

He pressed the button.

The device gave a little click, not unlike a light switch when first turned on, but no other sound. Elliot wasn't even certain it had been activated, but he wasn't about to start futzing with it or stick around. He was going to—how did Geary put it?—"get out of Dodge."

Elliot made his way back to the chasm where he activated the second device. Once again, crawling on his belly, crawling on hands and feet, walking hunched over, walking upright. Sometimes carrying and sometimes pushing his rucksack, now lighter, without Geary's devices weighing it down.

He had just returned to the spot where he'd placed the first device when he heard the sound.

It was a low rumbling which could have been anything from thunder to a low growl. Elliot remembered that the weather was starting to get more ominous on his trek to the cave. The sound might be the angry muffle of a thunderstorm in its earliest stages, or the angrier sound of a hunter whose home turf was invaded.

Elliot aimed his helmet light toward the interior of the cave. With its new batteries, the reach of the beam was considerable, and it reached quite a distance into the cave where the passage began to narrow.

From where he was standing, Elliot could see no sign that he was sharing the immediate vicinity with anything else. Still, he had no desire to stay in the cave any longer than he had to, no desire to retrace his steps back into the cave. With as much speed as he could muster without being careless, Elliot removed the gun from the ruck, and aimed it toward the interior.

"If you're there, come on out," Elliot whispered. "You bastard."

Nothing moved.

This was no time to linger. Elliot located the third device and pressed the button and edged back to the wall leading to the outside, and contemplated a logistical problem. He knew he could climb his way out of here with the ruck on his back, but what to do with the gun? What if he wasn't alone? What if the thing attacked him while he was climbing his way out?

There weren't a lot of alternatives, so Elliot selected the one which made him the least uncomfortable. He unbuttoned his flannel shirt and tucked the gun into the waistband of his jeans. He supposed that if he were attacked during his climb, he could relinquish one hand hold and shoot the fucker if there was no other choice. Of course, he could also shoot off his balls, but based on what he knew of the thing's handiwork, he'd take the risk.

The climb was slower than usual, since Elliot spent much of the climb with his back to the wall. This was so he could have a vantage point from which to view the passage out of which anything might come bounding. There were enough holds for his hands and feet for him to make progress. Only once did Elliot have to face away from the cave interior and that was when he was at the exit.

Outside was dark and Elliot couldn't tell whether it was because the thunderclouds had rolled in or because night had fallen. Still, it wasn't so dark that Elliot couldn't make his way back. He replaced the helmet in the ruck, wondering how much time he'd actually been down there, what with his escapade in that watery side chamber. Whatever. It was time to make tracks.

Elliot worked his way out of the crevice leading to the cave entrance. He crawled from the cleft in the rock which led from the crevice. From here on in, it would be smooth sailing. The rumbling of thunder overhead reassured him that this was indeed the sound he'd heard earlier. The hot summer air was a blessing to his skin, which had known nothing but bone-numbing cold for who knows how long? He'd run like hell to get as far from the escarpment as possible, as fast as possible, make his way back to the trail. He'd pick up EJ from his folks, head home, and enjoy a nice cold brew. Hell, make that a six-pack; he'd earned it.

He had just emerged from the crawlspace and was about to stand when something hard struck him on the head from behind. He went down, sprawling, tried to rise, when another blow struck him at the side of his left knee. He collapsed face down on the ground. Through a haze of whirling lights dancing across his vision, he became aware of footsteps. As his vision cleared, he raised his head to see a pair of construction boots before him.

He heard a voice.

"Hiya, fuck-head. Remember me?"

22

The Bronco that followed Elliot from Geary's began to sputter.

"MotherFUCKER."

"What's the matter?"

"Starting to stall out on me. Come on you, whore. All RIIGHHT."

The Bronco stayed behind Elliot's van, which was signaling a turn into Taylor Square.

No sooner had Elliot made the turn when the Bronco began to sputter again. It stalled and this time, it wouldn't start.

"Shit!"

"So what are we gonna do?"

"You know how to hot wire a car?"

"No. You?"

"No. Never mind. We're getting a ride."

The woman seemed to be lost in thought. She wasn't aware of anything until the gun was pressed against her ribs.

"Get in the car, bitch. Scream and you're dead."

Like most of Taylorville, Cheryl knew the Coreys by sight and reputation, and she had no illusions about her current situation. It was bad, major bad.

The older one, Howard, was sitting next to her in the front passenger seat, his gun pointed at her, just below dashboard level. The heavyset one, Desmond, sat behind her, but not before displaying an enormous hunting knife and placing it at the nape of her neck.

"What are you going to do?' she asked.

"Shut up, bitch," Desmond snarled and flicked the knife upward, just behind her right ear, drawing blood. She gave a little squeal, as Howard pushed the gun into her side, told her to shut up, then turned to his brother.

"Put that away, fuck-head. What's the matter with you? You want someone to see us?" Desmond glared at Howard, but said nothing. Howard turned to Cheryl. "You see that van over there?" Cheryl, too terrified to move, sat motionless. "I said do you see it?" Howard shouted, prodding her again with the gun. This time, she nodded.

"When the guy that owns it comes out, you're going to follow him," Howard said in a low voice, no less threatening for all its softness. "Don't try anything, or you're dead. You got that?"

Cheryl nodded again. She believed him. Every word.

Her cell phone rang. Instinctively, she reached for her pocketbook. LEAVE IT," Howard ordered.

"It's—it's my husband," Cheryl protested. "He always calls me this time of day. He'll be worried if I don't pick up. He—he's a cop," she added, knowing she was rambling, knowing how lame that must have sounded.

"LEAVE IT."

Cheryl withdrew her hand from the pocketbook as the phone continued to ring. Finally, the automatic answering feature kicked in, and the ringing stopped. The only sound in the car was Cheryl's frightened breathing.

They waited.

The cell phone rang again. This time Cheryl didn't move, just sat there, waiting for the ringing to stop.

A few minutes later, it rang again. Again, no one moved.

Then it rang again, and fell silent.

Howard grabbed for the pocketbook and upended it. The cell phone tumbled out and he made ready to stamp on it with his boot.

"Hey man, what are you doing?" shouted his brother.

"Fuckin' thing's getting on my nerves," the other snarled.

"Hey, man, if her old man's really a cop …"

Howard stopped. He reached down and picked up the phone. "OK, bitch. Next time your old man calls, just tell him you're having car trouble. Don't try anything funny or you're dead, you got that?" For emphasis, he pressed the gun into her side. She also felt the point of the knife press into the back of her neck. The touch was gentle, but with enough pressure to draw blood.

Cheryl nodded. For an instant, she wondered whether she should make a run for it. Would these two actually kill her in a public place such as this? She decided they would.

The phone rang. She picked up.

"Hello?"

It was Jeff, as she supposed. "Cheryl, you OK?"

No, Jeff. I'm not OK. I'm being carjacked by two madmen. One's holding a gun on me, the other a knife. I'm scared, I'm bleeding, and oh yes, I'm pregnant, so it's not only me they're going to kill, it's our child. No, I'm light years from being OK.

But instead, she said: "I'm having trouble with the car; I don't trust it; it's making funny noises." She paused, waiting for a response.

"What was that?"

"I said I'm having trouble with the car; I don't trust it; it's making funny noises. I'm OK, though. Really."

"You don't sound OK. You want me to come get you?"

"No, no. I'm just upset about the car is all. I called the road service. I'm waiting for a tow. Don't worry, honey. I'll be home soon. I'm OK."

No response at the other end. Was he buying it? If he didn't, would he say something to that effect? She was sure the brothers could hear his end of the conversation. If he said something to make them suspicious, what would they do? Please, Jeff, believe me. Please.

Finally, he said, "OK, babe. I'll see you when you get home. Love you."

"I love you too," she answered, as she clicked the End Call button. No sooner had she done so when Howard grabbed the phone, threw it on the floor and stomped on it.

"You done real good there, bitch. Keep it up and you might get to live through this."

That, she doubted.

#

Ten minutes later, Elliot Ryan returned to the van, carrying two full bags. As soon as he got into the van, Howard nudged Cheryl with the gun and she started the Honda.

"You stay with him, hear?" Howard ordered. "Don't hang too close, but don't lose him."

"And don't try anything," Desmond added.

"Right. Get going, bitch."

Elliot pulled out with Cheryl behind him. They continued on Route 29 for another few miles, then Elliot turned off onto a series of side streets. Cheryl was surprised; she figured Elliot would be heading back to Crow's Nest Pike. It was late in the day, the sky was darkening even as they were driving. She assumed that his work day was coming to an end. But he was going the opposite way, clearly with some other destination in mind. She had no doubt what would happen to him when he reached that destination.

Or to her for that matter.

They drove for another twenty minutes, past the McSweeney farm when Elliot pulled his van to the side of the road across the street from the boarded-up Dunbar's Wharf.

"Stop the car," Howard ordered.

She pulled over to the side of the road about a hundred yards behind the van.

"Let's get him," Desmond urged.

"No, wait. I want to see what he's gonna do."

After a brief wait, Elliot got out of the van and walked over to the start of a trail and made his way into the woods. Howard grinned. Perfect. He'd follow the little fuck-head into the woods and settle his scores with no one around. No one watching. "Come on!"

The three of them got out of the car, Howard and Desmond running, forcing Cheryl to keep pace between them. When they got to the trail head, Elliot's back was still visible, as it receded among the trees. Howard started walking on the trail, then stopped when Desmond began to follow.

"What the fuck are you doing?"

"I'm going with you."

"Hell you are."

"But Howie ..."

"You stay here and take care of the bitch." Howard grinned again. "You can even have a little fun with her if you like."

It was Desmond's turn to grin. "I can live with that."

225

Howard disappeared up the trail after Elliot. Desmond grabbed Cheryl's arm. "Come on, bitch."

"What are you going to do?"

Desmond wrenched her arm, and she cried out. "I said, come on." He half led, half dragged her across the road toward Dunbar's Wharf. She hoped a car, preferably a police car, would come by and see what was happening, but luck was not with her. It was a side road, one not frequently traveled, and no cars appeared.

They approached the abandoned restaurant and Cheryl recognized it as the place Jeff had taken her for their senior prom. It was called something else back then, but her mind was too occupied with her own survival to try to remember so trivial a detail.

Desmond dragged her to the back parking lot. He removed the knife from its sheath and for the first time, she got a good look at it. It was an ugly looking thing, nearly a foot long, and it looked like it could gut a rhino.

"This doesn't have to hurt, bitch. Don't scream, don't cry, and you won't get hurt."

This too, she doubted.

Desmond put his ham-sized hand on her breast and pushed her. She stumbled backwards, tripped over a discarded car bumper, pivoted and landed on her stomach. From behind, she heard the sound of something being unzipped.

Cheryl knew she was going to die. She knew that this bastard, this animal was going to have his way with her and be extremely violent about it. He was carrying a very formidable weapon, he was bigger than she was, he outweighed her by God knows how much. She was going to die. So was her baby.

That was when Cheryl decided that she was going to fight him. She would go for his balls, his eyes, anything she could. It wasn't much of a chance, but if she didn't do even that much she'd have no chance at all. Neither would her baby.

She heard footsteps as he started to approach her and she tensed her muscles, making ready to attack him as soon as he came within reach.

Cheryl turned, and what she saw changed everything.

23

Jeff pulled out of the parking lot, dissatisfied.

Part of him wanted to write off Baumann's words as the ramblings of a sick and confused old man. He rejected doing so as soon as the thought occurred to him. Didn't Baumann call him by name as soon as he walked into the room? What was even more significant, didn't Baumann make the association between him and *a room without light or sound?* It was possible that someone might have mentioned Jeff's name to Baumann; when he saw an unfamiliar face come into his room, he made a lucky guess. But didn't the doctor say that Baumann had Jeff's name on his person when he was admitted to the hospital? Why? How did he know about the room? Jeff never told *anyone* about that.

No, he couldn't just write off what Baumann had said. Baumann had been on target about the room; therefore he had to believe that Cheryl was in some kind of trouble. If she wasn't, so much the better; at least he'd be erring on the side of caution.

He pulled the car off to the side of the road and tried calling her cell phone number. Again he got the voice message.

He tried again. Same result.

Again. Same result.

Again. This time, she answered. "Hello?"

"Cheryl, you OK?"

"I'm having trouble with the car; I don't trust it; it's making funny noises."

Something clicked. It wasn't a loud click in his mind's ear; it was barely audible but there was something definite about it. Not only Cheryl's tone of voice, which was tense, almost tearful, indicating that things were *not* OK, but her words. Something about them.

"*What was that?*"

"I said I'm having trouble with the car; I don't trust it; it's making funny noises. I'm OK, though. Really."

"You don't sound OK. You want me to come get you?"

"No, no. I'm just upset about the car is all. I called the road service. I'm waiting for a tow. Don't worry, honey. I'll be home soon. I'm OK."

I'm having trouble with the car; I don't trust it; it's making funny noises.

This wasn't the first time he'd heard those words. There was something familiar about them, something meaningful. If only he could place what it was.

Finally, he said, "OK, babe. I'll see you when you get home. Love you."

"I love you too," she answered and rang off.

He sat there, more frightened than he'd ever been.

She *was* in trouble, he had no doubt of that. Cheryl was too self-contained to let mere car trouble upset her. Something else was going on and there was something about the words she'd used ...

Jeff's vision began to swim before him. The road before him, the darkening sky, the interior of his car—all of these seemed to fade away as if a gossamer curtain was being drawn before him. He put his hands to his temples, trying to clear his eyesight which was becoming fuzzier and fuzzier, even as he fought to restore clarity. It was no use. Every object which had been in his line of sight seconds before was hidden by a gauzy haze his eyes could not penetrate.

The next instant, he was no longer in his car on the side of the road. He was in a dark room, watching a shape. Sometimes it danced, sometimes it floated.

When it took form, Jeff recognized it, recognized where he was.

In a room without light or sound.

The shape was a Cheryl-vision, not as she looked now, but as she was years ago, smiling in that short cheerleader's outfit. She came closer to him and as she approached she changed. She aged to the still beautiful woman she was now, her cheerleader's skirt and sweater merging into the pantsuit she was wearing this morning. She was no longer smiling, instead she looked terrified.

"I'm having trouble with the car; I don't trust it; it's making funny noises. I'm by the landing. I want you Jeff, please come.

"Please come.

"Please come."

The vision faded. The gauzy haze faded. The gossamer curtain was withdrawn.

He was back, sitting behind the wheel of his car, on the side of a Massachusetts road.

The nonsensical *non sequiturs* of that Cheryl vision years ago were finally beginning to make sense. They were not the meaningless ramblings of a dreaming mind. "Please come" did not have the sexual significance he'd assumed at the time. In the context of what was happening right now, it was an urgent cry for help.

Jeff also understood the meaning of *the landing*. There was only one place with that name which would have any meaning for her.

He pulled back onto the road, tires squealing, and drove like a bat out of hell. He was going to *Help Cheryl*. He was going to *The Landing*.

Jeff got onto Route 29 then turned off onto a series of side roads, just as Elliot had done. He had just gone past the McSweeney farm when he saw his wife's Honda behind Elliot's van. He pulled in behind the Honda and ran to it. Was she in the car? Was she hurt?

The car was empty.

Then he remembered the boarded-up restaurant. Dunbar's Wharf. Where he and Cheryl went for their senior prom.

Back then, it was known as The Landing.

He ran to the restaurant and was about to call her name when he heard voices from the back. A male voice saying "This doesn't have to hurt, bitch. Don't scream, don't cry, and you won't get hurt." The sound of a zipper.

Jeff ran to the back and what he saw filled him with an equal mix of fear and fury.

Cheryl was face down on the ground. Over her was standing a large man holding a large knife in one hand. His other hand was just below waist level and Jeff could only imagine with disgust what that hand was holding.

229

He ran forward, stopping only to grab a two-by-four that was lying in the debris.

#

The last thing Cheryl expected to see was her husband looming over her attacker, wielding a two-by-four like a baseball bat. Jeff swung the two-by-four, connecting with the side of Desmond's head and the big man went down. Jeff stepped forward, and swung the board again, catching Desmond on the other side of the head.

To her amazement, Desmond was still conscious and still holding the knife. He got up on one knee with the knife held out in front of him, ready to lunge at Jeff. Before he could, however, Jeff brought the edge of the board down on Desmond's wrist. There was the sound of bones cracking, mingled with Desmond's wail of pain and rage, as the knife fell to the ground.

Desmond was still ready to make a fight of it. He began to rise, and Cheryl feared that in his rage, if he got those massive hands on Jeff, it would be all over.

"Jeff, look out!" she shouted.

But Jeff held his ground. As Desmond lurched forward, Jeff sidestepped and swung the two-by-four, connecting squarely with Desmond's hip. The big man screamed and went down. Jeff brought the board down again, this time with such force that it cracked Desmond's collarbone as well as the board itself.

Desmond screamed again.

Jeff, now with only half the board in hand began pummeling his wife's attacker with it. On the head. On the torso. On the hip. On the hip again. The head. The knee. Again. Harder. Even when the son of a bitch was no longer stirring, Jeff continued to rain blows on the unmoving form

"Jeff, stop it!"

His wife's voice brought him to his senses. What he saw in her face disturbed him almost as much as the scene he'd walked in on.

She was seeing her husband in the throes of a savagery she would have thought unimaginable in so placid a man. The fact that she herself would have delighted in administering such a beating to this beast was immaterial at the moment. That this gentle man could be transformed into an engine of such viciousness, such brutality, terrified her.

At the sound of his wife's voice, he dropped the remains of the two-by-four and broke into a spasm of sobs. The crazed look in his eyes gave way to one of fear and concern and love. "Are you OK, babe? Did he hurt you?" He raced over to her, helped her up, and hugged her with a fierceness to which she could only respond with an embrace of like intensity.

"It's OK, Jeff. He didn't hurt me. He was going to but …. Oh, thank God you're here!"

They stayed that way for a long time. Then Cheryl broke the clinch and said, "Jeff, we have to call the police. The other one went into the woods after Elliot Ryan. I think he's going to kill him."

"Other one? What other one?"

"There were two of them Jeff. This one and another one. The other one went into the woods after Elliot."

Jeff remembered seeing Elliot's van by the side of the road. Elliot must have gone back to the cave, not realizing his danger.

Help your friend.

Jeff started walking in the direction of the trail head leading to the cave. Cheryl ran after him. "Wait, where are you going?"

"I'm going after Elliot."

"No, Jeff. The police …"

"The police won't be able to find the place. I know where Elliot's going. I've got to help him."

"Jeff, the man had a gun!"

"I'll be all right."

"How can you say that?"

Don't be afraid.

"Trust me, babe. I'll be OK."

"How can you possibly know that?"

"Same way I knew where to find you."

That stopped her. How *did* he know that she was in danger? How *did* he know where she was?

He looked at her bewildered expression and gave her a little smile meant to convey reassurance. "Long story. Just call the police. Tell them what happened." He gestured toward Desmond, prone, but still breathing. "I don't think you'll have to worry about this lump of shit, but keep your distance anyway. I'll be back as soon as I can." He ran off toward the trail head.

SEP

Cheryl stood there, torn. She knew she should do as Jeff said, call the police and wait for them. Then she remembered the trashed cell phone. She couldn't call the police. On the other hand, her husband, the man she loved, *the man who'd just saved her life* was rushing headlong into danger. Rationally she knew she should stay where she was, flag down a car, and get to the police. It was the safe thing to do, but in good conscience, she couldn't just leave things as they were.

She picked up the knife, gave the prone form of Desmond Corey one last look, whispered "Fuck you," and ran after her husband.

24

As soon as Jeff hit the trail, he broke into a fast jog, then a full-fledged run. He kept running until he'd reached a clearing with a road in sight. He then realized that he'd overshot the point where he needed to leave the marked trail and make his way through the woods to the cave.

He stopped to get his bearings and tried to remember some landmark telling him precisely where that point was. Having run, concentrating more on speed than location, he realized that he didn't know where to deviate from the trail. Panting, he turned around, retracing his steps in a slow but deliberate walk until he got his second wind. Breaking into a steady trot, he focused on the scenery alongside the trail. Hopefully, he would spot something which would tell him to how to proceed toward the cave.

If only he'd been more attentive the first time he'd been here. But then again, he didn't expect to make a return trip without Elliot to guide him.

Jeff looked up at the sky and saw that it was divided in two. Half the sky was a blanket of light gray, the other half was pure black. Yin and yang. The division was even, but it would not remain so for long. The black was moving to overtake the gray. A storm was coming, it was coming fast, and it was going to be a fierce one.

Jeff took a few deep breaths and quickened his pace.

#

No sooner had Cheryl reached the trail head, than she lost sight of her husband. She shouted for him, but did not get any response. For a moment, she contemplated whether she should turn back or continue, then decided on the latter.

She found herself at a definite disadvantage. She was wearing comfortable shoes, which were designed for easy walking on pavement, in a mall, or some other civilized setting. A rutted trail did not qualify. Even so, Cheryl prided herself on her athleticism, and soldiered on. She had an obligation to fulfill, to keep her husband alive and safe.

For reasons she could not understand, Jeff was walking blindly forward to face a crazy man with a gun. For some reason, he felt that he was impervious to the danger. Much as she admired his loyalty to Elliot, she intended to overtake him and dissuade him running headlong into further danger. She knew just the card to play.

She was, after all, pregnant. With his child. Surely Jeff would recognize his obligation to her and to little Jeff or Cheryl as his highest priority.

Whatever happened, she'd deal with the emotional consequences of her actions and decisions another day. Right now, she wanted her husband back, alive, and out of these woods.

Cheryl quickened her pace, then started running, the discomfort from her shoes notwithstanding. She was starting to feel certain that she could talk Jeff into seeing things her way.

#

Jeff found what he thought might be the turn-off into the woods Elliot had taken on their last trek when he heard footsteps. He turned to face the last person he'd expected to see.

"Cheryl, what are you doing here?"

She stopped, out of breath. It took her a few seconds to respond. "Jeff, you've got to come back with me."

"I can't, I've got to ..."

"Will you just shut up and listen! That man has a gun! He's crazy, Jeff. He'll kill you! You've got to come back!"

Don't be afraid. Help your friend.

"Cheryl, no one's going to kill me. Now will you please go back?" He turned and started to walk into the woods, away from the trail.

She grabbed his arm, and shouted at him, "Jeff, you've got to listen. There's something you have to know!"

Before she could finish, two gunshots echoed through the woods in rapid succession. Then a third.

25

"Enjoying yourself, fuck-head?"

Howard Corey certainly was and the knowledge that Elliot Ryan was not, heightened Howard's enjoyment.

Elliot tried to rise by propping himself up on one elbow. Howard responded by leveling a vicious kick at the elbow. He felt a surge of satisfaction on hearing it crack and hearing Elliot cry out in pain.

Howard made sure that Elliot saw his face before beginning his own special brand of festivities. Once he was sure he'd been recognized, he whacked Elliot again on the side of the face with his gun, and began walking around the fallen man, punching and kicking various parts of the body en route.

Another time, he stopped by the head, squatted down, and grabbing Elliot by the hair, raised his head up. As he did so, Elliot spat at him. It was a feeble gesture, but it enraged Howard. Still holding Elliot by the hair, he punched him square in the face. Again, there was a cracking sound, and again, Elliot spat; this time his discharge was red.

Howard released Elliot's hair, but not before slamming him chin-first into the ground. Whether Elliot cried out or not, Howard couldn't say. A peal of thunder drowned out any noise Elliot might have made.

"Years spent pushing dope down south, because of you," Howard snarled and kicked Elliot in the ribs again.

Howard scrunched down, grabbed Elliot's hair again, this time taking care to hold Elliot's head out of range should Elliot attempt to spit again.

"Did us good, though, man," Howard went on. "Met some good ole boys, showed us the ropes. Crazy motherfuckers who went to the bathroom armed, ready and willing to shoot anybody who looked crossways at 'me. They needed guys like us to run all kinds of good shit between *Meh-hee-co* and the back roads of Dixie.

"Life was good. We were on top of our game." Howard's voice suddenly took on a dreamy quality Elliot was surprised to hear, coming from such a thug. "Then one day, we just decided to come back. We didn't talk about it or nothin.' We just did it. The two of us. Just like that. Like it was important for us to get back at you. Funny, ain't it? In all them years, we never gave you a moment's thought."

The thunder recalled Howard to his normal self. The dreaminess melted away, replaced by the usual meanness.

It thundered again, which meant the rain was going to start soon. The fun and games were about to end.

Howard stood up. "You're dead, fuck-head," he whispered. "You are *so* dead."

Elliot tried raising himself up again, and Howard started forward to knock him down again, but another roll of thunder changed his mind.

Howard went on, almost conversationally, "I hear you got a kid now. Well, after I waste your sorry ass, you know what I'm gonna do? I'm gonna pay your kid a little visit. Me and my brother. Yeah. We're gonna have a lot of fun together, you know what I mean?" He grinned when he saw the hatred in Elliot's eyes change to something else.

Howard laughed. Fuck-head was really mad now and really scared too. He could see it in his eyes. But he couldn't do diddly about it. Howard had messed him over good. Fuck-head was hunched over, writhing on his knees, clutching his stomach. Well, good. Howard's only regret was that Fuck-head would be out of his misery all too soon.

"'Course it ain't gonna be fun for your kid." Howard was getting ready to aim his gun at Elliot's head. "But don't worry. It'll hurt him only a little while."

As Howard aimed the gun, a thought began to take slow shape in his Neanderthal brain. Why was Fuck-head holding his stomach like that? The gut was one of the few parts of Elliot's anatomy that Howard hadn't assaulted.

The answer came even before the question could be formed. Elliot's hands came away from his waist holding a gun. Instinctively, Howard started back as he fired. The motion was slight, but just enough to turn what would have been a lethal shot into a miss by inches.

Howard screamed at the flaming agony that struck his kneecap. He fell and the last thing he heard was the second shot that blew most of his face away.

26

Elliot knew he had to get moving.

He didn't know how much time he'd spent being Howard Corey's plaything. What he did know was that the charges in the cave were due to go off at any time. Earlier, he'd worried whether they'd go off prematurely while he was still in the cave, or even if they'd go off at all. Now his concern was the nature of the explosion itself. He'd had no experience with explosives. He had no idea whether the resultant explosion would merely collapse the escarpment or send boulder-size missiles in every direction.

The clock was ticking; he had to move.

Still on his knees, Elliot reached into the ruck to pull out the light/helmet he'd used in the cave. He donned it and immediately threw it off, crying out in pain. The helmet itself was lightweight, even with the flash taped to it, no problem under other circumstances. Now, however, the weighted helmet rested on the spot where Howard has brutally pistol-whacked him. The pain was unbearable. Gritting his teeth, he threw off the helmet and grabbed one of the Maglights. He was able to hold it in the hand that was attached to the arm that Howard kicked, while he put weight on the other arm to get to his feet.

Every movement, no matter how slight, brought its own measure of intense pain. It was pure hell standing on the knee where Howard had leveled so vicious a blow. Elliot had to put most of his weight on the other leg. His upper torso and shoulders had also been pummeled and he found it agonizing to maneuver his arms through the straps of his ruck. As a result, he held the ruck with his good arm and used his other hand to hold the Maglight steady and aim the beam forward.

Thunder boomed overhead.

He tried walking, and found that the best he could do was a cross between a limp and a shuffle. Feeling like an arthritic old man, Elliot made for the trail. His bad knee throbbed with every step and his head felt like it was ready to burst.

Elliot had gone only a few feet when he misjudged a step. His ankle went out from under him, and he tumbled onto the ground, landing on his bad knee. The force of the fall jarred the Maglight from his grip and it rolled away out of his reach.

His cry of pain terminated in a series of sobs. A fine rain began to fall as Elliot lay there, sure that he'd never get out of these woods. He wondered if it wouldn't be easier to lie there and just wait to die.

#

Jeff ran toward the point from which the shots emanated. He was heading in the right direction, and only had to make a minor adjustment in his route when the cry sounded. He was aware that Cheryl was behind him trying to keep up. Several times, he yelled for her to go back. Whether she couldn't hear him over the thunder and wind, or whether she simply disregarded his pleas, he couldn't be sure. He shouted to her again and continued to run forward.

A second cry came from somewhere up ahead and this time, Jeff saw what looked like a point of light from somewhere up ahead. He ran toward it.

#

Elliot had heard something that sounded like shouting in the distance, something that sounded like "Go back!" It didn't make any sense under the circumstances, therefore he dismissed it as the product of his own imagination. When he heard footsteps, he knew that his luck had changed either for the worse (Desmond Corey) or for the better (rescue).

He prayed it was the latter.

\#

The point of light Jeff saw was a small Maglight lying on the ground. He picked it up and did a quick sweep of the area. Someone had to have dropped it. That plus the cry he'd heard earlier told him that someone was in the immediate area.

The light fell on a supine figure on the ground, one Jeff recognized. "Elliot?"

The figure raised its head. "Jeff? That you?"

"Yeah." Jeff ran to where Elliot was lying. Jeff could see that the other man was in bad shape. "You OK? Can you stand?"

"You're going to have to help me up. No, the other arm," Elliot said as Jeff reached for the arm whose elbow Howard had kicked. Painfully, bracing himself against Jeff, Elliot was able to stand.

"Jeff?" Another voice. A woman. Elliot squinted into the darkness, and saw Cheryl Strickland emerge into the Mag's aureole of light. As soon as she saw Elliot, her eyes widened and her mouth dropped.

"Elliot! My God! Are you OK?" Before he could answer, she went on: "There's a man with a gun after you. You have to …"

"It's OK," answered Elliot, holding up his free hand. "We've met. He's history." Then turning to Jeff, he said, "We got to get out of here or we'll be history too."

"What are you talking about?"

"This place is liable to go up any second." Noting Jeff's perplexed look, Elliot looked back in the direction of the escarpment.

This conversation meant nothing to Cheryl, but it obviously meant something to Jeff. He nodded.

"What's going on here?" Cheryl demanded.

"Long story, babe."

"You keep saying that, Jeff. *Just what's going on?*"

"Tell you later, babe. Promise. Right now, we've got to get out of here."

Another flash of lighting lit up the area, and Cheryl realized that her husband was right, at least about getting out of there. Aside from the threat of the storm, Elliot was in obvious need of medical attention. Nonetheless, she made a mental note to hold Jeff to his promise later.

Right now, they needed to address logistics. Elliot was in no condition to shoulder the ruck. Nor was Jeff, who would be half-supporting, half-carrying Elliot, so that responsibility fell to Cheryl. At Elliot's request, she undid the straps to get flashlights for all of them. In the process, her hand touched the gun. She now understood what Elliot meant when he said of Howard Corey, "He's history."

The three proceeded in the direction of the trail just as the drizzle gave way to a downpour within a matter of seconds. The thick canopy of leaves overhead shielded them from a thorough drenching, but enough of the rain got through to make the going difficult. Elliot's good arm was slung over Jeff's shoulder; Jeff had one arm around Elliot's waist and torso to support him. Which left one free hand for each of them, in which they were able aim their flashlights, but not shield them from the rain. Cheryl was the only one who could do this, as she was wearing the ruck and had both hands free.

In this fashion, they formed a procession moving toward the marked trail.

They had gone about a hundred yards when Cheryl cried out, "What was that?"

"What was what?"

"That noise! Back there!"

"What noise?"

"I don't know! I couldn't make it out! It came from back there!"

"I didn't hear anything!" Jeff shouted. Indeed, it was almost impossible to hear anything with the wind, the thunder, and the rain. "Must be the storm. Let's move!"

They walked on, making as much speed as they could, which, under existing conditions, wasn't much. Elliot was able to move his good leg with no effort, but the knee which Howard had assaulted gave him a great deal of pain. Also, his head throbbed with every step. Still, he set as fast a tempo as he could, with Jeff and Cheryl staying with him.

Soon they'd be at the trail. It would be quite a while before they reached the main road, and until they got there, none of them would feel safe.

In the shadows, something moved.

27

"Are you sure we're going the right way?" Cheryl shouted. They'd gone another few hundred yards and Cheryl had expected to be at the main trail by now. Though visibility was poor, even with the three lights beaming straight ahead, it was obvious that they were looking at a vast expanse of woods on all sides.

"Pretty sure," Jeff answered.

"No, I think she's right," Elliot said. "I think we've gone off to one side. I'm pretty sure the trail is that way," jerking his head to the right.

"Tell you what," Jeff said. "If Cheryl can switch places with me, I'll take a run ahead and check things out in that direction. If it looks familiar, I'll holler. You OK with that, babe?"

"Let me do it," Cheryl suggested.

"No, I've been here before and I'll recognize the spot."

"OK," replied Cheryl, still shouting. "Just holler loud. Even better, wave your light over your head. I have enough trouble hearing you as it is."

Cheryl positioned herself next to Jeff and gradually, Elliot shifted his weight so that she was could support him. *My wife, the Amazon*, Jeff thought, with a touch of pride. Her Nordic features radiated strength and determination. Despite being drenched and bedraggled, she was ready to do battle with the elements themselves. The urgency of the situation notwithstanding, he couldn't resist kissing her before starting out.

"For luck," he said.

"Good luck."

He started off in the direction that Elliot indicated and she watched his light recede in the darkness. It got smaller with distance and a few times it went out, briefly, then shone once again. She assumed this was because he'd turned in the other direction or went behind a tree. She squinted, looking for a waving motion to tell them that he'd found the way back to the trail, or better yet, the trail itself. She was so focused on her husband that she was only half aware of Elliot's weight leaning on her. She wanted to ask him a thousand questions (obviously, he was more in the loop about the strange goings-on than she was). She didn't, though; she didn't want to divide her attention and possibly miss a signal from Jeff.

Suddenly, a bolt of sheet lightning lit up the sky for a split-second, but that split-second was enough to reveal a large dark shape moving ahead of them. She wasn't sure what it was, or even if she'd actually seen it until Elliot yelled out, "Come on!" and began to move in that direction, enduring what must have been a world of pain.

"Did you see it?" she yelled and saw him nod as they hobbled forward. There was a look on his face of extreme fear. Yet fear and pain notwithstanding, he was hobbling toward the movement with a speed she would have considered impossible for him, injured as he was.

The next thing she knew, there was a loud cry up ahead, the light from Jeff's flashlight was extinguished and a horrible realization dawned on her.

The thing had been heading straight for Jeff!

#

Finding a familiar landmark was impossible, but Jeff strained his eyes for something that would tell him he was getting closer to the trail. He knew, worst case, that if they continued heading in the same direction, sooner or later they'd find the trail. Problem was, they might hit it at a point miles from the main road and they needed to get to the main road as soon as possible. Their main priority was Elliot. The guy was in bad shape and needed to get to the emergency room. He had no idea what had happened to the poor guy. Both he and Cheryl had said something about a man with a gun, but there wasn't time to go into the details.

So many unanswered questions.

When this was over, he resolved to back to the hospital and see Baumann again. Hopefully, the old man would be in better shape and more lucid. Somehow, Baumann was the key. Jeff didn't know how or why. But up to now, the old guy had called it, straight down the line.

Help Cheryl Help Friend Don't Be Afraid

Cheryl needed help, all right. So did Elliot. There was nothing to be afraid of. He was able to accomplish those tasks without danger to himself.

Then, it occurred to him that Baumann did a very strange thing. He crossed out *Don't Be Afraid* on the writing pad and in its place wrote *Eye*.

What did *Eye* have to do with anything? Why did Baumann cross out *Don't Be Afraid*? Did that mean that there *was* something to be afraid of?

Suddenly, he stumbled and found himself up to his waist in water. Cheryl had been correct, they weren't going the right way. There had been no body of water when he and Elliot came to the cave that first time. This must be a stream which had swollen to a rushing river, what with all the rainfall.

Jeff pulled himself out of the water, and he aimed his light directly ahead. He saw a marker painted on one of the trees. Shifting the light to one side, he could see the trail itself. He almost shouted with joy and was just about to signal the others when a flash of sheet lightning struck. Out of the corner of his eye, he sensed movement off to the side, coming up fast.

His first thought was that it was Cheryl and Elliot approaching, but it took only an instant for him to see how wrong he was. Whatever it was, was moving fast, faster than Elliot could possibly move. There was also a smell—it was a dead smell, and he flashed back to the time a woodchuck had crawled under house on Crow's Nest Pike and died. Dad had managed to remove it, but not before the whole house was permeated with that fetid stench. It had sent Rusty into an outbreak of whimpering howls and himself into protracted fits of gagging.

This was the fetor of a thousand dead woodchucks, and this time, he didn't have the chance to gag before it was upon him.

Jeff had only a split second for his eyes to register the shape that zoomed out of the blackness. The light was knocked from his hands with such force that it went out altogether. What he saw in that split second looked like a man, an *enormous* man, bigger and broader than Chief Parsons. It looked like it was wearing, of all things, a shiny black wet suit.

But a wet suit didn't have scales like a reptile's. Nor did a wet suit have spines coming out of it.

Nor did a man make those snarling guttural noises.

The shape had been a good twenty feet away from him when the lighting subsided and the darkness returned. Even so, it stood out in the surrounding darkness as it leaped at Jeff.

Jeff cried out.

His reflexes kicked in and he turned and ran. The shape landed where Jeff had been standing only fractions of a second ago. Had Jeff not moved, it would have handed on him squarely, snapping his spine. As it was, he felt something sharp grip his shoulder, whirling him around.

Although he was now face to face with his attacker, he could make out very little other than its shape, and that only dimly. He could discern none of its features, but he didn't need to see them to know they were hideous. He could see an armlike appendage coming down at him in a motion somewhat like, but not quite like, a roundhouse punch. Jeff put his arm up to block it. He would have blocked it successfully if his opponent were human, with only a single elbow joint. But this thing, its manlike contour notwithstanding, had multiple joints in its appendages, like an insect or a crustacean. Jeff's defensive motion prevented the full force of the limb landing on him, but it was still able to connect. A knifelike claw slashed his skin and penetrated to his shoulder blade.

Jeff screamed and the thing screamed with him, a sound more terrible than the snarls and growls it had been making.

In spite of his terror, Jeff knew that once this horror got through with him, it would go after Cheryl and Elliot. This realization lent him a physical rush and he fought back with the same ferocity that took Desmond Corey down. Each punch was like hitting stucco. Every time he connected with his adversary's carapace, his fist came back drenched and bloody. Also, it burned; the thing was emitting an acid-like excretion with the consistency of drool from its pores. Nevertheless, Jeff kept punching with all his strength.

At best, he knew that his efforts were merely delaying the inevitable, and not by much.

#

Although Cheryl and Elliot couldn't see what was happening, the sounds of a struggle were audible, drawing them to the site of that struggle. When they got close enough to see what was happening, Cheryl screamed and a terrified, "Holy shit!" escaped Elliot's throat as well.

Their lights revealed Jeff held in the death grip of something shiny, black, and grotesque. It had bulbous yellow eyes, protected by scaly beetling brows. Its epidermal covering reminded Elliot of the spiny protrusions on EJ's plastic toy dinosaur figurines. It was alternately rearing up and squatting down. It never relinquished its hold on Jeff, who was being shaken like a chew toy in the mouth of a playful dog.

As they watched, the thing slipped and they heard a splash. They hobbled closer as fast as Elliot's injuries could allow. When they saw what had happened, Cheryl screamed again.

Jeff and that thing had tumbled into a gushing stream. The thing was standing semi-upright, but Jeff was being held underwater!

#

When he was first attacked, Jeff had been remotely aware of Cheryl and Elliot's presence nearby. He had heard Cheryl scream and Elliot shout. Intermittently, and only for instants at a time, beams of light illuminated them.

In those instants, though, he got a clear look at his assailant. It had bulging yellow eyes, with no pupils. Its jaws jutted forward with sharklike teeth which, when open, looked like a bear trap; when closed, resembled a death-grin. Its claws, like its semi-human limbs, were multi-jointed, and where they gripped him, he could not wriggle free or break their hold.

Something connected with the side of his head and he fell back onto the wet ground, a tremendous weight on his chest, and he felt himself being pulled down. In another burst of lightning, he saw that he was sliding toward the rushing stream. The thing was still on top of him riding him like a sled. Sharp teeth, raptor claws, the reeking stench, all of these loomed over him.

They both hit the water.

Instinct borne of years of swimming and coaching kicked in. Jeff filled his lungs with air. He struggled as a long forgotten-voice echoed, "He's a mean one and once he gets hold of you, he won't ever let go."

Jeff redoubled his struggles without success and he felt himself losing air as he was being shaken from side to side. In a few moments, it would all be over for him, one way or another. He'd either be drowned or shredded.

#

"Hold still." Cheryl realized that this command was directed at her as she felt Elliot make his way in back of her and start fumbling at the ruck.

"What are you doing?" she yelled. Elliot's response was lost in a burst of thunder, but she thought she heard the word, "Gun."

Yes! He was going for his gun!

It seemed like forever when it was really only a few seconds that Elliot was kneeling beside her holding the gun with both hands in a shooter's stance. "Keep the light steady!" he shouted as she aimed the light on the combatants.

But her elation was short-lived. Even if Elliot were a champion marksman, there was no way he was going to get a clear shot as that *thing* reared out of the water as it was mauling and drowning her husband. It was thrashing too fast. No sooner would she get it in the light than it would move somewhere else. She'd have to re-aim the light toward the struggle all over again, where it was visible only briefly, instants before melting back into the darkness.

The only opportunity Elliot would have to kill that thing was after it finished with Jeff and came after them.

No matter what, she was watching her husband die.

#

The thing was now underwater with him and Jeff knew he was seconds away from losing consciousness. He knew that the last thing he'd see were those eyes, those abhorrent yellow …

Eye.

In a final futile effort, Jeff's clenched his hand into a fist and found he could not close it fully. Something had made its way into his hand, perhaps a stone, or maybe a thick twig. Whatever it was did not matter. The eyes, the teeth were coming closer and he was going to make one last, probably fruitless attempt to save his life as well as the life of his wife and his friend.

With the last ounce of force he could marshal, Jeff stabbed upward toward one of those bulging yellow eyes.

To his amazement, the weight was lifted from his chest instantly. He flailed his way to the surface and sucked in gulps of delicious, life-giving air as a barrage of sound assaulted his ears.

A high-pitched scream.

A succession of gunshots amidst bursts of lightning in which he saw his attacker for the last time.

He also saw something else.

The thing thrashed in pain away from him and the others, in the direction of the escarpment.

Jeff stood where he was, in the water, gasping in air, over and over again. His legs were sore and bleeding from myriad puncture wounds from the thing's claws. In spite of his pain, he managed to crawl out of the stream, get to his feet, and walk. His back was the worst and he could feel the blood soaking into his shirt, already drenched. He began removing the shirt, with help from Cheryl who had run up to him as soon as he emerged from the stream. She was crying with relief, and he was glad to see Elliot, still holding the gun, hobbling a few feet on his own.

"Oh, Jeff, are you all right?" Cheryl was sobbing with relief and Jeff hugged her, then let go abruptly when the shoulder started to throb.

"It's OK, don't move," Cheryl said. She removed his shirt and began to tie it under his arm and around his shoulder in a makeshift pressure bandage to staunch the bleeding.

"You OK, man?" said Elliot as he hobbled up to where the other two were standing.

"Yeah. Thanks."

"You lucked out. I couldn't get a clear shot for nothing. Then that thing just jumped up and let you go."

"I got it in the eye."

"Whatever. As soon as it threw you down, I let it have it."

"Thanks, Elliot. You think you killed it?"

"I got it dead center. More than once. It was hurt bad, I could tell. If it's not dead, it soon will be."

"I hope you're right."

"Yeah. Me too."

The three of them made for the trail, Cheryl supporting Elliot, Jeff walking slightly ahead of them, pondering something he knew he'd never fully understand.

In that final burst of lightning, he'd gotten a good look at the thing that assaulted him. He'd gotten a good look at its *Eye* from which protruded something he thought he'd lost long ago and that he would never see again.

Something sharp with the initials JSS taped to the handle.

AFTERWORD

Taylorville; Present Day

By the time Cheryl, Jeff, and Elliot had gotten back to the road, three thunder-like booms, which were not thunder, occurred. By then, it was after 10 pm and Jeff was in worse shape than Elliot. The shirt that Cheryl had wrapped around him as an improvised bandage/tourniquet was supersaturated and the wound was becoming increasingly painful. Cheryl wanted to make a beeline for Mercy Hospital, but Jeff balked at the suggestion. There were a lot of questions he didn't want to answer. It was Elliot who found the middle ground.

They got into Cheryl's car and drove to Doc Pressman's.

What Elliot whispered to Doc when they got there, neither Jeff nor Cheryl ever found out. All they knew was that Doc, blanched and wide-eyed, led Jeff into his examining room, disinfected his wounds, and stitched up his back.

When he was done, he said to Jeff in a low voice, "I imagine you want to keep this quiet, am I right?" Jeff nodded in agreement, and Doc nodded in understanding. "OK," he continued. "Ordinarily, I wouldn't do this. Hell, I could get my butt in a sling for treating you, but I guess this is a special case, right?" Jeff nodded again. "OK, I think you'll be all right. It looks and probably feels a lot worse than it actually is, so don't worry. Just relax, take it easy, don't exert yourself. You come see me in about a week, or sooner, if it gives you any trouble, OK?"

"Sure. Thanks, Doc."

"No problem, son." Doc put his finger up to his lips and Jeff nodded again.

Meanwhile, Elliot and Cheryl had called Chief Parsons' office on Doc's insistence. They told the officer that they were on their way to Mercy Hospital (courtesy of Doc who also provided a clean T-shirt for Jeff). They had a statement to make regarding two assaults and an attempted rape. Could someone meet them there?

At the hospital, Elliot's head was bandaged and his leg, arm, and shoulder X-rayed. All three locations sustained fractures which, thank God, were not severe, though the arm was broken. He'd be wearing a cast, carrying a cane, and walking with a limp for a while, but he was expected to make a full recovery.

While Elliot was being treated, Jeff and Cheryl spoke to the young officer who met them there. Afterwards, they spoke to Chief Parsons himself who drove out when he learned that the Corey brothers were involved. The Stricklands limited themselves to the attacks from the Corey brothers; nothing was said about the *other* assailant.

It wasn't until after midnight that Elliot had the opportunity to call his frantic parents, who were sitting for EJ, long asleep. He told them about the encounter with Howard. In the morning, he was to do something he hated to do: lie to his son. EJ was upset enough to see his father in a cast and limping, so Elliot told him he'd been injured on the job. He felt the truth was too close to EJ's nightmare and he didn't want his son to dredge up that particular memory.

Once back in their home in Dandridge, Cheryl feared that her husband was going to be a difficult patient. For a high-energy type like Jeff, inactivity was impossible to endure.

"Jeff, relax and let me take of you."

"I'm OK, babe. You don't have to …"

"I *do* have to." Then she realized that with all the excitement, she'd neglected to give him the big news. "Besides, in a few months you'll have to wait on me, hand on foot. So we'll be even."

"What are you talking about?"

"Oh," she grinned mischievously. "Didn't I tell you? Daddy."

#

Elliot Ryan knew he was near death the moment he opened his eyes.

He had vision in only one eye; the other throbbed in agony. His torso felt like it had gone ten rounds under a trip hammer.

He knew where he was: entombed beneath a massive pile of rock which once housed a cave.

With his good eye, he was able to make out those funky uneven shapes he'd seen before, on some occasions, up close and personal; he was seeing them now through eyes that were not his own.

Horrified, Elliot knew he was having another one of those out-of-body experiences. He knew because he could feel coolness all over his body, a moist, subterranean coolness. It was not the type of chill that comes from a drop in temperature.

Elliot knew that the being through whose eyes he was seeing was feeling excruciating pain. This being was dying.

Somehow, it had made it back to the cave before the explosions went off. Somehow, it knew that Elliot was responsible for its pain and imminent demise. Somehow, it reached out for him, one last time, to merge its consciousness with its own prior to its moment of death.

These things Elliot knew. What he didn't know was what would happen when it died. Would he die with it?

Elliot tried to break that hold with a supreme effort of mental exertion.

He could still make out dim irregular shapes. He knew from experience that his own eyes could not distinguish such shapes in the dark of the cave. He was still trapped.

Elliot tried again. This time, he focused on breaking that hideous hold by thinking of EJ. He concentrated on EJ. He fixated on EJ with all the mental force he could marshal …

… and found himself in his own bed.

I've beaten you! You're going to die, you scum-sucking piece of crap, but I'm not. You hear me? I've beaten you!

His body was no longer surrounded by cool air; it was drenched in sweat, hot and feverish. Elliot no longer felt the pain in his eye and trunk. Instead, he felt pain in his head, arm, and leg.

It was the most wonderful feeling of his life.

Elliot turned on the light and hobbled downstairs. He couldn't sleep anymore. By tomorrow, the thing would be dead, and he could sleep again, but for now, he was going to stay awake.

He stopped to look in on his son. EJ was sleeping peacefully with Garfield sprawled at the foot of his bed. Elliot smiled. All was as it should be.

In the kitchen, Elliot brewed himself a pot of strong coffee, sat at the table, and gulped it, unmindful of its scalding temperature. His eyes fell on the bottle of Percocets that they'd prescribed for him at the emergency room. They told him it would help deaden the pain and help him sleep.

Elliot took the bottle in his hand and stared at it. So that was how his consciousness found its way into the brain of that other, if indeed it had a brain. He was doped up, not like when he was smoking weed, but still doped up.

Elliot Ryan took the Percocets into the bathroom, and flushed them. He'd have to endure the pain with just the help of Advil.

As soon as he was fully healed, he and EJ were going to pick up stakes and leave Taylorville. For good.

#

Days passed. Dust settled. Wounds healed.

The day after the storm, Chief Parsons led a team of four men and two women from the police department, coroner's office, and ambulance rescue team into the woods to retrieve the body of Howard Corey. Howard was found holding the gun Elliot described with blood and hair caked on it. Forensic lab work would reveal that the blood and hair were Elliot Ryan's, proof that Howard had attacked Elliot and Elliot had acted in self-defense.

No charges were brought against Elliot Ryan for the killing of Howard Corey.

Desmond Corey was found in back of Dunbar's Wharf with severe damage to his legs and hip plus a concussion. From Cheryl Strickland's statement, the police determined that Desmond Corey had assaulted and attempted to rape her. Her husband, driving by, saw what was happening and attacked Desmond Corey with a handy two-by-four.

No charges were brought against Jeff Strickland for the assault on Desmond Corey.

Rand Corey was in no position to assist his surviving son or avenge his dead one. The State Attorney General had launched an aggressive investigation on organized crime in which Rand Corey's name cropped up often. Also uncovered were the inappropriate dealings between Randall Corey and an underage boy.

Two nights after Desmond Corey was brought to Mercy Hospital, Randall Corey went home and swallowed a bullet.

In going through the Coreys' personal effects, Chief Parsons uncovered a formidable cache of weapons. There were guns (illegally obtained) plus an array of knives from the traditional (switchblades) to the exotic (machetes, scimitars and an eighteen-inch kris). It was this assortment of weaponry that prompted Chief Parsons to put two and two together and get five.

The summer passed into fall and there were no further animal killings. Even better, there were no further human killings, which led Chief Parsons to submit this inventory, with specifications and descriptions, to two individuals. The first was the coroner who conducted the Coleman, Murchison, and Bascom autopsies. The second was Doc Marvin Pressman. Parsons posed the same question to both of these men: was it possible that these knives could have been used to affect the killings?

The coroner said yes, possibly.

Doc said yes, definitely.

This led to the, biggest and most glaring mistake of Parsons' career.

Chief Parsons, along with all the tri-county area, more than anything, wanted to see an end to the sporadic killings that had long plagued the area. At long last, fate had complied. The Coreys were a pair of sadistic human monsters. Although they had never, to anyone's knowledge, engaged in murder, such a possibility was certainly not out of character for them. Why had no one thought of it sooner? It had to be *the Coreys* who were responsible for these atrocities.

Besides, didn't Baumann hint that Jeff Strickland had a major role to play in the case? Jeff Strickland who was associated with water? Baumann was right. If not for Jeff Strickland, Desmond Corey might still be gutting squirrels and deer and worse.

Chief Parsons, of course, could prove nothing. Desmond Corey, when questioned, shed no light. The blows Jeff Strickland administered to his head had left him more addled than usual. This meant that Chief Parsons could not, *in any official capacity,* close any of the cases related to the killings. But the general consensus among the police was that the killings were a thing of the past and their perpetrators dealt with. The official opinion trickled down into the community at large. The resultant closure was not as complete as the Coleman, Murchison, and Bascom families would have liked, but it would do. Taylorville breathed a collective sigh of relief.

Perhaps the realization occurred to some that many of these killings had taken place while the Coreys were away. If so, the response to that realization was outright denial. The Coreys were responsible and that was that; it's over. Don't let a little thing like facts disrupt the comfort zone. Those not in denial might have another explanation. The killings that took place in the Corey's absence were either copycat killings or the work of the Coreys' confederates. They would either be found or they would slink back into the woodwork forever. With the head cut off, the body would die. The comfort zone remained intact.

Linus Parsons, with that particular case no longer hanging over his head, was able to give thought to his retirement. Renee was gleeful when he made the decision; she had long been looking forward to joining her sister, who'd moved out to California and raved about the climate. Linus was not averse to the idea. It was close enough to Taos, where Peter Strickland had relocated. Who knows? Maybe he'd look Peter up.

He wondered what the fly-fishing was like in that part of the country.

#

POINT OF VIEW SHOT: A campfire at the Taylor Creek Campgrounds around which three young men are sitting. They resemble Jeff, Neil, and Andy. Across the screen are superimposed the following words: "A Dramatization. Names Changed Upon Request". The boy resembling Jeff is speaking. If we listen very closely, we can hear that he is telling a ghost story about Isaac Dunbar and the Backwoods Demon.

ANDY (voice-over, speaking over "Jeff"): Every so often, these friends would get together for a camp-out and try to outdo each other with the scariest spook tale. More often than not, the stories elicited laughs rather than shivers. Until one night, when something very out of the ordinary occurred.

CLOSE UP shot of "Jeff," still speaking.

ANDY (voice-over, still speaking over "Jeff"): Steve Jackson decided he wasn't going to stick with the stories that had been told over and over again year after year. He was going to make up one of his own.

STEVE/JEFF: I'm going to tell you the true story about Isaac Dunbar and Dunbar's Massacre. Isaac Dunbar was a *warlock*. A wizard. A male witch.

ANDY (voice-over, still speaking over Steve): Steve told how Isaac Dunbar had been cast out of Salem years ago, during the time of the witch trials for devil worship. How, over a hundred years later, he surfaced in what's now the town of Taylorville.

STEVE: Isaac Dunbar learned about the British, and called upon the dark gods to accept his blood sacrifice if they'd send a servant, a familiar. In answer to his call, they sent the Backwoods Demon to do his bidding.

CAMERA pans to the other actors who are looking sufficiently entranced, as STEVE continues talking.

ANDY (voice-over): In most polite circles, such a story would be considered sacrilege. After all, Isaac Dunbar has been traditionally regarded as a local hero, a brilliant military strategist. What could inspire such a blasphemous variation on so revered a local legend?

STEVE (close-up, speaking to the camera): I don't know, it just came to me. I wanted to scare the [deleted] out of those guys, so I just told the most outrageous story I could think of. (Grins). It worked.

ANDY (voice-over): But was it a story? Recent investigations have turned up the existence of a Joseph Dunlap who escaped from Salem at the time of the witch trials. Physical descriptions of Dunlap are sketchy, but they describe him as gaunt, gray, fierce looking—all adjectives used to describe Isaac Dunbar.

CAMERA switches to a close-up of an eighteenth-century style engraving of a man, thin-faced man of uncertain age, but probably in this late forties or early fifties, piercing black eyes, and a stern, forbidding expression.

ANDY (voice-over): But there's more to the story.

Shot of Steve and the boy resembling Andy poking at the campfire. The third boy, resembling Neil, is absent from this scene.

"YOUNG ANDY:" - So how late do you want to stay up?"

STEVE: I guess till the fire goes out.

"YOUNG ANDY:" - OK.

Suddenly, both boys are staring in one particular direction, looks of shock and amazement plastered on their faces.

ANDY (voice-over): What did you see?

QUICK SHOT of the engraving seen earlier, then a CLOSE-UP on STEVE.

STEVE: It was an old man in Revolutionary War style duds holding an old-fashioned gun. Man, did he look mean; really pissed.

ANDY (voice-over): You both saw this?

STEVE: Oh, yeah.

Jeff took the remote from the end table and fast-forwarded.

AERIAL SHOT from a small plane flying over the Ridge.

ANDY (voice-over): Geologists tell us that the Ridge is the result of glacial activity predating the Jurassic era. The Native Americans who inhabited this region spoke of great rumblings in the earth and spirit beings that walked in the forest. But perhaps the oddest tales of this region are the ones you've just seen by people who live here today, your neighbors, people you might pass on the street or stand next to in line at your favorite shopping mall. You may not believe their stories, chances are you don't. But they all have one thing in common in regard to a place called Dunbar's Ridge. A belief that there's magic here ...

Jeff clicked the "Stop" button on the remote and stared at the blank screen.

It had been nearly five months since that stormy summer night. For most of that time, he'd had to swallow inactivity, at Cheryl's insistence. It galled him, but it gave him time to think.

He thought of something he'd read once in a James Bond novel. Something to the effect that: once is happenstance, twice is coincidence, the third time is enemy action.

The things that happened to him over the years went beyond happenstance and coincidence.

Like what were the odds of his non-smoking, aerobically healthy dad coming down with emphysema?

What were the odds of his dad's illness being so severe that his parents had to pick up stakes for a warmer, drier climate and rent out their house?

What were the odds of their tenant being the only other person in the vicinity who'd had visitations over the last ten years? Jeff didn't count the people in Andy's video. Their experiences were one-shot deals; his and Elliot's were consistent and ongoing.

What were the odds of the Coreys showing up at the exact moment they did? Or of their truck dying when it did? Or of them carjacking not just anyone, but his own wife? Or of them all ending up at The Landing?

Beyond happenstance. Beyond coincidence. Which left only …

"Honey?"

Jeff looked up and saw his wife, her belly beginning to protrude, enter the room.

It was once again a dark and stormy winter night, with icy shards pelting the windows. Soon, it would be Christmas, their last Christmas as a couple. The thought warmed him and he stood and guided Cheryl down onto the couch with him, where she leaned into the crook of his shoulder.

"Is that OK, honey? Does it still hurt?"

"No, not really."

Satisfied that she wasn't causing him pain, Cheryl cuddled up to him. "You know, it's still so hard to believe."

Jeff nodded. It was hard to believe, and he'd been going through it since he was a kid. Now, he realized that the improbable events he'd just been contemplating were orchestrated and that people were manipulated.

Andy was right, there *was* magic here, and it wasn't good magic.

Like Elliot, Jeff decided to leave the area. He'd gotten a job offer from a school in Pennsylvania about which he and Cheryl were enthused. Cheryl now knew everything with two exceptions. There were Elliot Ryan's OBEs (Jeff did not consider that particular secret his to tell). Also, he never told her of the Cheryl-vision which had pleasured him the night she appeared.

Cheryl now understood the associations that Jeff carried with him of Taylorville, Crow's Nest Pike, and the Ridge. She was just as happy to know that their baby would not grow up in proximity to any of these things.

Jeff pressed the "Eject" button on the remote and the DVD popped out. It was a good film and well-received, Andy had told him.

At first, Andy had been miffed that Jeff had changed his mind about participating in it, but he accepted his friend's decision. Instead, he got a couple of students at the university to recreate that night at the campsite where they might have seen Isaac Dunbar. Jeff even helped with the dialogue, but that was as far as he was willing to go. Andy attributed Jeff's decision to stage fright and Jeff let Andy think that. Andy never brought it up again, for which Jeff was grateful.

His one regret was that he never got to speak with Henrik Baumann again. It was such a shame about the poor old guy.

#

During the night of the big summer storm, Henrik Baumann lost consciousness. Over the few days of life remaining to him, he kept mumbling something that sounded like "Maw wah."

The hospital staff assumed he was asking for "more water," which made no sense. He was being hydrated via an IV. Besides, in his current state, it was highly unlikely that he felt the pangs of thirst. So every utterance of "Maw wah" was written off to delirium.

They had no way of knowing that what he was trying to say was "More than one."

Taylorville, Massachusetts; September, 1771

He might have been a statue.

He only moved to lift the glass of ale and bitters to his mouth and take a swallow. Other than that, he sat motionless and alone.

Men entered and exited John Taylor's Tavern and Ale House. Most of them, upon noticing him, turned their eyes elsewhere. A few, those who had gotten word of, but did not bear witness to the Massacre, greeted him with the most perfunctory of nods before turning their eyes elsewhere.

He acknowledged none of them.

It had been nearly a fortnight since he'd performed the necessary rituals; squatting naked and inscribing the ancient incantation and arcane symbols on the carriage house floor.

He'd almost laughed in maniacal delight when he felt the earth grow warm beneath him. It was then that he knew his efforts would be rewarded.

This would be no Salem. He would not be charged or held in chains here. Many would regard him with reverent awe as the man who saved their town from the onslaught of General Burgess. Those who were with him in the forest that night and who had seen the hordes of black shapes rise from the ground would regard him with a different type of awe. They had seen bloodshed beyond anything of which Burgess was capable. And they would hold their tongues forever.

Forever.

That was how long those he had summoned would exist. As long as they existed, so too would he. As long as he existed, so too would his unquenchable hatred of all things mortal.

They would become one with the forest. They would find dark hidden places they could make their own: hollows, lakes, gorges, caves. They would emerge and prey on native fauna and woe betide the luckless Indian or wayward traveler who ventured too close to their dwelling places.

There they would lie in wait and linger, gaining strength over years innumerable.

People would come. Already John Taylor's town was growing as were other settlements.

He knew it would be a matter of time, and time held not the import for him or for them as it did for others.

It had begun.

THE END

C. I. Kemp is a lifelong horror buff currently living in the wilds of New Jersey with his neurotic cat. By day, Mr. Kemp works in the Information Services; by night he is an avid reader and writer of horror, dark fantasy, and occasionally erotica and humor. He is a member of the Garden State Speculative Fiction Writers. When not engaged in pursuits which involve scaring the pants off his readers, Mr. Kemp enjoys hiking, biking, and various outdoor activities. He is the author of the novel <u>Autumn Moon</u> (Hartwood Publishing). His work has also appeared in <u>K-Zine</u>, <u>Cover of Darkness</u>, <u>State of Horror; New Jersey</u>, <u>Isotropic Fiction</u>, <u>Horror Garage</u>, <u>Allegory</u>, <u>Under the Bed</u>, <u>Encounters</u>, <u>Everyday Fiction</u>, and the anthology <u>Speculations from New Jersey</u> (Create Space Independent Publishing).

www.ingramcontent.com/pod-product-compliance
Lightning Source LLC
Chambersburg PA
CBHW031055020726
47495CB00007B/1883